About the Author

INGRID FRY was born and raised in Berkhamstead in the UK but spent much of her childhood commuting with her family between England and Austria. Emigrating with her parents to Melbourne, Australia many years ago, she has called Australia home ever since.

A business development consultant, writer and minder of a husband and a beagle with superpowers, she lives in a leafy suburb on the outskirts of Melbourne. Lakes Entrance is her second home, and it was from there, much of the Crystal Sphere series was developed.

In her spare time, Ingrid enjoys pistol shooting at the local gun club, dancing her socks off at The Caravan Music Club, and is a passionate karate nerd, well on her way to a black belt in karate. Ingrid models the belief that it is never too late to achieve your dreams, and age is definitely just a number.

You can find out more information about Ingrid via her website www.ingridfry.com.au
Email: Ingrid@ingridfry.com.au

Content Warning: The Crystal Sphere Series is intended for mature readers and contains sexual situations, violence, and other representations that may cause some readers distress. Please prepare accordingly.

National Library of Australia Cataloguing-in-Publication entry:
Creator: Fry, Ingrid, author.
Title: Search for Truth: Crystal Sphere Book 4
/ Fry, Ingrid.

ISBN: 978-0-6486816-4-9

Tale Publishing
Melbourne, Australia

Tale

For Bruce and Maggie
and my dear friends
Cate Hutchings and Chris Chandler

Follow Maggie's music playlist on Spotify!

Type *all* of the following ridiculously long code
into the Spotify search bar:

spotify:user:z s 8 x y x p x z b t 1 m j c i r 5 9 q z 1 j z w

Click the Follow Button for Crystal Sphere

Morning sun filtered through the surgery window, illuminating three plastic bags filled with skin. The contents resembled translucent plastic shards, which glittered with a soft, oily opalescence. Frank's scribbly writing was scrawled across each label: Epidermis/Tapakah.

I picked up a bag and memories of the night flooded back. The feel and sound of it reminded me of a bag of prawn crackers. The skin inside even looked like prawn crackers. I used to love prawn crackers. Not anymore.

The image of Tapakah's skinless body, all raw meat, interwoven muscles, and glistening tendons and ligaments would never leave me. I shuddered and quickly packed the bags in a cardboard carton, along with other medical bits and bobs. We were bugging out, as Tapakah called it.

I heard little footsteps thumping along the corridor of the old homestead. Billy's head appeared around the door. 'Come on, Maggie. We have to hurry. The truck's ready to go.'

'Coming. I had to get this stuff for Frank.'

We raced along the cool, dim corridor, through the internal courtyard, and out the front door into the sun. Nulla and Dee, the station dogs, jumped around us generating eddies of red dust as we made our way to the waiting four-wheel drive.

Tapakah stood hands on hips in front of the truck. Black jeans, black T-shirt, black hair, black eyes. Black was his happy colour. He'd muscled up even more since the accident, and my heart quickened at the sight of him.

'What kept you? We have to leave.' His tone was urgent, almost angry.

I handed him the carton. 'Keep your shirt on. Frank asked me collect stuff from the surgery.'

'The plane's on the runway ready to go. Come on!'

The station managers, Hugh and Elizabeth, were waiting. I hugged Elizabeth, and patted the dogs, quickly saying my farewells. Elizabeth's eyes filled with tears and so did mine.

Hugh drove Tapakah, Frank, Billy and me to the plane. He gave us all a hug and we boarded Tapakah's jet. The engines roared, and we were rocketing down the dusty runway before I'd even had a chance to put my seat belt on. A slight drop in my stomach and we were airborne, the red dirt and scrub spreading out below us. As we passed the ridge, my head buzzed with a powerful humming sensation and then it was gone.

Farewell, beautiful outback. You were all I knew; all I could remember. Everything in my past, other than the last few months, was a mystery to me. My life had started here, and now we had to leave.

Tapakah said I would love Victoria, and the old townhouse he had in East Melbourne. I didn't know if I'd like living in the city. I knew I loved outback Western Australia, but the people who'd tried to abduct me from Tapakah knew where we were, so we had to run.

Billy sat quietly. His diminutive form looked even smaller in contrast to the large aircraft armchair. He pressed his nose against the window. 'I don't want to leave. I'll miss the dogs. And the red dirt, and the big sky, the flowers and the animals. It was the best thing ever. I'll miss it.'

'So will I, Billy. So will I.'

He turned to face me, and his eyes filled with tears. I reached out, and he cuddled up and sobbed into my shirt.

'It'll be fine,' I said. 'At least you've been to Melbourne before. I don't know if I've ever been there. It'll all be new to me. It's not as scary for you as it is for me.'

He shuddered and sobbed even more.

---

[1] *Maggie's Playlist: The Beginning of The End — Klergy, Valerie Broussard*

"The truth is rarely pure and never simple." — *Oscar Wilde*

Three hundred pens of naked human females stretched out below me. My son, Cafard, had recently doubled our capacity. The pens were half the size now, but the women still had enough space to stretch their legs and lie down. They had feed, water, heating, artificial light and medical attention twenty-four seven. We needed to ensure their pregnancies would come to a healthy and robust fruition. Their hybrid offspring would be the start of a new world.

The laboratory control room afforded me a three-hundred-and-sixty-degree bird's-eye view of my operations, all of which were ticking along nicely.

Cafard had really stepped up whilst I'd been away with Maggie. He was turning out to be a chip off the old block, or more accurately, a clone off the old DNA.

Cafard was identical to me, apart from his eyes. He had different coloured irises, one black, one yellow, and he had more lenses than me, 2,562 per eye, to be exact. Our hybrid physiology had benefited from the superior aspects of cockroach DNA. The additional lenses enabled us to form multiple images of what was occurring around us. Our skin was particularly sensitive to air currents, pressure and other movements, providing a superior ability to detect human predators.

Cafard was as smart as me too. Neurons are packed into a roach brain ten times more densely than in a human brain, so we had a significant advantage in brain power. We used our cells in a more flexible way, with several tendrils of a single neuron having the ability to act independently. The bottom line was we got more brain power out of our brain cells. Homo sapiens thought bugs were dumb. Think again, suckers.

Thanks to Cafard helping me manage operations, I could focus more of my time on the big picture, Project BLOOD, and Maggie.

I loved to move, so when I left the control room, I ran down four flights of stairs rather than take the lift and headed along the dimly lit corridor to catch up with Frank, my Chief Medical Officer and unofficial 2IC.

He was in his office, sitting in his fancy leather chair behind a minimalist glass and steel desk. The floor to ceiling window behind him provided a fortieth-floor view across Sydney Harbour. The wall mural was so realistic it made me forget, just for a second, he was in the basement of a four-storey, windowless, totally secure, off the radar, secret laboratory.

I pulled up a chair and waited for him to look up from his laptop.

He brushed back a strand of hair that had escaped from his comb-over and met my gaze. 'What's up?'

'I'm going to tell Maggie the truth.'

Frank sat bolt upright. 'What truth would that be?'

'Absolutely everything. I'm going to ask her to marry me. Before I do that, I want her to know all about me.'

Frank leaned back in his chair and ran a hand through his thinning hair. 'And that conversation is going to go how? Let me see ... um ... Maggie, before I ask you to marry me, I need to tell you the truth about a few things.

'I'm actually not human, I'm half cockroach. I used to be all roach until I turned mutant from radiation and crawled into the mouth of a pregnant woman and merged with her fetus.

'I'm aligned with an entity called the Dark Force, which feeds off and creates negative human energy. It's responsible for most of the evil you see in the world.

'I run a genetic engineering laboratory that's kidnapped hundreds of women and men to use in experiments, and a breeding program to create a hybrid race based on my DNA. I have infiltrated the minds of hundreds of humans and turned them into compliant zombies, ready and willing to do my bidding.

'My ultimate mission is to eradicate five billion people from the planet to restore it to its former glory and populate the earth with hybrids.

'I've tried to stop you from working against me and destroying the Dark Force by sending my henchman to steal your crystals, the very crystals required to restore balance to this fucked up planet.

'I've hurt you, chased you, kidnapped you, imprisoned you, harvested your eggs, humiliated and tortured you to the extent you tried to commit suicide. I kidnapped, roached, controlled and eventually killed your lover, the news of which sent you into such severe catatonia you lost all memory of your past life.

'I have hurt and killed your friends, taken you away from your family, murdered nameless amounts of people and basically ruined your life. But, Maggie, aside from all that, I'm basically one helluva nice guy. I love you with all my heart. Will you marry me? Yeah, that will *really* work, Tapakah. Good one.'

Frank was a brave man. No one else dared to speak to me that way. I knew by the look on his face even he thought he'd gone too far.

'I've changed, Frank. I'm not the same. I'm evolving.'

'That may be, but it ain't going to win you Maggie's heart, that's for sure. She will walk, one hundred percent guaranteed.

You would too. Put yourself in her shoes.'

'I have and I'm sick about what I've done.'

'So what? You're going to close shop, live in the burbs and start a family? You're going to give up the plan?'

'Not entirely. I'll make modifications.'

'What? Eliminate two billion people rather than five?'

'Watch your mouth; you're pushing it.'

'I know. Sorry. But you need to give up this obsession with Maggie. If you're prepared to let her go, then let her go. Get your focus back on Project BLOOD. She'll only stay with you until she finds out the truth. Then she'll be gone. The only way to keep her is to keep her in the dark.'

The words Maggie's lover, Jason, had said to me before I'd had him killed echoed through my mind. 'What's the saying, Frank? If you love something, let it go. If it comes back it was meant for you, if not...'

Frank shook his head. 'Jesus, I liked you better when you were pure evil. Now it's like having a lovesick teenager around.'

'Why don't you say what you really think?'

Frank grinned. 'If I did, you'd kill me. But really, Maggie is a distraction for you. You are a genius, Tapakah. Nothing like you has existed before. This is cutting edge science, and the whole team is excited to be involved in the plan. You can't lose focus.'

'You think I'm pure evil?'

'No. You're like a two-year-old finding your way in the world. As you said, you're evolving. Let her go. Get back to the work.'

'The two aren't mutually exclusive. Get used to it.' I turned and left.

I knew Frank had it in for Maggie. He wanted me to concentrate solely on the work. He denied it vigorously, but I'm sure he played a part in Maggie losing her life-force blocker. That's how her friends had finally found her. They'd locked onto her life force, located us in the outback, and taken us by surprise.

I still couldn't believe she'd chosen to stay with me. How things changed. This time, she would have taken her life to save me, not because of me.

It was Jason who'd given her the means to slash her wrists. I'd made sure he paid the ultimate price for it. I didn't regret getting rid of him.

I did regret what I'd done to Maggie, but I would make it up to her.

And I'd make sure her friends wouldn't be able to find her again.

She was mine now.

Chapter 2: Found & Lost

"The most sublime act is to set another before you." — *William Blake*

'Ashley, stop trying to hit us,' Fox yelled as he ducked my fist. '*Stop it!* We're your friends, for Christ's sake.' I clipped the side of his ear, and he let rip a string of expletives.

Drom leapt in and jammed my arm up behind my back. I kicked his legs out from under him. He hit the dirt hard, raising a cloud of red dust. There was no shortage of that stuff, here, in outback Western Australia.

The Maestro stared me down with her violet eyes. 'Ashley, if you don't stop this, I will sedate you.'

'Yeah, with what, sweetheart?'

'The Maestro device has a stun function.' Her manicured fingernail hovered over a copper coloured button on the gadget around her wrist.

'Then why the hell didn't you use it on Tapakah?'

The Maestro rolled her eyes at me. 'You know why. Maggie would have blown her head off with the shotgun.'

Tapakah, that self-satisfied piece of alien scum-sucking shit. They'd had to drag me away from Maggie, and the smile on his face as they did will be forever etched into my brain. The image burned inside me so much I wanted to vomit.

I couldn't believe it. Finally, we'd found her, tracked her

down, and now we were leaving her there. With *him*.

The Maestro anticipated my next question. 'No, we haven't lost our minds. You know we had no choice. She wanted to stay with him.'

'But he's brainwashed her. This is wrong.' My voice cracked. 'We may never find her again.'

'We can discuss this later. We need to get out of here. Tapakah will be coming after us. Are you ready?'

'No. You go. I can't. I can't leave her. I'm going back.'

A second before it hit me, the Maestro mumbled, 'Sorry. Not happening.'

My body was torn apart in space, blitzed in a blender, microwaved, thrown against a wall and my brain yanked out my arse. My feet hit ground, and I opened my eyes and threw up.

The loud groans of Fox and Drom came from nearby. They'd obviously found re-entry just as taxing.

'Oh, Christ. Just shoot me now,' Drom moaned.

'Holy crap,' Fox said. 'That's got to have long-term side effects. Surely.'

The three of us stood bent over our vomit while the Maestro picked off a few fluffs from her skintight black shirt. 'You'll be fine, boys. It won't be so bad next time. A couple more jumps and you won't notice a thing.'

Fox grumbled as he straightened and wiped his mouth on his sleeve. 'That's what you said the first time.'

I brushed the red dust off my pants. 'Seriously, next time I'm taking a plane. Melbourne to Western Australia, five and a half hours. That's fine with me. I don't give a rat's arse if teleporting only takes one second; the pain ain't worth it.'

'Don't be such a wuss. Maggie would've been long gone. Speed was the only reason we caught up with her. Teleporting is the only way.'

The smile on her face told me she might just be enjoying our suffering. Or at least mine. Perhaps payback for that time I

10

patted her down and gave her a body search. But then, she'd already paid me back for that. I winced at the memory of her steel capped knee smashing into my balls.

The Maestro wasn't vindictive; I don't think she had a vindictive bone in her body. She was more mischievous — an alien who needed sex and sound waves to survive. I wanted to go to Sonus, the planet where she and Christos came from, but she said it would kill me. She said the sex and sound would do me in. If I ever wanted to commit suicide, that's where I'd go.

I looked around to see where we'd transported. My eyeballs still vibrated in my skull, but I recognised Maggie's front yard. 'Good work, Maestro. At least we didn't reintegrate into a brick wall or something.'

Drom was still doubled over, so I picked him up and carried him to the front door.

'Hey, put me down for Christ's sake.'

'No. Suck it up, little buddy. You look like shit.'

'I feel like shit.'

The front door opened and Maggie's sister, Bella, ran out, closely followed by her father, the Professor, Luca, and the two dogs, Boo and Schmoo.

Bella looked around anxiously. 'Where's Maggie? Did you find her? How is she? *Where* is she?'

'Take a breath, Bella. Let's get in the house first.' I squeezed through the front door with Drom in my arms and dumped him into a wingback chair by the fireplace.

Fox staggered in and flung himself on the couch. 'I need something fizzy, fast.'

'Champagne helps settle post transmogrification sickness,' the Maestro said. 'I'll get us some.' She headed into the kitchen.

'Where's Maggie?' Bella said again. '*Did you find her?*'

The two lines deepening between her eyebrows, combined with her fixed gaze, told me her mood was frustration bordering on anger.

'She was in outback Western Australia, just as the Maestro's device indicated. She was having a picnic with Tapakah. They seemed to be having a lovely time.'

'*What?*' Bella, Luca and the Prof said simultaneously.

'Yeah, I know. Hang in there for the rest. Other than looking like an escapee from *Mad Max*, she seemed okay.' I paused, considering how to phrase the rest.

'What do you mean an escapee from *Mad Max?*' the Prof asked.

'Her hair was shaved, maybe only a centimeter long, with designs cut into it. I reckon she'd lost weight too. Her collarbones were pronounced. She had scars running from the inside of her wrists to halfway up her forearms. Nasty. Broke my heart to see them. She also had a Catherine wheel tattoo on her right arm.'

'*No!*' Bella shrieked.

Everyone took a breath to ask more questions, but I cut them off at the pass. 'Wait. I need to get this out. Don't interrupt.'

Bella looked taken aback. Her tone was curt. 'Well, go on then.'

'Maggie had no idea who we were. Absolutely no recognition. Zilch. She was scared of us. Terrified. She's lost her memory. All of it, other than up until a few weeks ago, according to Tapakah.'

'Oh, my God,' Luca said.

'Yep. According to Maggie, she tried to commit suicide and Tapakah saved her. Apparently, she entered a state of extreme catatonia, and Tapakah brought her back. All she knows is him. No memory of anyone or anything else. She told us she was free to go anytime, and Tapakah wasn't holding her captive. She said Tapakah was a good man ... and ... that ... um...'

'*What* for heaven's sake?' Bella said. 'Spit it out, Ash.'

I couldn't bring myself to say the words. I just couldn't. It was as though by saying them it would make it real. At this point in time, the only power I had was the power *not* to say those words.

Drom stepped in to save me. He spoke quietly, probably having the same trouble as me. 'Maggie said Tapakah was a good man and … she loves him. Wants to be with him.'

The colour drained from Luca's face. 'Holy *shit*!'

Bella started to sob. The Prof resembled a stunned mullet. Maggie's dog, Boo, looked downcast and miserable. Fox's dog, Schmoo, tilted his head and replicated Boo's expression. He didn't like it when Boo was unhappy.

'Yep. Against my will, we left her there.'

'But why? That's insane,' Bella said.

I gave the Maestro a death stare as she entered with a tray of glasses and champagne. 'I know.'

She returned my stare. 'Give it up, Ash.' She poured everyone a drink. 'This is what happened, and why we chose to leave.' She quietly explained the rest of the story and the rationale behind the decision to leave Maggie. 'We really had no other choice. As strange as it sounds, we left her with Tapakah in the interests of her well-being.'

'You're absolutely sure she has no recollection of her former life?' the Prof asked.

The Maestro nodded.

'Not true,' Drom interjected.

'What do you mean, not true?' I asked.

'She still has an unconscious memory of the crystals.'

'How the hell do you know that?' Fox asked.

'By the designs cut into her hair. Didn't you notice? The prisms, the notches — it was a replica of a crystal. She's the only one who could do that. Maggie cut the design into her head, not someone else.'

'Jeez you're good,' Fox said. 'You'd make an A1 detective. I didn't even pick that.'

'So, you think there's hope?' I asked Drom.

'Definitely. She's been traumatised to the extreme, but the crystals will bring her back. They have to.'

I looked at Bella and the Prof. 'That was going to be our next move. Go back and blast her with a crystal.'

'You said she had a Catherine wheel tattoo. Does it mean she's been roached?' Bella asked.

'I don't think so,' Drom said. 'I probed her mind and didn't get a sense of roach. All I got was complete lockdown.'

'She's really staying there of her own free will?' Bella asked.

Drom looked downcast. 'Appears so.'

I wanted to vomit. I picked up my glass of champagne, skulled it, refilled it and skulled that too. My nose buzzed with a fizz of flowers and orange peel.

Bella came over and hugged me. 'I'm so sorry, Ash. This is insane. It must have broken your heart to leave her there.'

I nodded mutely.

Fox rubbed the side of his head. 'We nearly lost our lives trying to drag him outta there.'

'Sorry 'bout that, mate.'

All our phones beeped as a text message came through.

Fox checked his screen. 'What the hell? Did you guys get this?' He read out the text. *Listen up. This is a warning. You heard what she said and what she wants. There will be consequences for you and your loved ones if you try to find her or come anywhere near her. No crystals. No contact. You have been warned.*

We'd all received the exact same message.

I held up my phone. 'Did you guys get a smiley face and a gun emoji at the end?'

Everyone shook their heads in the negative.

'Nice. Tapakah reserved that just for me. Don't I feel special.'

'What the hell are we going to do?' Bella asked.

Nobody answered. Probably because, at this point in time, we didn't have a bloody clue.

Frank looked puzzled. 'Why did you bring Maggie back to Melbourne, Tapakah?'

'Our location in WA was compromised. We had to get the hell out of there, thanks to the problem with her bracelet.' I gave him a look.

'I had nothing to do with her bracelet coming loose.'

'So you say.'

I still suspected Frank had something to do with Maggie losing her life-force blocker bracelet. He'd made it clear he wasn't happy about my focus on Maggie. Losing the bracelet enabled her friends to pinpoint her lifeforce and mount a rescue. Lucky for me she couldn't remember who they were.

Frank let out a sigh, and said, 'Maggie would be better off in WA. She loved the outback station. She recovered there, made friends, thrived in the nature and isolation.'

'You know it was too risky to stay. I had to get her undercover.'

'But Melbourne?'

'I've already told you. I chose Melbourne because her friends wouldn't expect me to bring her here. She can't remember anything of her past, so it doesn't matter. Everything is new to her.'

'Have your priorities changed?'

Frank was invaluable to me as a medical doctor, and he was a brilliant microbiologist, but he could be infuriating. I hadn't even had to put a roach in his head. He worked for me willingly. He wanted to be around for the new world.

I took a breath and attempted to control my impatience. 'No, my priorities are the same. Now I have Maggie, I can fully concentrate on my goal. I feel more focused with her around me. I can't let her back into the lab, but I'll come up with something to keep her busy. She won't get in your way.'

'Yeah, letting her back into the lab would be a recipe for instant catatonia.'

'The plan is to increase production of my hybrids, finish work on the DNA specific bio weapon and…'

'And?'

'Procreate with Maggie naturally.'

This time Frank sounded annoyed. 'Why the hell are you so obsessed with this? You've got her eggs. Just make embryos in a test tube like you did with the others.'

'Well, for one, she doesn't know I've harvested her eggs, and two, I don't have to do it that way. She said she loves me, and so I will have her. It's only a matter of time. No rush. I'm enjoying the courtship.'

'Humour me. Why her? You could have any female you wanted. You have hundreds locked in the lab. Is it because of the Dark Force atom lodged in her head? Or do you still want the crystals? *What?*'

'It used to be yes to the first question. Now it's no. Same for the second question.'

'If it's not the Dark Force connection or the crystals, what is it?'

'Things have changed. Now, I'd prefer she wasn't linked to the Dark Force; it could be dangerous. I need to keep her away from the crystals so she doesn't regenerate and regain her memory. I need to leave the Dark Force alone to do what it does.'

'You didn't answer the question. Why Maggie?'

'Because I love her.'

Frank put his face in his hands and muttered, 'How things change. I never thought I'd hear the word love come out of your mouth.'

'I didn't think you would either. Consider yourself lucky.'

[4] *Maggie's Playlist: Changes — David Bowie*

"The mystery of love is greater than the mystery of death."
— *Oscar Wilde, Salome*

The staircase creaked as I carefully navigated the steep incline from the bedroom to the hallway. I loved Tapakah's old East Melbourne town house, but lots of things creaked, and I think my knees were contributing a few creaks of their own.

A shadow appeared through the frosted glass of the front door. I froze and held my breath. The handle turned and the door slowly opened.

Tapakah stepped through it. 'You look like a deer caught in headlights.'

I exhaled. 'Sorry, I'm still so jumpy. How come you're home early?'

His expression turned serious. I removed the AirPods from my ears. 'What's up?'

'We need to talk.'

Oh, I didn't like the sound of that. A "we need to talk" talk usually spelt trouble.

'Yes?'

'Come into the lounge.'

Hand on my back, he guided me to sit on the couch near the open fire. The leather creaked as we sat.

'Maggie, if you had a choice, and it were possible, would you want to know about your life before you lost your memory?'

'I guess so.'

'What if it meant you would lose what we … you … have here, with me?'

'Then I wouldn't want to know.'

'But what if there were people, family, friends, out there who were missing you and loved you? Wouldn't you want to find out?'

'Yes, but I wouldn't want to lose you. What are you saying? Do you know something?'

'I'm afraid I'm not who you think I am.'

'But I don't know who you are. You're a mystery to me.'

'You know my feelings for you run deep. I want to be with you for always. But I need to be honest with you. Even if it means losing you.'

My stomach clenched. What on earth was he talking about?

'You're scaring me. What have you done that you would lose me?'

He looked at me earnestly. 'I need to get this out and then you can ask questions. Okay?'

'Okay, tell me.'

'I'm not who you think I am. I'm not human. You may have suspected something strange already. I'm a freak of nature, a mutation. I'm a hybrid. A cross between a human and an insect.' He paused, sat back and considered the look on my face.

My eyes felt like they were the size of dinner plates. After what happened in Western Australia, I knew he had a weird physiology, but a cross with an insect? He must have been playing a joke on me. He had to be. But his face … I knew his range of expressions, and this expression … this was no joke.

I started to speak but he raised his hand. He cleared his throat. 'We believe nothing like me has existed before. I run a secret genetic engineering laboratory producing more hybrids like me from my DNA. I have grown from an infant to what you see now in less than twelve months. I don't know if I will stabilise or continue to age at an accelerated rate. It currently appears I've stabilised. I am a combination of human and insect physiology. It seems I have the best of both species. Frank says I'm still like a child, finding my way, learning, growing and changing.

'I've made mistakes, done many things I regret. I'm different now, but you wouldn't have liked who I was. You may not like who I am now. I love you, but I want to be honest. If you are to love me, you need to know what it is you love.'

I waited for the film crew to come out and say, 'Surprise! You're on *Candid Camera*.' But no one did. Tapakah fixed his gaze on me in anticipation. *Was he for real?*

What he'd said did explain many of the strange events I'd witnessed. Frank had intimated things while Tapakah was ill. And there was the God-awful condition he had. And the transformation his body had been through after he'd been shot. The image of his skinless body still haunted me. It also explained why everyone was so secretive. But *really*? A human *bug*?

It certainly would explain the supernatural connection he had with animals, his heightened senses and extraordinary reflexes. I remembered watching his fluid, spiderlike movements as he'd effortlessly scaled the tower of the station to fix the satellite dish. His confession would also explain why people were after him.

I reflected on our time in the outback, and the four people who'd materialised out of nowhere and tried to take us. He'd run a long distance in a few seconds, scaled massive boulders and returned with barely a sweat raised. I'd reckoned he was super human at the time.

'*Maggie?*'

My mind was miles away and continued to play over what I'd seen and what he'd said.

'Maggie, say something.'

'Sorry. I was trying to process.'

His dark eyes wouldn't leave my face. I noticed his body was rigid, muscles tight, fists clenched.

I couldn't think of what to say. What *did* you say to someone who'd just told you they were half bug? But I had to say *something*. 'So … you're like Spider-Man, then? And … and you have all the … the human bits. You know.'

As I finished speaking, all the tension left Tapakah. He threw back his head and laughed. When he leant forward again, his whole body shook with it.

'What's so funny?'

I hadn't heard him laugh so heartily before. It was infectious, and I couldn't help but laugh with him.

He wiped the tears from his eyes and took my hand. 'Oh, Maggie. You make me laugh. After what I just laid on you, I wasn't expecting that. I hadn't thought of it before, but yes, I guess you could say I'm like Spider-Man. And …' he paused as he chuckled, '… and I do have all the "human bits".' He grinned. 'I think you'll find them most satisfactory.'

My face felt red hot. 'I'm an idiot. You're making fun of me. I'm sorry. It was ridiculous what I said.'

'It was the perfect thing to say.'

'So, are you crossed with a spider?'

He looked serious again. 'No. People generally aren't enamoured of spiders, but they like the insect I come from even less. In fact, they loathe them.'

An icy chill engulfed me. I knew immediately what insect he was referring to. I braced myself for the answer before quietly speaking the word. 'Cockroach?'

'Yes.' His body tightened as he waited for my response.

Oh, Jesus Christ. I hated cockroaches. Who didn't? I just wasn't sure if I hated spiders or cockroaches more. Thinking about it, I would have to go with cockroaches. I reckoned they were the creepiest. The way they scuttled. Ew. And they were harder to kill. I knew we needed insects and we'd be history without them, but why did they engender such revulsion?

But Tapakah didn't revolt me. He was as sexy as hell, brilliant, powerful, otherworldly. He fascinated me with his dark, brooding good looks. And those black eyes. They were hypnotic. He reminded me of a Spanish conquistador. Put a helmet on his head and he'd be there.

I thought of the time I'd saved his life. He'd been shot, and his body had transformed in response to the trauma. I remembered the scars across his torso and how they'd opened, allowing me to see into his body as air hissed out of them. He had shed his skin. Frank had bagged and labelled it. Tapakah's body had looked as though it'd been skinned alive. I still had nightmares about it. At the time, I'd mistaken him for a zombie and tried to shoot him. What if that process happened to him on a regular basis? Crikey. I mean, he seemed human enough to me. We'd kissed. Nothing untoward there. We hadn't gone any further, but I had a sense his accoutrements were in working order.

Hell. What about *that*? Could he procreate? And if so, what sort of creature would result from the union of a human and … and … a whatever the hell he was?

My head whirled with questions. Tapakah stared at me intensely like he always did when waiting for a response.

'Maggie?'

'Well … um … that's okay. Cockroaches are survivors. I've read they'll probably be the only creatures to survive a nuclear holocaust. They'll inherit the earth. That'll stand you in good stead. I think all creatures are important, and beautiful, no matter how we perceive them. It seems to me you're lucky. You have the best of both worlds.

'But, Tapakah, I must admit, I'm not enamoured of cockroaches *(major, major understatement there)*, or insects in general for that matter. I do like dragonflies though. They're beautiful. And butterflies. I believe in live and let live, and I try not to kill creepy bugs. Catch and release is my motto. Well, to be honest, that probably goes more for spiders. I haven't caught and released any cockroaches. I feel awful. I've killed many of your … your brethren over the years. Sorry about that.'

Oh, bloody hell. Would you listen to me? I was babbling, like I always did when I was nervous or under pressure. And hell's bells, did I feel under pressure. This whole thing must have been a joke. It couldn't be true. He was having a lend of me. But I knew it to be true. And I felt scared. Scared witless.

I looked at my hands and they were shaking.

He took them in his and held them still. 'Oh, Maggie…'

The mix of emotions whenever he touched me, or looked at me, were overwhelming. He was a drug. I was hypnotised and possessed by him, and I loved it. I loved him — it. And what else did I have? Nothing. No one. My past life was a mystery, lost with my memory. He'd saved me. Cared for me. Loved me. He was my world. I didn't realise what a brave new world it had turned out to be. I had no choice.

'Maggie? Tell me, you can be honest. I can take it. What's going on in that beautiful head of yours?'

'I have so many questions, and I know we'll work through them. To be honest, I'm scared. No, make that terrified. But you were there for me when nobody else was, and I want to be there for you. It must be hard for you, and I want to support you. I don't know if I'll be any good at it, but I'll try my best. You would have to be the most unique creature on the planet. I'm blessed to know you and be part of your life.'

Tapakah dropped his head. As his gaze disengaged from mine, I felt a sense of loss. His body shuddered.

Oh, great. I'd tried to be articulate, to say what I really felt, and he was laughing at me again. I was lousy at expressing myself verbally. I needed to write things down.

'I'm sorry if it sounded corny.'

He lifted his head. 'What?' He stood, turned away, and wiped his face.

Was he crying?

'Maggie, I can't tell you how much that meant to me. Your acceptance of me. I'm sorry, the sensations … emotions I'm feeling … it's all new.'

I stood and turned him to face me. 'Don't be sorry. It's all part of being human.'

'I don't know if I can handle it. These feelings … they make me feel out of control.' He trained his gaze towards the ceiling.

'That's what I do when I try and control my emotions, look up at the ceiling, focus on things, count things. But you know what? Emotions won't be trapped. They'll burst out when you least expect it. If you bury them, they'll come out in your body and make you sick. You have to feel them, acknowledge them, and then let them go. Emotions are energy, Tapakah, and energy needs to flow.'

He nodded. I sensed the emotion running through his body.

'Yes, you're right.'

'So, have you told me everything about the man I love?'

His eyes locked on to mine, and again I felt the intense connection. He appeared surprised. 'You're saying you *love* me? Really love me. After everything I've told you?'

'Yes.'

He closed his eyes and took a sharp breath. The sound seemed to emanate from his whole body. When he opened his eyes again, he was quiet for a while.

'Tapakah?'

I felt frightened. He wasn't being honest. I asked him again. 'Tell me. Now do I know *everything*?'

I was lost in his gaze. He seemed hesitant to answer, and I sensed an enormous internal struggle.

'I want to be honest. And the answer is … no. No, you don't know everything, and right now I … I'm not ready to tell you.'

I wasn't stupid. I could work it out. He did say I wouldn't

have liked who he was in the past. The things he'd done. How bad were they? Were we talking tax evasion or murder? Genetic engineering had possibilities for crossing the line. Big time. That had to be it. What he'd done must have been bad, and the reason he wouldn't tell me was because I would walk.

But where the hell would I walk to? The thought of remembering my past life filled me with fear. A terror so intense it led me to the conclusion my old life was best left dead and buried. Starting from nothing, I had the opportunity to be with this incredible creature. If he was pure human, then perhaps he wouldn't be able to change. I knew, for humans, past behaviour was the best predictor of future behaviour. But Tapakah wasn't human.

I took his hand. 'I know the reason you won't tell me is because you're afraid I'll leave. What level of badness are we talking about here, murder or tax evasion?'

'I can't answer that.'

'You just did. Christ. That means both and maybe more.'

'I've bought an apartment for you in Port Melbourne, and a home in the country. Simple, energy efficient, exactly what you like. They're in your name, no strings attached. You won't have to see me again. You can start a new life, maybe find your old one.'

'Hell. You've got it all worked out, haven't you? But I just said I love you. You said you love me. I can't go. What would I go *to*? There's nothing out there for me. No matter what your previous level of badness was, I must trust you're different now. You *are* different, aren't you?'

'Yes. I am.'

'I have a choice. I'm choosing to stay. To trust you. Tell me more when you're ready. There are so many unknowns on so many levels it's mind-boggling. I'm prepared to take it day by day, to go with the flow. I can't control anything, just how I respond to what happens. My head wants to spin out of control, with imaginings, but I'm reigning it in, bringing it back to right here, right now, with the you that I know. That's what I choose to do, until further notice. If that's okay with you … I mean if—'

Tapakah touched my arm to interrupt me.

'I'm babbling, aren't I?'

He nodded. His face filled with a soft joy, an expression I'd never seen on him before. Even his eyes changed; they were warm and alive. I'd noticed with each passing day his face had gained more expressive qualities.

'I love you, Maggie. I will honour your trust. We will take it day by day. I am humbled you love me after everything. It's incredible.'

After *everything*. The word rang in my mind. What *was* "everything"? I guess if Tapakah wouldn't tell, time would.

I extended my hand and smiled. 'It appears, until further notice, we are partners in crime.'

He took my hand, pulled me into his arms and kissed me. His passion was overwhelming. I matched it pound for pound. The world disappeared as I dissolved into his embrace.

How was I to know?

It was a kiss of consequence. A kiss and a choice that would decide my fate.

---

[5] *Maggie's Playlist: Bad Choice — Kathy Valentine*

Chapter 5: Boo Brainwave

With all the time I'd spent here, Maggie and Jason's house felt like home. I sat at their kitchen table staring into my cold coffee, and wished they were here. Fox leant back in his chair, feet on the table, and stared at the ceiling. Drom's eyes were glued to his phone, probably reading his second book for the day. Luca sat opposite me, elbows on the table, chin resting in his hands which were in a prayer position.

Ashley, I don't have a mobile phone. Boo's voice was in my brain.

I jumped. Crikey. I'd almost forgotten Boo could speak — in our heads, anyway. Not out loud, like a Disney dog, but telepathically. She still sounded exactly like Prince Charles. I didn't remind her of the fact, as it pissed her off. As a girl dog, she would have preferred to sound like the Queen.

Yeah, I know that, Boo. You're a dog. You can't use one. Your point is?

Well, I didn't get a warning from Tapakah.

Fox, Drom, Luca and I exchanged looks. They could hear Boo too.

Drom smiled. 'You goddamn beauty of a mutt. What a little pearler! That's it! That's the plan. It's *Boo*.'

I'm smart, aren't I?

Hell yeah, Boo. Tapakah is clueless regarding you and your powers. What harm can a dog do? You can keep tabs on Maggie. It's brilliant!

Fox looked happier than I'd seen him in ages. He grabbed Boo and kissed the top of her head. 'Boo could make like a stray and worm her way into Maggie's heart. Get adopted. She'd be our spy. Get right into the heart of things.'

Boo looked embarrassed. I'm sure she was blushing under all that fur.

I've always wanted to be a spy. Boo Bond. License to kill.

'But do you choose to accept the mission, Boo? It'll be dangerous,' I said.

I certainly accept the mission, and I don't think it will be dangerous.

'Are we sure Tapakah isn't wise to Boo?' Drom asked.

'Hmmm. Not one hundred percent sure, now I think about it,' I said. 'If he did, I don't reckon he'd be savvy to her powers and ability to fly. She'd be just a dog to him.'

I'm willing to take the risk. We have no choice. If he sees any of you lot go near her, there's no telling what he'd do. And it probably wouldn't be to you, it would be to someone you love. That's his MO.

'No doubt there,' Fox said.

I think it's a win-win all round. I can't wait to see Maggie. I miss her so much.

We nodded in agreement.

'It would be therapeutic for her to have you around, Boo. It may help restore her memory,' Luca said.

'Maybe Boo could bring Maggie a crystal,' the Prof suggested.

Drom looked straight at me as he replied. 'Yes, but we need to find her first, and we'd have to be careful. If her memory is restored, she could freak out, and if Tapakah finds out, who knows what could happen. We may not like it, but she's probably safer right there with him, than she was with us.'

I reluctantly acknowledged the truth. 'Yeah, yeah. I get it, Dromski. I just worry if she says she loves him … I hope he … they … don't, you know … haven't.'

Bella looked horrified. 'Oh jeepers, don't even go there.'

'I go there all the time.'

The Maestro put her hand on my shoulder. 'Don't be miserable, Ash. They haven't. At least when we saw them, they hadn't.'

A rush of adrenaline coursed through my body. 'How the hell do you know that?' I tried to restrain the excitement in my voice.

'Sex is our food, you know that, and I didn't get a sense of any recent coupling between them. I can smell it, sense it. I'm never wrong.'

Bella turned red. 'Jesus.'

The Maestro laughed. 'You have nothing to worry about. There's nothing going on with you lot either. Well, most of you.' She gave the Prof a wink. 'Beats me how you survive.'

Fox sighed. 'Ain't that the truth.'

The relief must have shown on my face. The Maestro hugged me and kissed my forehead. My whole body tingled. She had that effect on everyone.

'You're not messing with me are you, Maestro? Just saying it to make me feel better?'

'I wouldn't do that to you,' she whispered. 'I know what Maggie means to you.'

'I can't tell you how happy it makes me feel. I may even be able to sleep tonight.'

The Maestro rubbed my back. She loved touching people. I reckon she sucked energy from us that way as well. I didn't mind; it felt good.

She chuckled to herself. 'You humans and your sexuality. I still can't relate. I mean would it *really* matter if the two of them got it off together?'

'That question is so wrong on so many levels that I'm not even going to bother going there. But actually, yes, it would bloody well matter. A human and an insect hybrid. What would be the result of *that*?' I removed her arms from around me and walked away.

Christos entered the room looking sleepy and dishevelled. 'He has a point, Maestro.'

Christos was still trying to adapt to planet Earth. He'd had to learn how to eat food for energy, instead of screwing anything and everything in sight. The only thing he could tolerate, food wise, was Bella's lasagna. He would've liked to tolerate Bella, but the Maestro had warned him to stay away from us. We were a no-go zone. Except for Luca, who had just come out of the closet, helped by a passionate encounter with Christos. Bella was more than willing to give herself to Christos, as it seemed her marriage to Liam was on the rocks. We'd taken bets they'd hook up, but Boo had foiled Christos just in time.

Christos parked his massive frame on a kitchen chair. He was solid muscle, not an ounce of fat on him. The chair creaked in protest. 'I would need to smell him. Then I could tell.'

'Tell what?' Bella asked him.

'If DNA a bad match.'

I glanced at the Maestro. 'Wow. Can you do that too?'

'No, only Sonusian males have that ability. They can detect DNA matching in anything. I can only detect it for myself.'

'Why would that be?'

'Because they are the guardians of our DNA. No one couples with someone who doesn't have the right DNA match. If it does happen, and defective offspring are generated, they are eliminated.'

'Eliminated?' Fox said.

'Yes, eradicated. Destroyed,' Christos said.

Luca looked dismayed. 'What, *all* of them? Parents, children?'

'Yes. It is law. Through this, our race is vibrant and healthy, unlike yours.'

'Crikey,' Bella said. 'No one gets sick, has disease?'

'It's a rarity,' the Maestro said.

31

'Ha, can you imagine that happening here?' Drom said. 'Eighty percent of the planet would be wiped out. Our gene pool is trashed.'

'Yes, well, once upon a time someone did have a go at trying to create a pure race,' Luca said.

'Really, who was it?' Christos asked. He wasn't fully up to speed with Earth history.

'Adolf Hitler. World War Two,' Drom replied.

'What happened?' Christos asked. 'Good plan to make strong, healthy race?'

'The plan didn't fly,' Bella said.

'Anyone planning to try again?' Christos asked.

'We hope not,' everyone said simultaneously.

Christos looked confused. It tended to be his go to expression since arriving on our planet. He found Earth, or at least its inhabitants, extremely perplexing.

What I found equally bloody perplexing was the fact that, currently, our major weapon in the fight against Tapakah and the Dark Force was a beagle, cocker spaniel cross who spoke like Prince Charles.

---

6 *Maggie's Playlist: Me and You and a Dog Named Boo — Lobo*

Chapter 6: Secret Agent K9

It was our regular Sunday breakfast meeting at Maggie and Jason's house. All the musketeers were present — except Jason and Maggie, of course — and Bella and I had cooked up a storm.

Maggie would have loved it. We had all her favourite things — free range bacon, eggs, chipolatas, hash browns, grilled tomatoes, sautéed mushrooms with parsley and garlic, and homemade baked beans. Jason would've been in heaven too, if he wasn't already.

I peeked under the table and saw Boo and Schmoo snuggled up together between everyone's feet. Boo was resting her head on Schmoo's back. Their eyes were open, but their gaze was soft and distant as they relished each other's body contact.

I envied those two dogs. I thought back to the time when Maggie, Drom, Jasmine and I were hunting crystals in Gippsland. Exhausted and grieving, Maggie and I found comfort in each other's arms. Just simple human contact and affection. Though by God I would have loved to have … wanted to … but she'd just lost Jason. That moment together had got us both through. Now Jasmine was dead, and probably Jason too, and Maggie was in the clutches of that evil, alien roach. What a missed opportunity. I should've done it — loved her the way I'd always wanted to. But I'd been trying to do the right thing, and now she was lost to me — gone.

Bella looked at me worriedly. 'Penny for your thoughts.'

'You wouldn't want to go there.'

'I can imagine,' she said sadly.

Bella had made a fresh batch of lasagna for Christos. That woman had as much heart as her sister Maggie, and I'd happily die for the both of them.

Fox munched away on a piece of toast. 'How are we going to find Maggie? The Maestro device isn't picking up her life force, and we're not getting any radio waves. I try and tune into her mind constantly, but I get nothing.'

'Same here,' Drom said.

'Yes, we're all trying, twenty-four seven,' the Professor said.

Boo's voice sounded in our heads. *I can track her, but it may take a while, especially without a general area to start with.*

Drom leant back in his chair, balancing on two chair legs. 'It's an excellent idea to use Boo as a spy, but useless if we can't find Maggie to begin with.'

I reached over to the side table and picked up the ginormous Melway and plonked it on the table. 'She's in there somewhere. She's in Melbourne.'

Drom laughed. 'Hell, I haven't used a street directory in years.'

Everyone looked at me like I'd lost it. Bella stared at me sceptically. 'How the hell do you know she's in Melbourne?'

'I sat up last night with Jason's old atlas and tried to tune into her. I knew Tapakah could have taken her anywhere in the world, so that's where I started.

I looked at a map of every country in the world and nothing resonated like Australia. Then, I progressed state by state, narrowing it down to Victoria, and then suburb by suburb. She's somewhere in the CBD. I know it.'

'But you've never been psychic,' Luca pointed out.

'Maggie and I have a special connection. Something happened between us which created a link. It's not my imagination; I can feel it.'

'What happened?' Bella asked.

Drom looked at me knowingly.

I was deliberately vague. There was no way I was going to tell them *that* story, particularly as Jason was there at the time. 'I'm not exactly sure. It must have been during one of our mind melds, perhaps the time when I smashed into her brain and killed Tapakah.'

'Pity he didn't stay dead,' Fox said.

'Yeah, I wish. When I narrowed it to Melbourne CBD, I was sceptical myself. Why would Tapakah bring her back to her hometown? And then I figured, he would've thought it would be the last place we'd look.'

'I hope you're right,' Drom said. 'We have nothing else to go on, so we may as well follow your hunch.'

'Boo and I are going to start as soon as we've finished breakfast. We're going to make the CBD our home until we find her. With Boo's nose and my spidey sense we've got to get lucky. I've booked a hotel in the city, and I ain't coming back until I've found her.'

'How exactly are you going to proceed?' Drom asked.

'Once we're in the city we'll narrow it further, going street by street until we've covered every inch of the place.'

Bella pointed to a stack of photos I'd put on the sideboard. 'What are you doing with those?'

'I'm going to make an album for Maggie. If there's an opportunity, I'll get it to her, along with a note saying to keep it hidden from you know who. If she sees the photos of her with us, of her past life, it has to trigger something, even if it's just curiosity.'

'That's dangerous,' Bella said. 'You read the warning from Tapakah. You could be putting our lives at risk.'

'Well, what do you want me to do? Nothing?'

'No. Of course not. It's a risk we have to take, are willing to take. Just be careful.'

'I'm going to go in disguise, like we did in Gippsland. That worked a treat. I won't be strolling around advertising I'm there, no way.'

'Sorry, I'm just … terrified really.'

I knelt on the floor in front of her chair. Bella reached out and we hugged. Her tears ran down the side of my neck.

'Bella, I promise you, I will get your sister back, and I won't let anything happen to you, okay? I promise.'

She was probably thinking, *that's what you said to Maggie*. But of course, she didn't. Instead, she kissed me on the forehead. 'If anyone can do it, you can, Ashley.'

She was Maggie's blood all right.

Fox raised his coffee cup. 'Well, here's to Sleuth Berringer and Secret Agent K9, the dynamic duo.'

Everyone laughed and clinked cups. You had to grab a laugh whenever you could these days; they were getting as scarce as hen's teeth.

---

[7] *Maggie's Playlist: Secret Agent — Rory Gallagher*

I picked up the iPhone Tapakah had given me and looked at my contacts. I had three. Tapakah, Frank and Billy. That was the extent of my world.

No wonder I was lonely. Billy was at school, Tapakah and Frank were at work, leaving me to rattle around in Tapakah's huge terrace house in East Melbourne. I had no idea where Tapakah's work was. He couldn't divulge the location of his secret lab, otherwise it wouldn't be a secret, and he'd have to kill me. Well, he was joking of course. But there was only so much time I could spend keeping house. Everything was as clean as a whistle.

I opened my laptop and Googled "Maggie McLaine" to see if any images of me came up. Nothing. I searched Tapakah, Frank and Billy. Nothing. I hadn't forgotten the names of the four people who'd tried to kidnap us, so I searched for them too: Ashley, Drom, Fox and the Maestro. Same deal. Nothing.

Weird. Surely Tapakah would show up online. I made a mental note to ask him.

The walls started to close in on me. I had to get out. I pulled on my boots, grabbed my satchel and headed out the door.

I walked to the corner of the street and saw a tram coming. I dashed across the road to the stop and hopped on. Destination CBD.

As I looked out the window, everything seemed strange but familiar at the same time. Tapakah said they'd found me under a bridge in Melbourne, so I must've lived here. Maybe. Maybe not.

It was going to take time to build a new life, make friends, discover the world again. Learn who I was. The tram stopped and I decided to jump off at random. I stood at the busy intersection pondering which way to go.

Up the hill. I needed exercise. People rushed past me. City commuters clutched mega jumbo coffees in one hand and phones in the other. Corporate suits, shiny leather shoes, high heels clicked by. The herd stopped at the lights. Heads down. Fingers flicked over phones. Their faces reflected disconnection, despite everyone being connected. They shared a homogenised, fixed expression of grim blandness as though no other countenance was available. The children accompanying their parents weren't immune either.

Crikey, had I worked here once? Was I like them? No wonder I'd tried to commit suicide.

The bleakness drove me down a laneway. Coffee. That's what I needed. I'd find a nice spot in a coffee shop, and just sit in the corner while I tried to get my bearings. I wouldn't order a mega jumbo coffee in case it turned me into one of those robots out on the street.

I stood in the doorway of a café and peeked in. It felt warm and welcoming, decked out with plenty of wood, distressed paint and a smiling barista. He caught my eye and beckoned me with a nod of his head. I stepped through the door, and the ceiling made me laugh out loud. A jumble of chairs hung from the roof and ran the entire length of the building. Wooden, painted, metal, wire, square, round, old new — all shapes and colours. It was as if a giant had sneezed and the chairs had landed on the ceiling.

I loved this. I could sit and count them.

Why the hell would I want to do *that*? I had no idea, but the urge was strong.

'What can I get you, sweetheart?' the barista asked.

'Flat white, please.'

'I'll bring it over. Grab a chair.' I looked up at the ceiling and he laughed. 'Those are off limits.'

The barista was friendly, the café was lovely, and I started to feel better. If the coffee was as good as it smelt, this might well be my new home. I wonder if I'd been here before.

'How long has this café been here?' I asked the barista as he put my coffee on the table. The coffee looked perfect, and he'd drawn a love heart in the crema.

'Three years, but it's under new ownership. I've had it for six months.'

'I love the chairs.'

'I hope you like the coffee too.' He smiled and headed back to the counter.

Six months. If I'd been here before, probably no one would know me now.

It was obvious I loved coffee. Maybe I could spend my time going into every coffee shop in the city. Perhaps one day, someone would say, 'Hey, Maggie, great to see you! Where have you been?' I would tell them what happened, and maybe they could tell me about myself.

On the other hand, the idea of finding out my past filled me with fear, yet I had no idea why. Perhaps I should just push through the fear. At least it would give me something to do, and I so needed something to occupy myself.

A coffee shop search wasn't such a silly idea. How else could I find out who I was? I had to get lucky at some stage. People ran into each other all the time. Surely, it was only a matter of time before I bumped into someone who knew me. Decision made. That's what I'd do. I felt happier. I was obviously a woman who liked to have a plan, a mission.

The café was so lovely I decided to have another coffee. Jeepers, if I did that in every café, I'd be wired as hell by the time I arrived home.

Outside the window, the world rushed by as I flicked through a newspaper. It was all bad news — murder, mayhem and every variation thereof. I threw the paper to one side in disgust and stared out again.

A small dog poked its head through the café door. Holding its nose high, it sniffed the air, fixing large dark eyes on the tiny lemon tarts on the counter.

It resembled a beagle with the long soft ears, but it was prettier than a beagle. More petite. It was black, white and tan, shorthaired, except for its ears, which sported a fringe of long hair at the ends. The fringes fluttered in the breeze and caught the light. What a gorgeous creature.

The dog sat in the doorway, two mournful eyes glistening under raised eyebrows, as it slowly raised a paw.

'Is that your dog?' I asked the barista.

He came out from behind the counter. 'No. Never seen him before. Check out the sad face. Looks like he has a sore paw.'

I slowly approached the dog. 'I think he has his eye on your lemon tarts.' I bent down and gently examined his paw.

'Phffft!' The dog gave a loud sneeze, jumped and pushed me over. I landed on my bum on the floor, and it licked me all over my face.

I laughed and pushed him away. 'Yuk! Bleah! Dog Germs.'

The barista extended a hand to help me up. 'You've won a heart there. I don't blame him.'

Oh wow. Was he flirting with me, even though I looked like an escapee from *Mad Max?*

A grin spread across my face. Maybe I'd found a new friend. Well, I'd definitely made one new friend, I decided, looking down at the dog sitting on my foot.

The barista patted him. 'No collar or ID. Must be a stray. He's in top notch condition, though. Maybe been microchipped?'

I bent and stroked the dog's silky ears. 'I'm going to take him to a vet and see if I can find the owner.' The dog jumped up again and licked me right in the earhole.

'Would you like one of those little lemon tarts?' I asked it. The dog looked intently into my eyes. 'I know they're not good for you, but just as a special treat. You've had your eye on them, haven't you?'

The dog's face broke into a crazy grin, revealing a pink tongue and perfect white teeth. He sat up in a flawless beg.

I giggled. 'He's a canine meerkat.'

He had big paws for a small dog, light tan fur with perfect black nails. His back was as straight as a ramrod, and the fur from his white chest came together in a cute little curl in the middle. I swear he made his eyes grow even bigger as he pricked his ears and tilted his head slightly to one side.

The barista took out a tiny lemon tart and gave it to the dog. 'Oh my God. How could you resist that?' He grinned at me. 'It's on the house.'

The dog took the tart gently from his hand, and its eyes closed in delight as it savoured the sweet morsel.

'That went down a treat,' I said. 'By the way, what's your name?'

'Ben.'

I held out my hand. 'I'm Maggie.'

He shook it. 'Pleased to meet you.' His grip was warm and firm. Always a good sign. I liked him.

'I have a piece of rope out the back you can use as a temporary lead.'

'That would be helpful. We have a vet nearby I can take him to.'

Ben checked out the dog's nether region. 'I think it's a she, not a he.'

The dog immediately sat. I giggled at the expression on her face. 'She looks embarrassed.'

'What are you going to call her?' Ben asked.

I wanted to link her name to the coffee shop somehow. 'I don't know. What about, Beans?'

'Okay, Beans, I'll go get some rope.' Ben headed off out the back.

Beans wiggled her bum and made herself more comfortable. She was using my foot as a chair. What a funny creature.

Ben returned and tied the rope around Bean's neck. He handed me the end. 'There you go.'

I gently extracted my foot from under her bum. 'Come on, Beans, let's see if we can find out who you belong to.'

Beans stood and hobbled to the door.

'That's a bad limp,' Ben said. 'She wasn't stacking it on.'

'Yes, there's no way I can walk back to my place with her limping like that, and you're not allowed to take dogs on trams. I'll have to carry her.' I scooped her up and took a few steps forward. 'Crikey, you're bloody heavy for a little dog.'

'How far away do you live?' Ben asked.

'Well, the tram ride to the city took ten minutes, and then it took another ten to get here.'

'There's no way you can carry her that far.'

'I know, I'll get a taxi.'

'They're not keen on dogs in cabs either. Tell you what, if you wait five minutes, I have two more staff coming in. I'll give you a lift back. My car's outside.'

'Really? That would be fantastic.'

'No worries. My pleasure.'

As soon as the staff arrived, Ben, Beans and I headed off.

Outside, Ben opened the door to a beautifully restored old Holden.

'Oh my God, what a cool car. I used to go out with a guy

who had one of these, same colour, yellow with black stripes.' I froze on the spot, stunned by the memory that had flashed into my barren mind.

'It's a 308 Holden HQ GTS two door Monaro.' Ben stared at me. 'Are you okay?'

'Um … yes. It's a long story. I'll give you the potted version on the way.' I picked up Beans and slid into the front seat. Ben jumped in and started the car. It burst into life with its classic, throaty rumble, and we roared off down the road. Beans sat on my knee; eyes fixed on the road ahead.

Ben grinned. 'She's into it.'

I laughed. 'So am I.'

Who'd have thought a car would trigger a precious memory. It wasn't much, a mere snippet, but something had flowered in the bleakness of my brain.

'So, what was with the shocked expression back there?' Ben asked, after I finished explaining where our house was.

'I have amnesia. Something happened to me, and I've no recollection of my life. Who I was, where I lived, family, friends, nothing. My memories go back a few weeks. That's it. The extent of my life. Your car, it triggered a memory. Just a flash. It's the first memory I've had.'

'Jesus, I'm sorry. I can't imagine what that would be like. I feel honoured my car gave you back a memory.'

'Yes, it gives me hope. The car is amazing, by the way. Did you restore it yourself?'

'Yes, it's a hobby. I'm a bit of a petrolhead.'

'A barista and a mechanic. Good combo.'

'Yeah, the mechanical genes come from Dad, and coffee is in our blood.'

'Italian?'

'Yep.'

'Here will be fine, Ben, there's a car park right outside. Thank you so much.' I fiddled around, trying to open the door. 'I'll let you know what happens with Beans.'

'I'll get the door for you,' he said, leaping out.

Ben opened the door, took Beans, and gently put her on the ground. He offered his hand, which I took it, and he pulled me from the car.

I stood rubbing my leg trying to encourage the circulation. 'My leg's gone to sleep from Beans sitting on it.'

The sound of raucous voices interrupted us, and a group of six drunken yobbos wandered around the corner from the pub nearby. They staggered past and one of them bumped into me. He patted my head and ran his hand over my hair. 'Groovy haircut. Love the fuckin' designs.'

He hung over me, his breath reeking of alcohol. He could barely stand, let alone speak. I pushed him away in disgust. 'Get off me!'

He flew back quicker than a boomerang. 'Hey, girly, don't be like that.' He lunged at my groin. 'You bald there too?'

A fist flew past my ear, and I heard the sound of bone hitting flesh. Drunk man's face rattled with the G-force of Ben's punch. His mouth flattened out across his face, and his bottom lip exploded, spraying me with blood.

The man's mates turned around, and from the looks on their faces, they were up for a fight as they stumbled towards us.

'Oh shit. We're in trouble now,' I said.

Drunk man staggered to his feet and came back for seconds. 'You said it, sweet cheeks. Nuffin' better than a bit of a rumble. You got nice tits, girly.'

'Back off,' I said.

He reached out to grab me. 'Come here, little darlin'.'

I delivered a hard, swift kick to his groin. Snapped it out. *Bang!* He hit the asphalt like a sack of spuds. He wasn't getting up anytime soon.

The other men surrounded Ben, circling warily around him. No one was game to make the first move. I scrabbled in my bag for a phone to call the police, but then stopped. There was no point. By the time they arrived, it'd be too late.

The men pressed in closer. Ben made a move and lashed out with a backwards kick to the guts of Drunk Number Two. An elbow to the head took out Drunk Number Three.

Drunk Number Four whipped out a knife. Quick smart, Ben kicked his legs out from under him. The bloke's head hit the pavement with a sickening thud, and the knife clattered across the concrete.

Drunk Number Five wasn't as drunk as the others, but he was one big mother. He grabbed Ben in a chokehold while Drunk Number Six moved in for the kill.

I ripped out a star picket from the nature strip and whacked Drunk Number Six across the head. As he crumpled faster than an old lady on a hot day, it occurred to me I could possibly play a mean game of baseball. Maybe I did. Who knew?

Drunk Number Five was ramping up the pressure on Ben's neck. I had a feeling of déjà vu. This was a no-win situation. I couldn't get at the guy to do any damage. The bloke was so mammoth Ben's blows had little to no effect. Judging by the colour of Ben's face, he was ready to black out.

There was a peculiar low rumbling noise, and Beans — with rocket-powered haunches — launched herself at the big drunk, landed on his shoulder and latched onto his ear. How a little dog managed to jump so high I had no idea.

The drunk's broad shoulders provided a stable platform for her to do her work. And her work, it seemed, was to try and detach one large ear from one large, Neolithic head. The guy screamed in agony as Beans played tug of war with his ear. He raised an arm to deal with the attacker, and it was all Ben needed to extract himself from those massive arms. Ben dropped to the ground, turned and delivered a powerful flick kick to the man's groin.

He folded over in agony, clutching at his shattered

appendages, then lurched forward, pitching Beans off his shoulder at speed.

Taken by surprise, Beans neglected to disengage her teeth, and took his rather large ear along with her for the ride. The cartilage cracked as it detached from his head.

My hands flew to my mouth as she fell. It was a long drop for a little dog. Time slowed — it had to be the adrenaline — and she appeared to float gently to the ground. Alighting softly on the pavement, she sat with the bloody ear hanging out of her mouth. Head cocked, she met my gaze and displayed her trophy. She appeared extremely pleased with herself.

Was she going to eat it? She had a look in her eye that made me think she might scoff it down any minute. Really, the bloke would want his ear back. They could sew it on. I'd better retrieve it.

I spoke sweetly. 'Come on, Beans. Good dog. Give Maggie the ear.'

Beans gave me a look and turned her head. The look said, 'There ain't a snowball's hope in hell you're taking my prize off me.'

'Good dog, come on. I'll get you another lemon tart. It'll be much nicer than a yucky old ear.'

Bean's head spun around and her ears pricked up when she heard the words *lemon tart*. Ah ha. I'd found her weakness.

'We can do a trade, Beans. One lemon tart for one ear.'

Ben ambled over to us, rubbing his neck. Beans tilted her head to one side and showed interest in my offer but was still reluctant to part with the ear.

I knelt in front of her. 'How about *two* lemon tarts for one ear? Now that's a really good deal.'

'I have two lemon tarts in the car,' Ben said. 'I was going to give them to you for "ron".' He opened the car door and took out a brown paper bag.

'Excellent! Okay, Beans, we'll do the trade?'

Beans hesitated for a second and put the ear on the ground. I placed the two lemon tarts nearby.

Beans sprang into action, leapt on the tarts, and then tried to grab back the ear. I must've had a dog before, so I knew that move. Way ahead of Beans, I snatched the ear from under her nose and raced over to felled Drunk Number Five, who was still on the ground groaning. I tucked the ear into his jacket pocket and yelled, 'Hey, mate, *focus*! Your ear's in your pocket. Tell the paramedics.'

Ben was on the phone calling an ambulance. I opened the gate to Tapakah's house. 'Come on, let's get out of here before the others come to.'

Beans skipped ahead of me, ran up to the front door and stood there wagging her tail. She was busting her chops to get inside. Ben was somewhat slower. He'd taken a couple of solid whacks.

'Come into the kitchen and I'll clean you up. Are you okay?'

'Yeah, I'm fine. Those karate lessons finally came in handy. I was a bit rusty though, slow on my feet. You look like you've taken the brunt of it. You're covered in blood.'

'It's not my blood. I'm fine. You were amazing. You've saved my bacon. Thank you.'

'I couldn't have done it without Beans stepping in.' Ben gave Beans a good scratch behind the ears. She closed her eyes and scrunched up her face as if he'd really hit the right spot.

'I know. I still can't believe what she did.'

He grinned. 'Well, we know her currency of barter now. Lemon tarts. One ear is worth two of 'em.'

I laughed. 'It's hilarious. Well, not for the drunk bloke. At least I know a reliable supplier of lemon tarts now.' I picked up a clean cloth and began wiping the blood off Ben's face.

He checked his watch. 'Shit. I've got to get back. They'll be wondering what's happened. 'Here, let me.' He took the cloth and gently wiped the blood from my face and neck. He screwed up his face. 'I think I'm going to have nightmares about the ear.'

'Oh, that's nothing.'

He seemed shocked. 'What do you mean that's *nothing*? It was bloody awful.'

I paused, trying to find something in my brain I could reference. Why the hell had I said that?

'I have no idea why that came out of my mouth. Of course, it's awful. What could be more awful than seeing someone's ear ripped off?'

A feeling of dread washed over me.

Ben studied my face intently. 'I get the feeling you've seen much worse.'

'You may be right.' The wail of sirens drowned me out. 'The ambos are here. I think you should wait until the coast is clear. Call the café. It shouldn't be too long. I reckon the thugs will clear off ASAP. They're not going to hang around in case the cops show up.'

'Good idea.' Ben tip-toed to the window and peeked through the blinds.

'Can I get you something to drink?'

'What have you got?'

'Pretty much everything, I think.'

'A beer?'

'VB?'

'That'd be great. I've worked up a thirst.'

'No wonder.' I opened the fridge and handed him a cold one. 'Glass?'

'No thanks.' He drained half the stubby in two seconds flat. 'Hey, you knew how to handle yourself out there. What's with that?'

'I don't know.'

'Oh yeah, of course, sorry.'

'It's weird. I know things, but I don't know how I know them. I found out I can use a gun too.'

Oh shit. I shouldn't have said that.

Ben looked taken aback. 'How on earth did you find that out?'

Alert. Alert. Emergency subject change required.

I hightailed it over to the window. 'Look, everyone's gone. It's safe to go. Take these paracetamol tablets with you; you might need them.'

'Thanks. Will you be all right here, on your own?'

'Fine. They didn't see where we went. Plus, I have attack dog Beans. Thanks again, Ben. Sorry for all the trouble.'

He opened the front door and regarded me with gentle green eyes. 'Hardly your fault.' His dark hair fell in soft waves around his face. He had well-formed lips, which turned up slightly at the corners. His gaze made me feel self-conscious.

'What?'

'Will I see you again?' he asked.

'Definitely. I'll need more lemon tarts.'

He flashed me a cheeky grin. 'Anytime you need a lemon tart, come and see me. I'll fix you up. Ciao, Bella.'

'Ciao, Ben.'

I closed the door and leaned back, taking a deep breath. At my feet, a little dog stared up at me with large, intense eyes. All the talk about lemon tarts must've got her hot under the collar. I felt that way myself. The Monaro thundered off, and my heart rattled with the windows.

I wandered back to the kitchen to make a cup of tea. I could really go a lemon tart right now.

---

[8] *Maggie's Playlist: Barista — Pamela Machala*

"One who has no love in his heart will try to possess everything for himself. One who has love in his heart is ready to sacrifice everything, including his own body, for the benefit of others." — *Thiruvalluvar*

'Beans! Beans, come!' I yelled down the hallway. 'Beans?'

Nothing. Silence.

Where the hell had she gone? I checked downstairs, upstairs, in every nook and cranny, but Beans was nowhere to be found.

The doors and windows were closed, except for the door to the upstairs balcony, and I'd looked out there. There were no gaps, and the iron lacework balustrade was too high for her to have gone over the edge.

It was a mystery. She must be in the house, hiding somewhere. She'd probably come out when she was hungry.

I yelled out once more. 'Lemon tarts!'

Nothing.

Oh, well. Now what?

I heard the rattle of a key in the front door and then footsteps along the hall. My heart started to thump, and I seized a knife from the kitchen bench.

A tall figure appeared in the doorway. He eyed off the large knife in my hand. 'Hell, Maggie, that's some greeting. Man comes home after a hard day's work to be faced with a knife wielding woman.'

'Tapakah! You're early. Sorry 'bout that. I didn't know who it was.' I returned the knife to the bench.

'Who else would have house keys?'

'Just Billy. I'm a bit jumpy is all.'

'I understand.' He strode over and held me tight. I could hear his heart beating in his chest. It felt so wonderful to be in his arms that I wanted to stay there forever. 'Why home so early?'

Tapakah's hands moved over my body. 'I wanted to see you.' He held my face and kissed me deep and hard. The blood rushed from my head and I felt faint.

I held the side of the bench to steady myself, and as I came up for air Tapakah said, 'You like?'

I fanned myself with my hand. 'Oh, my word, I like.'

Going back for more, I pushed him up against the fridge. His body was taut and muscular, and his bum was tight under my hands. I wanted him and I wanted him now. I undid his belt and tried to undo the button on his trousers. Tapakah grabbed my wrists and moved my hands away.

'*What?*' I was going to die of frustration. My body ached for him.

'No. I want to wait.'

'Wait for what?'

'The right time.'

'And when would that be, exactly? It's a good time right now. Billy won't be home for hours.' I opened the buttons on his shirt and ran my hands over his flesh. He had just the right amount of chest hair. I nuzzled my face against his chest and inhaled his scent. I sucked his nipple and he gasped, arching his back.

'Maggie, no. Not now.'

'You don't want me.' I felt rejected as he gently pushed me away. 'You're a tease. This is killing me. I think I should report you for cruelty.'

'I want you more than anything. More than you know.' His face was flushed. He ran a hand through his hair.

I moved in to try again. 'So, what's the problem? You want

me. I want you. Simple.'

He took my hands away from his body and held them tight.

'I want to wait for the right time.'

'So you said. And when the hell would that be?'

'When we're married.'

'You've got to be kidding me. I can't wait that long! And what if I don't want to marry you? I'm not even sure I'm the marrying kind. And say we do tie the knot and find out we're not sexually compatible. What then?

'Maybe you want sex once a month, and I want it every day. Or vice versa. You might be lousy in bed, or maybe weird. I mean, you are only half human. And you might find I don't really do it for you. You may need a lady bug. I mean it's old fashioned. We're not Christians or living in the Victorian era. I don't mean to be rude, Tapakah, but waiting is a crazy idea. I do love you, and I'm flattered you want to marry me and everything, that's lovely, I'm not saying it's a bad thing, it's just—'

Tapakah put a finger against my mouth.

I mumbled through the finger. 'I'm babbling, aren't I?'

He nodded, took me by the hand and sat me at the kitchen table. He pulled up a chair. 'Maggie, listen, don't talk. Let me explain.'

'Okay.' I ran a finger and thumb across my lip to zip it.

'As I've said before, I've made mistakes. I've done many things I regret. Too many. With you, I want to do the right thing. I love you, and I want it to be special. It may seem old fashioned, but I want to court you. Give you time to really get to know me. After everything I've … after everything you've been through, it needs to be perfect. It's why I want to wait until we're wed. Until you're my bride. Does that make sense?' His dark eyes fixed on mine and he was silent.

Well, that was all very lovely, but he hadn't answered my concerns regarding compatibility. I wasn't sure if I wanted to be a bride. I had a vague feeling I wasn't that sort of girl. I couldn't be sure, but the whole wedding thing didn't set my pulse racing. Whereas, he definitely did. And what sort of time frame were we talking about? A twelve-month engagement, two years? Jesus Christ, I'd go insane.

'Maggie?'

'Can I talk now?'

He nodded. I would make a special effort not to babble. To keep it short and succinct, to condense what I had to say to its most important elements. I took a breath. 'Can you clarify exactly what it is I have to wait for?'

Tapakah looked puzzled. 'What do you mean?'

See, that was what came from trying not to babble. He didn't have a clue what I was talking about.

'You said you want to wait until after we're married. I need clarification on exactly what it is we have to wait for.'

He looked at me like I'd lost my mind. 'To make love, of course.'

'Okay, and your definition of making love is?'

'What the hell are you on about?'

'I'm sorry, Tapakah, I was trying not to babble, but I need to. You said we should wait until we're married. Does that mean I must wait until then … for the whole consummation thing and everything else that goes with it, or is there stuff we can do before, like share a bed, sleep together, meaning *sleep* only, lie naked in each other's arms, explore each other's bodies, have oral sex, or use sex toys on each other. I mean we already kiss and touch, so are we allowed to kiss and touch lying down, with no clothes on?'

His eyes grew bigger as I spoke. His Adam's apple moved as he swallowed. He took off his tie, undid the top buttons of his shirt and pulled the material away from his body. He swallowed again as I continued.

'If we're in the kitchen, can I unzip your trousers and, you know, make you happy like I wanted to do before. Or what if we're driving in the car, could I unzip you and perform oral sex. Well, we'd have to pull over, be safety conscious, of course. Or could I dress up in a maid's outfit with suspenders and no knickers and clean the house in front of you, bending over to dust under cupboards. Or what if I undress in front of you, and you watch while I pleasure myself. So, you're not touching me at all … you know, that sort of thing.'

Tapakah cleared his throat and stretched his neck to one side. He moved in his chair and rubbed his forehead. He inhaled deeply. It appeared as if he wanted to say something.

'Shall I go on?'

He rubbed the back of his neck and nodded. He seemed breathless.

'Okay, where was I? Oh yes, or what if I watch you masturbate. You know, looking not touching. Is that allowed? Then there's cleavage sex, you know, I engulf you with my breasts until you come. Or what about tying me up, bondage, that sort of thing? Am I allowed to tie you up to the bed and dominate you, spank you, do stuff to you, other than penetration, which I'm assuming is the issue here, and drive you crazy until you come? Can I do that? Or can I be your slave, collared and leashed? Or you mine? The list is endless, I guess. And if we get engaged first, does that mean we're allowed to do more stuff? The devil is always in the detail, Tapakah, and that's what I need clarification on. I need something in writing. A list.'

Tapakah's jaw clenched. He stared at me, and his nostrils flared slightly, and his mouth twitched. I waited for him to say something.

Maybe I'd offended him. Jesus, I had. That was it. He really was old fashioned, and now he thought I was obsessed with sex and not interested in the whole courtship thing. I had gone on a bit, but I thought it needed to be said, and I'd pretty much covered everything I wanted to say. He'd seemed interested, concentrating on every word.

Tapakah stood, turned away from me, and leaned up against the kitchen bench. He gripped the back of the barstool. I didn't know what was going on in his head. I'd stuffed up, said the wrong thing again. Good one. Oh well, better to know now rather than later. Get it all out there.

'Um, Tapakah?'

'Yes?' he replied hoarsely.

'What about an "in public" situation? I forgot to mention that. Say, for example, we're sitting in a booth at the back of a dimly lit cocktail lounge, and I duck under the tablecloth and give you a surprise you'll never forget. You know, it's a bit risky, people are around, and you have to sit there looking casual like while I … you know. Can *that* go on the list?'

Tapakah swung around and slammed his fist on the bench. His expression was thunderous. 'Fuck the list!' He grabbed me by the wrist and yanked me up and out of my chair. Fear surged through me. Was he going to hit me?

No. He scooped me up, carried me to the staircase and bounded up the stairs two at a time.

He kicked open the door to his bedroom and threw me on the bed. He ripped off my T-shirt and bra, tore off my jeans and knickers, and stood looking down at me as he tore off his shirt and slipped off his trousers and jocks. His eyes never left mine. He was devouring me with them, and I him.

It was the first time I'd ever seen him completely undressed. I'd had concerns, given he was half bug and everything, but what stood before me was all man, no question about it.

I swallowed and felt extremely hot under the collar. He pulled me upright, so I sat on the edge of the bed. His eyes fixed on mine as he knelt between my legs.

I swallowed again as his skin brushed mine. My voice was a hoarse whisper. 'So, just to clarify then, what are we allowed to do?'

'Everything, Maggie. Everything and then some.' He kissed

the side of my neck and headed in a downward trajectory.

I gasped. 'Are you sure this is what you want?' I worried he'd given up on his resolution. 'I mean—'

He pushed me back on the bed and put his fingers over my lips as his mouth explored my body.

I groaned and mumbled. 'I assume that's a "yes" then?'

Tapakah's shoulders shook with gentle laughter as his mouth continued its journey. It wasn't long before he made me shake with ecstasy, throwing his long-term resolutions out the window.

Bang, bang, bang!

A racket broke into our consciousness, bringing our activities to an abrupt halt. Someone was hammering the hell out of the front door. For heaven's sake, it was as if the universe didn't want us to make love. We never seemed to have the opportunity to get past first base.

Bang, bang, bang!

Ding Dong. Ding Dong. Ding Dong.

'Damn it!' Tapakah looked furious. 'Who the hell is it?'

'Ignore it.'

'I can't.' He leapt out of bed, walked onto the balcony, leant over and shouted, 'Hang on. I'm coming.' Returning inside, he grumbled, 'At least, that's what I was trying to do.'

'Who is it?' I asked.

'The police. You stay here.' He whipped on jeans and a T-shirt.

Oh, crikey. This could be trouble.

The stairs creaked as he ran down to open the front door. I slid out of bed and listened at the doorway.

'How can I help you?' he said politely. 'Sorry for the delay. I was asleep upstairs.'

'Sorry to disturb you, sir, but we're investigating an altercation which took place on the footpath this morning, right outside your premises. We want to know if you or anyone else was home at the time, and if you saw anything.'

'What sort of altercation?'

'A street brawl. One man had his ear ripped off.'

'Nasty. But I'm afraid no one was home at the time. I'm mostly away. I'm sorry I can't be of more assistance.'

'Thanks for your time, sir.'

The door closed. I leapt back into bed as Tapakah raced up the stairs. It was odd he hadn't asked me if I'd seen anything.

He took off his clothes. 'Now, where were we?'

'I think we've lost the moment.' I snuggled up to him as he climbed back into bed.

'Maggie, when you were home today, did you see or hear a street brawl going on outside?'

Oh dear. If I told him what had happened it would worry him. Make him even more protective. Beans had disappeared, so really, I didn't have to tell him. What he didn't know wouldn't hurt him.

'No, I didn't hear or see anything.'

Technically, it wasn't a lie. I hadn't seen or heard the brawl while I'd been at home. Only when I was outside and fully involved in the whole bloody thing.

He hugged me and nuzzled my neck. 'So, shall we continue from where we left off?'

'I'm worried you've abandoned your plan. It was clearly important to you.'

'It was obvious my old-fashioned notions weren't cutting the mustard with you. I want you to be happy, so I made an executive decision to ditch them. And I couldn't resist you any longer. You and your request for "clarification" tipped me over the edge. It was a deliberate ploy, wasn't it?'

'No. No ploy. I just needed to know exactly what we had to wait for. I don't like to assume; assumptions get you into trouble.'

'So, are you happy now, Maggie?'

'Extremely. You're amazing. A consummate lover so far. I

guess you must've had a bit of practice.'

'None.'

'What do you mean, *none*?'

'Exactly that. None. I've had zero "practice" as you call it. You are my first lover.'

'You're a virgin? You're *kidding*!'

He was having me on. Pulling my lariat. There was no way this guy was a virgin. He was too good to be a novice.

'No, not kidding. Remember, I haven't been around for long. I grew to maturity in twelve months. With all the plans I've implemented, I haven't had time.'

'Wow. Well you certainly knew the right buttons to press for a complete rookie.'

He grinned. 'I guess I can only get better then.'

'Crikey.'

'Will you marry me, Maggie?'

'Is this an official proposal, right now?'

'Yes. I wanted it to be special, but I don't want to wait anymore.'

'Tapakah, we haven't discussed this properly. There are issues.'

'Such as?'

Oh hell, this wasn't going to be easy. I guess I'd just blurt everything out in my usual undiplomatic way.

'Well, for one, I've just found out you're a virgin. It's probably not smart to marry the first girl you come across. I'm not keen on the idea of you going out with other girls, but you should explore your options more broadly. Live a little. As you said, you're still young, still changing, learning. If you say you've changed so much in such a short time, then you could change again, even more. You could want totally different things, and I may not be one of them. Hell, if I'd married—'

'What?'

'I was going to say if I'd married half the guys I was with I would've been divorced five times over, but I couldn't remember who I'd been out with and, oh, never mind, everything came up blank.'

Tapakah looked directly into my eyes. The hypnotic power of them was strong. I loved it.

'Maggie, do you realise you are exactly like me. You have no past. Everything is new. As you said when we were in WA, you are essentially a virgin too. You can't remember having men. So, I'm your first and you are mine. I don't want to explore other "options". I don't need to. I want you and you only.'

'You're dead right. I am like you, and that's what worries me. I don't know who I am. I could change. I've obviously lived, but I've no idea what my life was like. I'm scared, Tapakah. Everything could change. I love you, I do, but I feel my foundation is built on quicksand, on … on … dust, and any second a puff of wind will blow it away again. And what we had … have will be gone.'

'It's the same for me. I feel you're a precious diamond ready to be snatched from my grasp. At any moment, someone, or something, may steal you from me and I will lose you forever. The thought breaks my heart.' His face was awash with emotion as he spoke. 'We can't give into trepidation. We can't not be together because we fear what might happen. It may never happen. If it does, then we deal with it. We have now, and now is all anyone ever has. The past is dead; the future exists only in our heads. Maggie, don't give in to fear.'

I'd never realised he felt that way too. He'd always seemed so confident and in control. Maybe that's the real reason he was keen on marriage; it would give him a sense of security, of permanence.

I decided to tackle the elephant in the room. 'The issue of children. I know you want them. I'm not sure I do. And what would be the result of our union, if indeed we were even able to procreate? To be honest, that scares the hell out of me.'

'Yes, I want children. My DNA has already been used to produce perfectly normal offspring.'

'Define perfectly normal.'

'They look like humans not insects, if that's what you're getting at.'

'And do they have the same medical issues as you? And how many "offspring" have you produced, for Christ's sake?'

'That's classified. I'm not at liberty to reveal such information.'

'Righty ho, then. If you were in my shoes, how do you think you'd be feeling right now?'

'Worried. Uncertain. Unhappy?'

'Bingo. You can't expect me to make such a huge decision without all the facts.'

Tapakah sat on the edge of the bed. The soft light accentuated his muscles and the tattoos on his right arm. They seemed to pulse and move in the shifting sunlight. He sat with his elbows on his knees, his clenched hands rested under his chin.

The minutes ticked by. I studied the plasterwork around the ceiling light to take my mind off things.

Finally, he cleared his throat. 'Forget marriage. Let's take it day by day. You okay with that?'

Funnily enough, I didn't know if I was okay with it or not. Marriage was the big thing for him. Now he didn't want it?

'What changed your mind?' I asked.

'You did, of course.'

'So, you don't want to marry me?'

'For fuck's sake, Maggie, I'm trying to make you happy.' He turned around to face me. Click. That connection as his eyes locked onto mine. It possessed me.

'You don't want to get married; you're not sure whether you want children, particularly with me. I *get* that. Everything you said makes sense. I must respect how you feel, what you want. It's too soon; I'm putting you under pressure.'

'Do you want me to leave?'

He shook his head in frustration. 'Hell no, I don't want you to leave. I love you. I don't want to spoil what we have. That's why marriage is off the agenda.'

'So, we take it day by day?'

'Yes, day by day.'

'Well, we could get engaged … given there are no restrictions now, and I'm not going to die of sexual frustration. It would be a compromise. I mean, I do love you, and you love me. It's unfortunate things are … are so *complicated*.'

He looked at me in astonishment. 'You want to get engaged? But you don't want to marry me.'

'It would be symbolic. A sign of our commitment to each other, to show we're prepared to take it day by day together. It would remind us to focus on what we have now. To enjoy each other and have fun together, as we both find our feet. It may or may not lead to marriage, but it's a start. Does that make sense? Would it make you happy?'

A smile crept across his face. 'It would make me very happy indeed. More importantly, would it make you happy?'

'Yes, it would make me happy.'

I really hoped it would. Fingers crossed I hadn't made a terrible mistake.

---

[9] *Maggie's Playlist: I Want Your Sex, Parts 1 & 2 — George Michael*

"Doubt thou the stars are fire. Doubt that the sun doth move. Doubt truth to be a liar, but never doubt I love." — *William Shakespeare*

The new day dawned with a bright blue sky and a soft warm breeze. Tapakah had left early to go to work, back to his secret men's business, and Billy was at school.

The traffic hummed outside. The sound of it made me wish we could leave and return to WA. I loved being at the Murchinson station, and so did Billy. I think Tapakah did too. He seemed relaxed there, surrounded by nature and all the animals and insects.

Billy wasn't his normal happy self these days. I made a mental note to have a quiet chat with him and see what was up.

I still felt out of place in the city. I missed having something to do and people to talk with. Time for a coffee. I needed to tell Ben that Beans had vanished.

I found my way back to the coffee shop. The chairs on the ceiling still brought a smile to my face. It was mid-morning and fairly quiet. A surfer dude sat in a corner near the window, staring into his coffee.

Ben bobbed up from behind the counter. 'Hey, Maggie.'

'Hi, Ben. Good to see you.'

'Flat white?'

'Yes, please.'

He lowered his voice and said, 'Are you okay? After everything?'

'I'm fine, but the police were going door-to-door asking questions. I was in bed when they came around, so didn't talk to them. I wanted to tell you about Beans. She ran away. I don't know how she escaped, but she did.'

'That's a bummer. She's a smart dog. Probably found her way back to her owner.'

'That's what I was thinking and hoping. Anyway, I'm going to get a few lemon tarts in case she turns up again.'

He fired up the machine. 'Take a seat. I'll bring you your coffee.'

'I want to watch how you make it. And I've changed my mind. Can you do me a latte please?'

He winked. 'I can do anything you want.'

He took a cloth, cleaned the coffee basket and pressed a button to flush the machine. Then he put the coffee basket under the grinder and ground some freshly roasted beans. He tamped the coffee. 'You have to make sure you tamp it flat and straight. Then you insert the coffee basket in the machine, like so, and press the button to brew, remembering to put the cup underneath, of course. The coffee that comes out shouldn't gush, or dribble, but flow, like honey.'

He pressed the button to stop the coffee flow and moved on to steaming the milk.

'So, clean jug, cold milk. I only put in enough for the coffee I'm making. I don't like waste, and I won't re-steam milk; there's a drop in sweetness and texture. You purge the steamer, steam the milk, then clean and purge again. When I pour the milk, I keep the rich brown of the crema and come closer with the white of the milk and, there you go, one perfect coffee.' He handed it to me.

He was a coffee artist. There it was, with a perfect floral heart design. Done in seconds with a flick of the wrist. Amazing.

'Thank you. It's a thing of beauty.'

He popped a tiny lemon tart on the side. 'I was hoping you'd come by again. The lemon tart is on the house.' He reached behind the counter. 'I have something else for you. It's very mysterious.' He handed me a package wrapped in brown paper.

'What is it?'

'I don't know. It feels like a book. An old man with a beard and hat came in and asked if I could give it to you when you came in next. I didn't see any harm in it, so I said yes.'

'Who was he?'

'He wouldn't say.'

'I hope it's not a bomb or something.'

Ben looked shocked. 'Why the hell would you think that?'

'I'm not sure.' I felt along the outside of the parcel. 'It sure feels like a book.' I held it to my ear.

Ben raised his voice. '*BOOM!*'

I just about jumped through the roof. 'Jesus. Don't *do* that!'

He laughed. 'Sorry, you're a bit jumpy.'

'I'm always on high alert for some reason.'

Ben looked at me eagerly. 'Are you going to open it?'

'I guess so.' Ben followed me to the table, and we sat. 'Here goes.' I gingerly peeled off the sticky tape and removed the paper.

It was a book, bound in red leather, and it didn't explode. *Maggie's Life* was embossed in gold on the front cover. My arms erupted in goose bumps. A strange shock wave buzzed through my chest.

Ben read the title and looked at me with wide eyes. 'Mamma mia!'

I bit my lip and stared at the book.

'Aren't you going to open it?'

'I'm scared my life was awful. It must have been; I tried to commit suicide. I don't want to go there. What if it makes everything come back? All the horrible stuff. I don't want to risk what I have now.'

'What if I look first? If I think it's bad shit, I'll tell you and we can burn it or something. If it looks okay, then I think you need to find out who you are.'

'All right. You look at it. Don't show me.' I stood the book up on its edge.

I flinched as Ben opened the cover. I really felt it could explode.

'I need to read the note inside, okay?'

I nodded.

'It says, Dearest Maggie, we made this photo book for you to help you remember your life, who you are, and the people who love you. Your family and friends miss you dearly and we want you to come back to us. Come back to your real life. Everything you've been told is a lie. Whatever you do, please don't take this book home or let it fall into Tapakah's hands. Our lives depend on it, and yours too. Leave the book here; it's the safest place. All our love, from your family and friends.'

Ben looked at me and I looked at him. My heart pounded in my throat.

'Do I keep going?' he asked.

I nodded.

Ben slowly turned the pages. He studied each page intensely, and I studied him. The suspense was killing me. His long dark lashes flickered as he perused each page. A curl fell across his forehead. He pushed it back with one hand.

I sipped my coffee and counted the passersby. The sun was streaming in through the window lighting up the café with a golden hue. The chairs on the ceiling cast crazy shadows over the walls. The surfer dude was reading the paper. He looked up and averted his gaze when I caught his eye.

By the time Ben was getting to the end of the book I couldn't contain myself any longer. My fingernails tapped the table impatiently. 'Well, what do you think?'

He looked up and fixed me with his soft green eyes.

'*Well?*'

'From the looks of these photos, it appears you had a good life. A *really* good life. There's nothing in this book that would upset you. They're pictures of you with family and friends, and you look happy.' He slid the book across the table.

'Should I look?'

He nodded.

I took a deep breath and opened the book. There I was. Me with long hair and a big smile on my face, in the arms of a handsome man with sandy hair and piercing blue eyes. The text said the man was Jason, my partner, who was now missing. There were heaps of photos of the two of us. For me, it was like looking at a stranger. I felt nothing.

I turned the page and gasped. I certainly recognised those faces. They were the people who held us at gunpoint in Western Australia.

Ben looked at me worriedly. 'Everything all right? Do you remember something?'

I pointed to the photo. 'Those people held me at gunpoint when I was staying at an outback station. They tracked me down, wanted to take me with them. That tall, tough looking guy's name is Ashley, this one is Fox, this one Drom, and that's the Maestro. They said they were my family and wanted to take me home. But they had guns. They frightened me.'

'When you look at the rest of the photos, it appears you were very close with them.'

'They said I'd been kidnapped and had my mind wiped.'

'Maybe it's true. I think you should look at these photos here.' He flipped over a couple of pages. Brace yourself.'

He showed me the page. 'Holy shit!'

'You know who it looks like don't you?'

'Beans. This dog is *Beans!* It's identical. But how?'

'It appears to be your dog, and its name is Boo.'

'Bloody hell.'

'Do any of the other pictures resonate? Your dad, your mum, your sister. What about Jason?'

'No. No they don't.' I wanted to cry or be sick. My bottom lip quivered as a surge of sensations splashed around inside me. I was a washing machine of emotions set to click into the spin cycle.

Ben moved his chair closer and put an arm around my shoulder. I gripped the book so hard my knuckles turned white. The warmth of his touch calmed me. I took a deep breath and let it out slowly.

'Shall I put the book away?'

I nodded.

He stood and tucked it under the counter. 'Let me make you something to eat. I think you need something to ground you, after all that. I'll keep the book safe, so anytime you want to look at it, it will be here, okay?'

'Thank you, Ben. I really appreciate what you've done for me. I think food would help.'

'Leave it to me.' He headed off to the kitchen.

It was lunchtime and the café started to fill up with people. I liked the hustle and bustle; it took my mind off things. What the hell was I supposed to do now? What was I supposed to think? The only people in the book I recognised were from my recent past. And that experience wasn't pleasant.

Tapakah, Billy and Frank were the only positive things in my life. Well, the only things in my life, actually. There was Hugh and Elizabeth from the station, and now Ben. They were all lovely people, but they were all I had.

And what was with the dog? That was uncanny. It couldn't be Beans. If Beans was Boo, and Boo was my dog, then Beans wouldn't have run off. Beans would have stayed. It was bullshit; it had to be. People could do anything with Photoshop these days. You couldn't believe what you saw anymore. I wasn't stupid.

I looked up and caught the surfer dude staring at me. He quickly looked away.

Suddenly the crowded café didn't feel so good anymore. I had to get out. Get air. Walk. Walking was good. I'd walk the streets until I couldn't walk anymore, couldn't feel anymore and couldn't think anymore.

'Ben, forget the food. I have to leave.' I blew him a kiss.

He waved back at me through the crowd of people. He wanted to say something, but I had to get out, and I had to get out now.

Walking city streets wasn't as soothing as walking in a park. Too many people, too many cars, too much noise. But I kept going because I needed to move. I'd walk along one street, right to the end of the city, and then walk back up the next street to the other end and so on until I'd covered the entire city, or until I couldn't take another step. That was the plan.

So, I walked, in a daze, one foot in front of the other. Sometimes I registered a nice shiny thing, in a shiny shop window, but generally I zoned out. I was in Zen mode. I enjoyed being in Zen mode. Things generally worked themselves out, became clear.

I checked my watch. I'd been walking for two hours. Where was I? I didn't even know. Beside me was a massive hotel. The Hyatt. That was where I'd go. I felt slightly better after the walking, and a drink could only improve things.

I entered through the revolving door and whisked up the escalators to the first floor. The bar and restaurant area was to the right. It was dimly lit; a fire was burning in a massive stone fireplace, and there were plenty of comfy chairs around and not too many people. Perfect.

I selected a chair by the fire giving me an extensive view over the whole area. I didn't want anyone sneaking up on me. There was a latticed screen behind me, allowing a sight through to the restaurant, but protecting me from an attack. God knows why I was always on high alert. It was driving me crazy. Why the hell did I think someone was always out to get me?

A waiter came over and I ordered a glass of champagne. It arrived in a stylish glass accompanied by a bowl of delicious looking nibbly things. I took a sip and closed my eyes as the scent of melon and citrus filled my nostrils. I was feeling better already. I sipped my drink and settled down, more able to concentrate on my surroundings.

I lost myself in the flames of the fire, watched the toing and froing of the wait staff, listened to the gentle chill out jazz, and sunk ever deeper into the soft leather of the armchair.

I wanted another champagne and turned around to hail a waiter. That's when I saw something that made my heart pound and the champagne rise in my gut.

Tapakah. Seated at a table for two. Opposite him an attractive blonde woman talked in an animated fashion, whilst twirling a strand of long blonde hair around her finger. Tapakah seemed mesmerised. He refilled her glass and spoke. She listened. His hands were on the table. She reached across and took his hand in hers. He put his other hand over the top of hers. She reached across and touched his face.

My heart pounded so hard I could hardly hear. A rush of adrenaline made my heart beat even faster. Their body language told me everything I needed to know.

I growled under my breath, 'The bastard.' My face became hot with rage.

So that was all it took. One suggestion to broaden his horizons and hey presto, he was on to it. He'd said he was *working*. He was a goddamn liar. A stinking, lousy cheat. Jesus, he barely had time to take me out since we'd arrived here, and there he was having lunch with some floozy. The photo book said everything was a lie. It *was* a lie. He was a liar. I'd been taken for a fool.

I turned away. I couldn't stand to watch. Should I walk up and cause a scene? I sure as hell felt like it. I wanted to punch his lights out.

No. I wouldn't demean myself like that. I would leave. That's what I'd do. Get the hell away from him. I checked my watch. If I left now, caught a cab, I could get to the house, pack and be out of there in a flash. Before he came home. That's if he was coming home. He often stayed away overnight. Now I knew why.

I left money next to my glass and bolted from the bar. I flew down the escalator looking for a cab. Five of them pulled away just as I arrived. Damn it!

In panic mode, everything was a blur. Across the road, a taxi stopped. I waved frantically. I stepped off the curb to make a dash for the other side. A car horn blasted in my ear. A vehicle rocketed past, a mere centimetre from my feet. Simultaneously I was hoisted backwards by someone grabbing my jacket. I landed on my bum on the footpath. A strong arm hoisted me upright.

My head was in a daze. Jesus, I could've been killed. Who had saved me?

I looked around and caught sight of a man walking swiftly away. I shouted out and he broke into a run, disappearing into the crowd. I wanted to follow him, try and find him, thank him, but I had to go. A cab pulled up and I leapt in.

Seven minutes later I was home. Tapakah would still be sitting there enthralled, if not already screwing her brains out in a hotel room. Still enraged, my heart pounded fit to burst. I paid the cab, ran up the steps and fumbled with the key in the lock. I slammed the door shut so hard a picture fell off the wall. I left it there and raced up stairs.

First things first; this thing *had* to go. I removed Tapakah's tracking bracelet from my wrist and tossed it in the wastepaper basket. I found a duffel bag in the wardrobe and stuffed in my clothes. I didn't have much, so packing was easy. Into the bag went toiletries, cosmetics, my laptop, iPad, AirPods, notebook with poetry, and what else? That's probably it. I went through the place faster than a whirlwind, took the bag and ran downstairs. Where the hell would I go? The only person I knew was Ben. He could help me. Maybe I could sleep upstairs in the café for a couple of nights until I worked out what to do.

I grabbed my handbag and checked my wallet. Two hundred dollars in cash. My credit card and bank account had been set up by Roach boy. He could shut it down in a snap.

I headed towards the front door and a key turned in the lock. I froze, my heart in my mouth. I dropped the duffel bag behind the lounge room door and watched the front door open. My mind raced through a million scenarios as I anticipated those dark eyes latching on to mine.

'Hi, Magster!' Billy threw his school bag on the floor.

I let out a sign of relief and felt peculiarly lightheaded. 'Huh, hi, Billy.' I held onto the coat rack to steady myself.

He studied my face intently. 'What's wrong?'

I hated myself for lying to my darling Billy. 'I've been running around a lot today. I have a cracker of a headache.'

There was a soft thunk as my duffel bag fell onto its side. Billy followed my gaze. 'What's that?'

'A bag.'

'What's in it?'

'Bits and pieces.'

'What sort of bits and pieces?'

'Stuff I'm taking to the op shop.'

'What sort of stuff?'

'Oh, for Christ's sake, Billy, just stuff, okay?' I fought back tears.

Billy raced to my bag and unzipped it. He took one look inside and yelled, 'You're leaving! This is everything you have. I know, because I remember all your things. You're not going to the op shop; you're *leaving!*'

The colour drained from his face and the sprinkling of freckles across his cheeks stood out in stark relief. He dashed over, flung his arms around me and sobbed into my chest. 'You can't leave. *Why* are you leaving? Where are you going? I'll come with you. Take me with you!' His voice grew ever more hysterical.

I quickly wiped the tears from my face and hugged him close. I stroked his head. 'It's okay, Billy. I'm just going away for a little while.'

He looked up at me with his tear streaked face. 'But *why?*'

I gazed into his big brown eyes. 'I'm only going away for one night. I'll be back.'

'But where are you going?'

'To see a friend.' My voice sounded hollow and flat.

I unwrapped his arms from around my waist. 'Billy, I have to go *now*. I'm late. There's milk and a snack for you in the fridge. I love you.'

'I love you too.' He looked straight into my eyes. 'You promise you're coming back?'

I picked up the duffel bag and headed for the front door. Turning back for one last look, Billy's little face was scrunched up with emotion. '*Maggie!* Promise you'll come back?'

'Yes.'

My heart was breaking. I turned and walked out. The wind caught the door and slammed it shut behind me.

---

[10] *Maggie's Playlist: Before He Cheats — Meg Birch*

Maggie **Chapter 10: Runaway**

"You left and I cried tears of blood. My sorrow grows. It's not just that You left. But when You left my eyes went with you. Now, how will I cry?" — Rumi

I hightailed it along the street, my duffel bag slung over my shoulder. I checked, but Billy wasn't following.

I loved him and was going to miss him terribly. Maybe I should've taken him with me. But it would've been all too hard. Billy loved Tapakah and Tapakah was good to him. He'd found him on the streets, like me, and looked after him like a son. It was for the best.

I dashed across the road for an approaching tram. As I crossed, someone called my name. A chill enveloped me, and goosebumps erupted on my arms.

It was Tapakah.

Billy must've phoned him. There was no way Tapakah would've left his floozy otherwise. They'd been having too much of a good time together.

The approaching tram was packed with people, and for a horrible second, I thought it wasn't going to stop. But it did, thank God.

I jumped on and it took off straight away. I made my way to the back and looked out the window. Tapakah was running across the road, dodging cars. He stopped in the middle of the tram tracks and his eyes locked onto me. His face was stony.

Escaping him was a lucky break. I couldn't think of anything worse than having to see him now. Someone stood, so I snaffled a seat. I could relax. I glanced back through the window and my heart caught in my throat. Tapakah was running along the tracks.

I couldn't believe it. He was coming after me, and he was gaining on the tram. His arms and legs pounded the ground like pistons. He was closing the gap at superhuman speed, his movements so fluid it was as though he ran on an invisible cushion of air.

I watched in horrified fascination as he drew ever closer. No, no, no. Not good. Really, not good.

I looked ahead and saw the next tram stop coming up. People stood, ready to disembark. The tram was going to stop. If it did, I was screwed.

I didn't want an altercation. I didn't want to confront him. I wanted to run away somewhere and lick my wounds.

The tram slowed to a stop and there was Tapakah, outside the back door, staring in at me. He mouthed, 'What the *hell*?'

I gave him a death stare.

As if I was going to stay with a two-timing bastard. I chose not to voice the choice expletives that came to mind.

The tram door opened, and he leapt up the steps and yelled, '*Maggie!* Where the hell are you going? Billy said you're leaving. Talk to me.'

I pushed towards the front of the tram, whispering, 'Please let me pass. Don't let him get to me. Please let me pass. Don't let him get to me,' to the people around me. The crowd opened to let me through and closed tight behind me. Tapakah pushed and jostled his way through.

I reached the front of the tram as the doors began to close. I leapt through the gap and someone grabbed my duffel bag. Tapakah.

I let go of the strap and it took him off balance as he yanked the bag towards him. The door closed and the tram took off.

I didn't stop to think. I ran. I ran as fast as my legs would go, and really, it wasn't that fast. I wasn't naturally athletic, and I certainly couldn't outrun Tapakah. The next tram stop was only minutes away. I had to make the most of my lead time. I had absolutely no doubt he would come after me.

My lungs began to burn. At least I didn't have the duffel bag to weigh me down. But now I had absolutely nothing. Just the clothes on my back. I turned left to head towards the café, but the street was blocked with road works. The workmen pointed to a detour sign directing foot traffic straight ahead. I had to get off the main road or Tapakah would see me. Panic rose in my gut. I checked behind but couldn't see him. I dug deep and cranked up my legs. I had to get away.

The extreme physical exertion made me sob, causing people to turn and stare as I ran by. The roar and rumble of an engine sounded out above the rest of the traffic noise, and a car horn blasted next to me. A flash of yellow and black appeared in my peripheral vision.

'Maggie! Get in,' a voice shouted.

It was Ben and his goddamn beautiful Monaro. He leaned across and flung open the door. I fell into the car, and he took off at speed before I could even close it. He looked at me as I gasped for breath. All I could do was nod.

He patted my leg. 'Don't try and talk.'

I sunk into the seat as he accelerated and sped off down the road. We hit the Hume Highway — he was heading out of the city to who knew where. A few minutes passed before I could finally speak. 'That was a helluva lucky break you happened by when you did.'

'It wasn't luck. I was told to go get you.'

My blood ran cold as I descended back into panic mode.

Jesus, he worked for Tapakah. He was taking me back!

Adrenaline flooded my body. When the car stopped at the lights, I made a decision and jumped out and ran, narrowly missing a car in the left turn lane.

My feet crunched across the gravel of an expansive verge as I headed for a wide brown paddock full of grass, rocks and thistles. I figured he wouldn't be able to get me there. Littered with wrecked cars and old concrete pipes, it would provide plenty of places to hide. As to where the hell I would go afterwards, I had no idea. My only friend Ben was working for the enemy.

The roar of an engine and the crunch of tires on gravel ripped through the air as a car spun in front of me. I was covered with a spray of dust and gravel so thick I couldn't see. My eyes stung with grit, leaving me flying blind as I turned to run in the opposite direction. The paddock was in front of me, and I ran flat out towards it. I heard the crunch of footsteps behind, and as I glanced back, I hit a barbed wire fence at full pelt.

The barbs shredded my hands and body, and then the momentum of the impact tossed me backward, right into the arms of Ben. Our skulls cracked together, and we fell in a heap in a puddle of stinking, oily mud.

It was a couple of seconds before we regained our senses. I leapt up and made a break for the paddock. Ben grappled me from behind and held me in a bear hug. He was wheezing. He must have been winded when I landed on him.

I let my knees buckle and slid from his grasp. I followed through with an elbow jab to the solar plexus. He hit the dirt harder than a ton of bricks. I took off again, but he grabbed my ankle and I fell flat on my face. I crawled up on all fours and tried to kick free. He launched himself on top of me and I collapsed back into the dirt. His entire body weight pinned me to the ground.

Our bodies heaved as we gasped for breath. I could barely get a breath under the weight of his body.

'For Christ's sake, Maggie, stop wriggling. Listen to me! I am *not* going to hurt you. I'm not the bad guy. I'll say it again; I'm not going to hurt you. I. Am. The. *Good*. Guy. I came to help.'

I wheezed. 'You said you were *told* to get me.'

'Yes, by the guy who gave you the book. He called and said, and I quote, 'I'm the man who gave you Maggie's book. She needs your help. She's running up Russell Street, from Flinders on the left-hand side. She's being chased. You must get her out of there. I can't get there in time.'

'I thought Tapakah had told you to take me back to him.'

Ben sounded hurt. *'Really?* You thought I was a bad guy?'

'I have paranoia issues,' I mumbled. 'Could you please get off me?'

'Promise you won't run or try and kill me or something?'

'I promise.'

Ben pushed himself up and plopped down on the gravel next to me. I groaned and rolled over onto my back. The mud oozed into my shirt. I took in Ben's disheveled state. 'I am so, so sorry, Ben.'

'No, I'm sorry. Look at you. You're covered in blood and dust. You look like something out of *Revenge of the Zombies*.'

I groaned. 'Thanks. I feel like it. I can't believe I doubted you. It's no excuse, but I was pumped with adrenaline and in panic mode, I—'

'Don't worry about it. Here let me help you stand. We need to get you cleaned up. Do you need a doctor? Your hands are cut.'

'I'll be fine. I definitely need a shower. But I have nothing. No clothes, no money, just what I'm wearing, and now that's trashed.' My eyes filled with tears.

'Don't worry about anything, okay? I'll take you back to the café. My studio apartment is upstairs; my sister stayed there for a while. You can get cleaned up, and there's bound to be some of her clothes that'll fit. We'll get you new stuff tomorrow. Food, drink and sleep, that's what you need now. Keep your head out of tomorrow. We'll work out what to do in the morning.'

I was too stuffed to think anymore. Running on empty, that's how I felt, as he helped me back to the car. Mud, oil, blood and dust covered me from head to toe. Same for Ben. 'We can't get into the car like this.'

Ben found a couple of blankets in the back. He bundled me up and helped me in. He covered his seat with the other blanket, and we were good to go.

He grinned at me through his dirt-streaked face. 'We sure do stink!'

I screwed up my nose. 'Like skunks.'

'There's never a dull moment with you around, Maggie.'

'So I've been told.'

I wished with all my heart for one, just one, dull moment.

* * * * *

It took a long, hot shower to get the oily muck off my body and out of my hair. As I dried myself, I considered how strange it felt to have nothing. And I literally had *nothing*. My clothes were in the trash, and I was naked except for a robe Ben had given me.

Putting it on, I wandered into the lounge area. The studio on top of the café was spacious and light. Tastefully decorated, it was clean, neat and tidy. There was a tall glass on the kitchen bench with a note beside it. The glass was full of iced coffee and the note said, "Drink Me".

I took a sip through the pink straw sitting in the middle of a mountain of cream and ice cream. The bitterness of the coffee and the sweetness of the ice cream was a perfect combination. I brought it back to the couch and sat savouring its deliciousness. I hadn't had an iced coffee in, well, I didn't know how long.

Having nothing was frightening. In a way, I had even less than nothing, if that was possible. I'd also lost my memory and my life. I felt like a refugee relying on the charity and kindness of strangers. But it also felt strangely liberating.

Nothing. No one. No memory. No past life. No money. No possessions. I'd lost everything. It was just me, here, now.

Peace enveloped me as I accepted where I was right now. A sense of gratitude overwhelmed me. Not many people in our affluent society got to experience having nothing. I suddenly felt it was a gift.

There was a knock at the door, immediately followed by, 'Relax, Maggie, it's Ben.'

'Come in.' Bless him. I'd hardly had the chance to go into panic mode.

He handed me a few shopping bags. 'Well, don't you look one hundred percent. And you seem happy.'

I held up my empty glass. 'It was the shower and your delicious iced coffee. You know, I don't even have the clothes on my back, and it's scary, but it's also weirdly liberating to have absolutely nothing. I feel surprisingly good, given the circumstances.'

He pointed at the shopping bags. 'I'm sorry to burst your nothing bubble, darling, but you do actually have clothes. I took the liberty of buying you some. I didn't want to put you in my sister's clothes, not really your style. I hope you don't mind.'

'Thanks so much. I hate wearing other people's clothes. I will pay you back. I'll get a job, and it'll be the first thing I do.'

'No stress. I hope you like them. I have the dockets if you need to change anything.'

I grabbed the bags and headed into the bedroom. 'Let me go try them right now.'

Skinny jeans, boots, a pair of flats, a couple of cute tops, a jacket, toiletries, cosmetics, a bag and two sets of gorgeous underwear, *Victoria's Secret*. Crikey.

I tried on everything and everything fitted. *Amazing.*

Returning to the lounge, I suddenly felt self-conscious, seeing Ben sitting there staring at me. 'Everything's perfect. Thank you.'

I stepped forward, caught my foot on the rug, wobbled, overbalanced, and Ben leapt up and caught me by the arm. He hauled me upright before I hit the deck.

'Jesus, that was lucky.'

'Saved me again! The clothes are spot on — even the underwear. Extravagant, but so beautiful. I can't believe you got the size right.'

He grinned. 'I have a good eye.'

I felt my face go hot.

'So, what actually happened? What were you running from? Can you tell me?'

I owed him an explanation, but not the whole story, not the hybrid cockroach bit. He wouldn't believe me; no one would, so it was pointless to go down that path.

From our previous conversations, Ben already knew how Tapakah rescued me and that he loved me, and how I came to love him. So, I told Ben about Tapakah's deceit and infidelity, and how upset I was he'd lied to me. I also told him how scared I was when he was chasing me, like a man possessed.

Ben listened intently. When I finished he sat quietly for a while.

'What?'

'I'm playing devil's advocate here, but how do you know he was unfaithful? There may have been a legitimate explanation for what you saw. I mean, who knows, he could have been meeting up with a wedding planner for all you know. If he was organising a surprise, then he obviously wouldn't tell you.'

'It was the intimate body language. If it was a wedding planner, then it looked like he was planning to marry her.'

'I still think you need to talk to him. Hear what he has to say. What if you're wrong? You said you loved him. How would you feel if you threw it away over a mistake? I don't think you should run off without giving him the chance to explain.'

Now it was my turn to sit quietly. Jesus. Ben had a point. A very good point. I suddenly felt foolish. I couldn't believe what I'd done.

'Maggie?' he said softly.

'You're right. You're absolutely right. I owe him that. The chance to explain. I mean, after everything he's done for me. I guess it's possible I could be wrong. I feel like a bad person now, the way I've behaved. But at the time I was so upset.'

'You're not a bad person. You were upset because you thought you saw the person you love betraying you. It happened to me. I jumped to the wrong conclusion in a relationship and it ruined everything. I don't want it to happen to you.'

'Oh, Ben, I'm sorry. I'll take your advice. But can I stay here tonight? I can't face a confrontation today. I'm not up to it.'

'You can stay here as long as you like. Truth be told, I don't want to push you back into his arms, but it seems the right thing to do. Everyone deserves a second chance, particularly as you can't be one hundred percent sure he deceived you in the first place.'

'You are a wise and wonderful man.' I leant over and hugged him.

He hugged me back. 'You bring out the best in me, Maggie.'

'Well, that's a good thing. I hope I bring out the best in Tapakah.'

There was a knock at the door, and I jumped. Frantically, I ferreted around underneath the cushions.

'What are you doing?' Ben asked.

'Um … beats me … looking for something? Don't know what. It was triggered by the door knock.'

'Who is it?' Ben asked.

A female voice said, 'Haley. I have a visitor for you. It's a surprise.'

'Who's Haley?' I asked.

'She runs the café when I'm not around, which is pretty much most of the time.'

Panic stirred in my gut. 'Shit. Do you think the visitor's you know who? Do you think?'

'If it is, what do you want me to do?'

'Deny all knowledge of my existence.'

'Really?'

'Yes!'

'Okay. Go hide in the bedroom.'

Once I was in the bedroom, Ben opened the apartment door. 'That's fantastic. Come on, come in. Let's go get Maggie.' The door closed.

Shit. He'd brought Tapakah in. It must be him. No one else would come looking for me. I had no one else. There was no way I wanted a confrontation here; I wasn't mentally prepared. I flung myself onto the floorboards and slid under the bed. The door opened. I held my breath.

'Maggie? *Maggie?* Where the hell's she gone? She was here a minute ago.'

I closed my eyes and tried to make myself invisible. My mind raced. If he looked under the bed on the opposite side, I could make a break for the door. If he checked the side near the door, I'd be trapped.

Something cold and wet touched my cheek and I shrieked. A whiskery nose tickled my face, and a rough tongue licked my ear. I jumped and cracked my head on the bed. Two big brown eyes peered in at me.

'*Beans!'*

Her face split into a wide grin as she returned to give me a few more licks.

I yelled. 'Ew! Help, Ben, stop her, I'm being licked to death.'

Ben laughed his head off as he dragged me from underneath the bed. 'You do have paranoid tendencies. What the hell were you doing under the bed?'

'Just because you're paranoid, doesn't mean people aren't out to get you. I thought it was Tapakah, and you were letting him in.'

'Bloody hell, you're kidding! You need to trust me. I wouldn't go against your wishes. You still don't trust me, do you?'

'I do. I *do* trust you. I'm a fruitcake is all. My mind's been messed with.'

'It's okay. I get that. Are you happy your little friend is back? Haley said she walked into the café by herself.'

'Very happy.' I gave Beans a thorough head and ear rub. She closed her eyes and looked completely blissed out.

'I'd like one of those. Check out the expression on her face,' Ben said.

I laughed. 'I'll do you later.'

He flashed me a cheeky grin. 'Promise?'

* * * * *

Ben opened a bottle of Sauvignon Blanc and we spent the whole afternoon chatting. Beans lay on the couch between us, her head on my lap. She had her eyes closed, but I had the feeling she was on high alert, ready to spring into action at the scent of a cat, or lemon tart.

'So how come you don't need to work in the café?'

'I make my money from restoring cars. I own the coffee shop, but Haley runs everything. I work as the barista whenever I want to, because I love doing it.'

'Where do you restore your cars?'

'Mum and Dad have a place at Woodend. Big property with a few large sheds. It's only an hour away, so I work from there. They love having me around. The other kids have left and gone overseas. I'm the only one in Australia now.'

'And your relationship recently ended?'

His eyes clouded over. 'Yes. Because of what I mentioned to you before.'

'I'm sorry. I will act on your advice. I promise.'

'Good. But whatever happens, know I'm here for you.'

'I can't tell you how much your friendship means to me, Ben.'

'Ditto.'

We sat in silence for a while listening to the buzz of conversation drifting up from the café. The light was falling outside, and a star was twinkling through the skylight. Eventually, Ben reached across and held my hand. 'I hope it works out for you.'

'Me too.'

'Hungry?'

'Ravenous.'

'Let's eat in the café. Beans can stay here. I'll bring her back a steak.'

Beans rolled over onto her back, chest out, legs in the air. She grinned up at him, her pink tongue hanging out the side of her mouth.

I laughed. 'She seems pretty happy with that plan.'

'Lemon tart for dessert, Beans?' he asked.

Beans stood on her hind legs and commenced her meerkat impersonation.

Ben chuckled. 'That'd be a yes then.' He hauled me off the couch, and still holding my hand, steered me down the narrow staircase. The hubbub of the café enveloped us as we opened the door.

He guided me to a chair facing out towards the street. 'I've reserved a table for two in the corner, Milady.'

'Perfect. I love people watching.'

After making our selection, Ben ordered dinner and I scanned the crowd. I didn't recognise anyone, and it appeared no one recognised me. I was still on edge, worried I'd run into Tapakah. I couldn't shake the adrenaline from my system, so every detail in the café stood out in stark relief.

A familiar figure sat in the corner near the window. It was

the surfer dude. Crikey, didn't he ever work? He was always here. He was probably thinking the same about me. He glanced up, and I caught his eye. He looked quickly away.

'Ben, don't turn around now, but the bloke in the corner by the window, he's always there. Do you know him?'

Ben pretended to turn around and look at the menu. 'He showed up around the same time you did actually. I don't know him. Keeps to himself. Doesn't talk much.'

There was something vaguely familiar about his persona, and I stared at him when he wasn't looking. Tall, well-built, rugged. Seen a fair bit of sun and hard work I'd say. He brushed the hair back off his face. My heart started to pound in my chest as adrenaline kicked in again. The scar on the back of his hand. I recognised it. And the shoes. I'd seen them before. They were unusual, but where had I seen them?

Then it hit me. When I'd accidently stepped out in front of a speeding car, the person who'd saved me had been wearing those shoes! It was the only thing I'd caught a glimpse of. I was positive they were the same shoes.

And the scar on his hand. It was the same as the one on the man in WA — the man who'd held me at gunpoint. The image in my brain was clear. It was a "Z" shaped scar. I remembered thinking at the time, it was as if he'd been branded by Zorro.

It was him. I was sure of it.

He was in my photo book. It was the man called Ashley. Stalking me. Maybe working for Tapakah. Maybe the whole thing was a twisted plot orchestrated by bug boy. Or could it be that Ashley was Tapakah's boss, and Tapakah was the crony in some grander plan? Maybe he owned the café, and Ben was really working for him. My head started to hurt as tentacles of paranoia wound their way through my neurons.

Ben leaned into my line of vision. 'Are you all right? You've turned a whiter shade of pale.'

I barely heard him as I stood. I had to get to the bottom of this once and for all. It was seriously doing my head in. I marched over to the surfer's table, pulled out the chair opposite, and sat down. He visibly jumped.

I reached across the table and yanked off his glasses. Leaning forward, I stared closely at his face. He sat back in surprise and then looked away.

'It is you! You're in disguise, but it's definitely you.'

'Who's you?' he said softly.

'Ashley. The Ashley who held me at gunpoint in WA. The Ashley in my photo album. The Ashley who dragged me from the path of an oncoming car. That's the "you". The you who saved my life. That's *you*.'

He looked at the tabletop and wouldn't meet my stare.

'It is, isn't it? I know it.'

He spoke in a whisper. 'Do you remember?'

This guy was pretty darn thick. 'I just told you what I remember.'

'That's it?' He still wouldn't meet my eyes.

'Yes. That's it.'

He sat silently looking out the window.

'Listen, I need to know what the hell is going on. Stop ignoring me. Why are you stalking me?'

Then another penny dropped.

'Jesus, and I'll bet "you" are the Ashley who made the call to Ben to pick me up in his car.'

He still said nothing. He still wouldn't look at me. It was as if he was trying to pretend I didn't exist. He moved his chair to get up and I grabbed his arm.

'No you don't, buster. Sit! You have to tell me the truth. And why won't you look at me, you gutless wonder?'

He plonked back in the chair with an air of sadness and defeat.

Silence.

'*Well?*

He took a breath. 'The reason I won't look at you, Maggie, is … is … because it breaks my heart.'

I jumped when he spoke my name. He kept on staring at the table as he said, 'It tears me apart when I look in your eyes and you don't see me. When I see nothing, no recognition of who I am, or what we had. That's why I can't look at you.'

I sat in stunned silence. The emotion behind those words was no act. I could feel the waves of it sweeping across the table as he spoke.

'I've lost my two best friends. You and Jason. Jason vanished, is presumed dead. And you're here, but you're not here. Having you here in body, not mind, is probably harder to deal with. After everything, we're strangers to each other and, worst of all, you're in love with the enemy. You're like the walking dead. The man you now love took everything from you, and you think he's a hero.' He shook his head sadly.

'But why are you here? You've been following me, haven't you?'

'Yes. I'm looking out for you because you're my friend. I was determined to find you, and I did. I'm not here to hurt you. I want to make sure you're safe. I will always be here for you, Maggie.'

I didn't know what to say or how to respond, because my mind had stopped. So I said nothing and stared at him staring at the tabletop.

I glanced at Ben over at the corner table. He raised his hands and shoulders in a questioning gesture. I shrugged my shoulders at him.

What should I do? What should I say? I didn't know what to make of his words. What I did know was he rescued me from Tapakah when he thought I was in trouble. And his words, they were so heartfelt.

I reached out and took his hand. He jumped at my touch but still wouldn't look up. Instead, he fixed his gaze on my hand.

'Ashley, thank you for looking out for me. I'm grateful for what you did. And I'm sorry. I'm sorry I don't know who you are. I wish I did.'

A lone tear trickled down his face. It splashed onto the back of my hand and he wiped it away with his thumb.

'I can't remember anything, and I'm scared of everything. I'm a shadow of myself.'

He placed his other hand over mine and held it. A spark of electricity ran through me as we touched.

'Did you feel that, Maggie?'

'The spark?'

'Yes,' he said, sounding hopeful.

'It's static.'

'It's *not* static. And, by the way, the dog is yours. It's not a stray. You don't have to look for the owner because the owner is you.'

'Really? So, her name's Boo?'

'Yes, her name's Boo, but she doesn't mind being called Beans.'

'How the hell do you know I called her Beans?' My heart started to pound again.

A faint smile played around his lips. 'She told me. Oh, and don't tell Tapakah about me, or the dog. He'll have us both killed.'

'I don't believe you.'

'Well, even so, please don't say anything.'

He still wouldn't look at me. He stood, plucked a fifty-dollar note from his pocket and handed it to me. 'That's for the bill, for Ben.'

'You're leaving?'

'Yes, but I'll be back.' He strode out of the café and into the night.

* * * * *

The encounter with Ashley left me feeling upset and confused. If it really was true, and Tapakah was responsible for what happened to me, then I could never forgive him. It was too terrible to consider.

I returned to Ben, who looked concerned. 'I'm sorry, it was rude of me to leave you sitting there, but I had to talk to that man.'

'Who was he?'

'Ashley, the man in my photo book. He was in disguise.' I told Ben the whole story and relayed what Ashley had said.

'Bloody hell. What if it's true? He didn't threaten you or make you feel uncomfortable?'

'Not at all. He was different to when they confronted me in the outback. They wanted to take me away with them. I was frightened, didn't know who the hell they were. If they really are my family, it must be breaking their hearts.'

'It would be your worst nightmare. I feel sorry for him, if what he says is true.'

'How am I ever going to know for sure? What on earth should I do?'

'Maybe you could see a doctor specialising in memory loss. You said Frank was fantastic, and he made you better, but a second opinion from someone outside of Tapakah's camp would be helpful. Perhaps you could get treatment to help restore your memory?'

'I'm actually scared of it coming back. I embraced the new start because I thought my past was horrible. It must've been, if I tried to commit suicide. I feel mixed up now, but happy, not suicidal, and I do love Tapakah. He's been nothing but good to me, well, until the incident today. That threw everything into doubt.'

'Maybe wait and see where things lead. You should talk to Tapakah and find out what he has to say. Just take it from there.'

'You're right, I can't solve this problem by thinking. It makes my head hurt. I need to take things as they come. Enjoy what's now. Like sitting here with you, enjoying your company and delicious food and wine. That makes me happy.'

Ben squeezed my hand. 'It makes me happy too. Whoever you end up with is a very lucky man.'

He regarded me with his green eyes and I felt myself blush. Ben smiled. 'Sorry, I didn't mean to embarrass you.'

'It's okay. I blush at the drop of a hat. It's so annoying.'

'You look hot.' He topped up my glass. 'Here, have some wine to cool you down.'

Funnily enough, I hadn't registered, until right that second, how handsome Ben was. Just went to show how distracted I'd been.

He was a classic Italian hunk. Thick black wavy hair, square jaw with a slight cleft, roman nose and a sensuous mouth. His lips were just right, and a five o'clock shadow highlighted his strong jaw to perfection. His eyebrows were strong and well-shaped, providing the ideal frame for his gorgeous, soft green eyes. A simple thin, black knit and well-fitting jeans highlighted his muscular physique.

Jeepers. I was starting to feel hot and flustered. I smiled to myself. It was lovely to feel cheerful, normal emotions and appreciate the attractive man sitting across the table from me. I felt extremely lucky.

I only realised I'd been staring when Ben said, 'Now I feel embarrassed.'

'Sorry, I didn't mean to stare. I was appreciating what a handsome bloke you are and thinking how lucky I am to have met you.'

He raised his glass. 'Ditto. Right back at you.'

We clinked glasses.

He smiled. 'Here's to happy endings.'

I giggled, as my mind took a trip to the gutter. 'To happy

endings.'

He shook his head and laughed. 'I didn't mean that sort of happy ending.'

'I know what you meant, Ben.'

'Well, since you brought it up—' he said, trailing off.

I laughed. 'I think we'd better stop right there.'

The wine had gone to my head, so I decided to call it a night before I said or did something I'd regret. My life was complicated enough as it was.

---

[11] *Maggie's Playlist: Runaway — Del Shannon*

We headed back upstairs bringing the steak Ben had lovingly prepared for Beans.

Ben put it in a bowl on the floor, and Beans wolfed the lot in two seconds flat, and then with pleading eyes begged for more.

'It barely touched the sides,' Ben said. 'You didn't even savour it, and it was fillet steak too.'

'She probably wants lemon tart for dessert.' Beans immediately spun around in circles.

I took one of the bite sized tarts from the fridge and gave it to her. It was down the hatch and she sat up and begged again.

'This can't be a habit, Beans, or you'll get fat. That's it. It's bedtime now.'

'I've put blankets on the floor,' Ben said. 'Hopefully, she'll like it there.'

Beans immediately leapt into a large comfy leather armchair. She walked around and around in slow circles before flopping down and curling herself into a tight ball. One eye slowly opened to gauge our reaction.

I laughed. 'That'd be a no. Come on, Beans, get off.'

'It's fine. She can stay there; she looks so snug.'

'You're a very lucky dog, Beans.'

Beans winked her eye, closed it, and was instantly asleep.

Ben shook his head. 'Wish I could drop off as fast.'

'Me too.'

'You can have my bed and I'll sleep out here.' He grabbed the shelf of what appeared to be a wall cabinet and pulled it towards him. The shelf rotated so the knick knacks stayed put, and a bed unfolded from the cabinet, the shelf becoming legs for the end of the bed.

'Oh, that's nifty! But I'm happy to sleep here. I don't want to put you out of your bed. The pull down looks very comfy. Plus, I'll be able to keep an eye on Beans if she needs to go for a wee.'

'All right, if you want. If Beans does need to go, wake me. I'll worry about you if I think you've gone outside alone.'

'Will do, and thanks, I appreciate your hospitality.'

'Anytime. Sweet dreams.' He kissed me on the cheek.

I would've so loved a sweet dream. Mine were mostly nightmares.

* * * * *

Even though we'd drunk a shipload of wine, it didn't serve to put me to sleep. It was hot, and as I tossed and turned, the sleeping T-shirt Ben gave me twisted around my body. I couldn't do clothes in bed, so I took it off and tossed back the sheets.

I lay there feeling the cool air against my skin and immediately felt better. Finally, my brain settled, and I drifted off listening to the soft snores of Beans in the chair.

I wasn't sure how long I'd been asleep when a low, deep growl rumbled nearby. There it was again. More menacing this time. And again.

I fumbled for the light switch at the back of the bed. Click. The light was one of those LED energy saving things which took forever to reach full brightness. I blinked, attempting to focus on what the hell was on my bed.

Beans was standing on the chair, her stance in attack mode. Hackles raised, tail stiff as a ramrod, lips drawn and teeth bared, she stared at the bed.

A six-inch-thick black line ran around the edge of the bed. What was it? A pattern on the sheet? I reached out to touch it and the line receded from my hand.

The light finally hit full capacity and I saw what surrounded me. Thousands of glistening black eyes fixed on mine. Thousands of antennae swept the air, and even more legs moved forward in a steady advance towards me.

Beans barked wildly, and I screamed my lungs out. The door flew open and Ben raced in, baseball bat at the ready. He looked back and forth for an intruder, ready to whack him to kingdom come.

'What is it?' He ran over to the bed, looking wildly around the room. He turned to face me and colour drained from his face.

I sat with my arms and legs scrunched up as far as I could get them, encircled by a pulsating mass of cockroaches.

'Holy Mother of God,' he whispered. '*Cockroaches!* I hate cockroaches.'

He dropped the baseball bat, grabbed a chair and pushed it next to the bed. He stood on it and held out his arms.

'Give me your hands. I'm going to pull you up and out of there.'

A loud, menacing hiss erupted from the roaches, and Ben nearly fell off the chair in fright.

Choice expletives erupted from his mouth, as he fought to regain his balance. He managed to save himself. 'On three, jump up and into my arms. I'll pull you out. One … two … *three!*'

I launched myself into a clumsy upward swan dive, and Ben grasped me under the armpits and pulled me towards him. I made like a koala and encircled him with my legs. The chair tipped and we wobbled precariously for a split second before hitting the deck. Ben took the full force of the fall, and the chair shattered beneath us.

He scrambled to his feet, hauled me up, and dragged me towards the kitchen.

'What are you doing?' I gasped.

'Bug spray.'

'No. *No!* You can't kill them. It's … there's … too many. We can barricade ourselves in the other room until morning.' I seized his hand and pulled him into the bedroom.

'Beans!' I yelled. *'Where's Beans?* Get in here. *Now!'*

Beans was already sitting on Ben's bed.

'No flies on you, is there Beans?' I slammed the door shut.

'Do you have any duck tape handy?'

Ben looked at me quizzically. 'Well, not in the bedroom.'

'You should never be without duck tape. We need to seal any cracks.'

'I think it's called *duct* tape.'

I ignored him and ran into the ensuite. I grabbed a towel and the bottle of *Dior Eau Sauvage* aftershave from the vanity.

'What in God's name are you doing?'

I rolled up the towel and jammed it in the crack under the door. Then I doused the towels with aftershave. *Phew!* Strong enough to repel anything. I could never understand why some men marinated themselves in aftershave. Such a turn off and played hell with my sinuses.

Ben ferreted around in the wardrobe. 'Bingo!' He held up a roll of masking tape. 'There was some in my sister's craft box.' He looked pretty happy with himself.

'Fantastic. Cover up the downlights. They can get in through those. And cover those ventilation strips too.'

I ran around the room looking for more entry points. Searching through the craft box, I found Blu Tack. *Perfect!* That stuff was as handy as duck tape.

There were numerous cracks in the skirting boards, so I knelt on all fours and sealed them up. 'Those suckers can squeeze through the narrowest of gaps. Make sure you seal up every nook and cranny.'

Ben had climbed on the bed and was busy taping up the ventilation slots. He turned and jumped off the bed. '*Whoa!* Maggie. That's a sight for sore eyes.' He looked away, picked up a blanket and threw it over to me.

My face spontaneously ignited into a blazing furnace. It felt the hottest it'd ever been, well, as far as I could remember anyway.

I'd been totally in action mode and hadn't registered the fact I was running around stark naked.

Beans lay on the bed staring at me. I felt myself turn even redder.

I tucked up my legs to conceal my nether regions, covered my breasts with one arm, and tugged the blanket over my head with the other. I sat huddled in the corner of the room under my blanket tent. I wasn't coming out anytime soon, that was for sure. My face burned so hot I reckoned it would probably take two hours for the heat to dissipate.

I didn't know why I felt so embarrassed. I was comfortable with my body and certainly wasn't a prude.

I heard Ben laughing. 'Maggie, what are you doing?'

'Um … nothing … just sitting,' I mumbled.

'Come out.'

'No. I'm embarrassed.'

'Why the hell for?'

'I'm not sure, but *duh*, probably because you saw me naked. And possibly in the most unflattering position. I mean, we hardly know each other; it's *embarrassing*.'

He laughed. 'Don't be embarrassed. I know you intimately now.'

'Oh, and that's supposed to make me feel better how?'

'Come out, or I'll have to come in there and get you.'

'No. I need to wait for my face to dial down to at least the colour of beetroot.'

'You're being silly. Come out. I have a robe here you can wear.'

'No. Not coming.'

'Go get her, Beans,' he whispered.

There was a thump as Beans hit the floor, and then the scrabble of nails across floorboards. Oh dear, scratches in the wood.

The blanket shifted as Beans snatched a corner and yanked. I yanked back. Beans growled and pulled harder. I hung onto the blanket for dear life, but Beans was determined. She was in tug of war mode, and she was winning.

How could it be? I gripped the blanket with all my strength. There was no way she could get purchase on those slippery boards. How the hell was she winning?

Ben was standing by with the robe as Beans yanked the blanket from my grip. He held it up and looked away as I stood up and slipped into it.

'I don't know why you're looking away,' I grumped. 'You've already seen everything there is to see.'

'I was trying to be respectful.' He sounded hurt.

'I'm sorry, I know you were.' I started to giggle.

'What's so funny?'

'Everything.' I began to snort with laughter.

Ben's shoulders shook as he joined in. 'I'm glad you can see the funny side.'

We laughed ourselves silly, until finally, wiping tears from our eyes, we turned our attention to the door. Something moved beneath the doorknob.

'The keyhole!' I grabbed a piece of Blu Tack and raced across to the door as a pair of spikey legs protruded through. I slammed my fist hard against the door. 'No, you don't, sucker!' The legs retreated and I plugged up the keyhole good and proper.

My lack of attention to detail disappointed me. 'Crikey, I can't believe I missed that.'

'So, what now? We're trapped. I must've left my phone in the other room.'

'Wait until first light. They hate the light, and the way the sun blasts through the skylight out there, I have no doubt they'll scarper.'

'I've never seen so many cockroaches. It's disgusting. The place is infested. The health department will close the café down.'

'It's not your fault. Trust me, after I leave here, you won't see them again.'

'What are you talking about? It's nothing to do with you. They're just cockroaches.'

What could I say? I couldn't tell him.

'It's just a feeling I have.'

He rubbed the stubble on his chin. 'Well, I hope you're right. Never a dull moment, ay?'

'Yeah, I wish.'

'Are you tired?'

'Exhausted.'

'Me too. You have the bed. I'll sleep on the floor.'

'No way. We can share the bed, it's huge. I promise I'll behave myself.'

He shook his head. 'It's not you I'm worried about. Sorry, but I can't get that image of you out of my head.'

Oh, good one, Ben. Thanks for that. The furnace in my face reignited, and I pressed my cold hands against my cheeks for relief.

'Hot under the collar, Maggie? Well, it's how I feel about you. To be honest, I don't think I could trust myself.

Oh Jesus. I didn't know what to say. So, I didn't say anything.

Ben had his head down and wouldn't look at me. I think he

was taking his turn at embarrassment. He twisted the corner of the sheet into a tight, coiled snake of material. He had beautiful hands, and the veins stood out underneath his olive skin as he worked. To be honest, it wouldn't take much persuasion to let him run those hands over my body. In fact, I wouldn't need any persuasion, particularly as sexual activity seemed to be one of the few things that made my overloaded brain switch off.

The sexual tension in the room was so thick you couldn't cut it with a knife. You'd need a chain saw.

I suddenly realised how easy it would be to be unfaithful, put in the right circumstances. A naked woman, rescued from hordes of cockroaches by smoking hot Italian man, locked in a room together until morning, with a bucket load of alcohol still flowing through their veins. I mean, really, no one would stand a chance. You wouldn't be human.

I thought about Tapakah. Maybe he was in a similar situation, well, he wouldn't fear roaches, but perhaps, somehow circumstances conspired to put him in a compromising position he couldn't resist. Maybe he still loved me, like I still loved him.

If he'd had a fling, it could be because of extenuating circumstances. Like the extenuating circumstances here. And really, my life was just beginning, same as Tapakah's. I hadn't experienced other men, that I remembered anyway, and he hadn't had other women, so wouldn't it be better we had, before committing ourselves to one person. Wouldn't it? *Wouldn't it?*

'Maggie? You haven't said anything. I've upset you.'

'No, you're honest. I love that. I was just thinking.'

'What were you thinking?'

'About everything. Every angle, every possibility, every which way. Up, down, inside and out. I think about things so much it makes my head hurt. But you know what? Right here, right now, I'm tired of thinking.

'I'm tired of thinking about what's right, what's wrong, the what ifs, the whys and the wherefores. I'm really attracted to you, but I want to do the right thing. The problem is, I'm not sure what the right thing is anymore.'

'I know how that feels,' Ben said softly.

No more thinking. I scooped up Beans and kicked the blanket across the floor as I carried her into the bathroom. I placed Beans on the floor and closed the door behind me. I used the blanket to make up a bed on the floor. It would be comfortable enough. Decision made.

Ben talked to me through the closed door. 'What's going on?'

I came out of the bathroom and closed the door behind me.

'I can't do it, Ben. I just can't. Not with Beans watching.'

He looked at me in astonishment.

'What? You're saying you want to sleep with me? *Really?* What about ... I mean ... do you think?'

'I'm done with thinking. It makes my head hurt.'

He ran both hands through his hair and pressed them hard against the sides of his skull. It had the effect of pulling his eyes back, making them look slightly oriental, and somehow even sexier.

'You're sure?'

I nodded.

'But it has to be no strings. Given everything that's going on, it must be string less. No strings, no knots, no complications.'

'I'll try, but I don't know if I can do no strings.'

'Me neither. But I'm willing to give it a go.'

'I can undo one knot for you then.' He gently undid the tie around my robe and slid his hands over my shoulders. The silk robe caressed my skin as it fell to the floor. He took a sharp breath as his hands caressed my back and slid over my hips. He whispered. 'You look spectacular from every angle.' He pulled me in close. 'I wanted you from the first minute I saw you. I never thought it could happen.'

His warm body was hard up against mine, my breasts pressing into his chest. He slid his hand up my spine and cradled my head in his hand. 'I'm going to kiss your sweet mouth until your knees go weak.'

I put my arms around his neck. 'They already are.'

'Then they won't know what hit them by the time I've finished with you,' he whispered throatily in my ear.

That did it.

All doubt retreated as my body exploded with desire. I leant up to kiss him, and as our lips touched something else exploded. An almighty crash reverberated above our heads as the skylight window disintegrated. I screamed as a shower of glass splinters rained on our naked bodies.

An enormous black crow zoomed in through the shattered window and flapped madly around the room. It dive-bombed our heads and targeted Ben, trying to peck out his eyes. Ben shielded his face. The crow screeched with furious intent and pecked viciously at his arms.

I yelled and threw a cushion at it. 'Bugger off!'

The crow alighted on the bedside lamp and cocked its head, staring at me with black eyes. Beans barked hysterically in the bathroom, scratching and thumping on the door, frantically trying to dig her way in.

The crow took flight and swooped at Ben again. He ducked but couldn't run. Broken glass surrounded us, and we had bare feet. I picked up a pillow. 'Here use this to cover your head. I'm going to get shoes.'

He yelled, swatting wildly at the crow with his pillow. 'You can't walk over the glass!'

I picked up another two pillows. 'I don't intend to.'

Thank God Ben had a well-dressed bed with a top-notch bedding scheme. He had a mountain of pillows. There were plump European squares, sleeping pillows, standard pillows with standard shams, boudoir and accent cushions. I'd bet he never thought his flair for interior design would save his life one day.

'Watch and learn.' I placed a pillow under each foot and

ploughed my way through the broken glass to the wardrobe. There, I extracted a pair of shoes and threw them to him. I chucked a spare shoe at the crow who was having another go at Ben and slipped on a pair of his rather stylish brogues.

Ben bent over to put on his shoes and the crow flew up from behind and pecked him a beauty on the arse.

'*Vaffanculo!*' He rubbed his buttocks and examined his blood-stained hand. 'The bastard's drawn blood. Thank God there's only one of the mongrels.'

No sooner were the words out of his mouth than another four crows flew in.

He grabbed my hand. '*Che palle!* Come on, I'm getting you out of here.'

I stared at the roof. 'Um … we've got trouble.'

A thick black cloud followed the crows in through the window and swirled in the middle of the room.

A deep humming filled the air as it spun faster and faster, drawing in more of the black through the window. A shrieking willy-willy from hell had blocked our escape.

Ben's deep voice shouted out strings of Italian expletives. Well, I assumed he was swearing. Maybe he was praying. I couldn't speak Italian.

'Jesus Christ, what the hell is it?' he yelled.

I wasn't sure, but I certainly wasn't going to hang around and find out. 'Grab as much bedding as you can. I'll get clothes. Get your sister's craft box.'

'Why?'

'We're going to hunker down in the bathroom.'

The willy-willy had expanded to fill three quarters of the room. The edge of the black tornado was inches away from my face. I squinted to try and make out what comprised it.

'*Moths!*' I yelled. 'Bogong moths.'

'I *hate* moths!'

The tornado split apart, scattering thousands upon thousands of moths around the room. Frantic, fluttering, swarming, crazy moths bombarded us with kamikaze ferocity.

Their wings beat against our bodies. Ben's arms spun like windmills as he tried to bat them away. Amongst it all, the crows flapped and screeched around our heads. My eyes stung with moth dust and I could barely breathe. Ben disappeared in a cloud of moths. The visibility reduced to zero as the room reached maximum moth capacity. The moths were suffocating us. We were going to die. Murdered by moths.

The humming noise vibrated in my ears as I made a frantic dash to where I figured Ben was. Moths enveloped me. Millions of wings fluttered wildly against my body, millions of tiny legs scratched and tickled against my skin. They crawled up my nose and poked into my ears. The room smelt of honey and old socks. Sweet and disgusting.

I ran smack into him, caught hold of an arm and pulled him to where I estimated the bathroom door to be. Fumbling around, I finally found the handle.

I yelled into his ear. 'On *three*!'

I tugged at his hand. 'One — two — *three*!'

I flung open the door, shoved Ben inside and slammed it shut behind us. A few hundred moths had followed us in, but we could handle that.

Beans jumped up and down and spun around with joy at the sight of us. Bloody paw prints decorated the white tiles, and streaks of blood covered the bottom of the door. She had worn out her paw pads from trying to get to us.

Grabbing hand towels, we brushed the moths off our bodies. A thick layer of moth dust covered us from head to foot. The remaining moths flew up to the ceiling and fluttered annoyingly around the bathroom light, but they left us alone.

'Before we tend to Beans, we have to get this stuff off. It could be toxic.' I stepped into the shower and turned on the water.

'Right behind you, if that's okay.'

It was a double shower, so we had plenty of room. Ben stood politely with his back to me as he showered, and I to him.

The water blasted the moth debris off our bodies. 'Oh, my God, that feels so good.'

Ben coughed. 'I'm going to have to stay in here for twenty-four hours before I feel clean. And I'm going to have nightmares forever, I reckon. I think I'm gonna need counselling or something.'

'Me too.' I turned to glance at him.

Water ran over his back and buttocks, cutting through the dust to reveal streaks of olive skin. His broad muscular shoulders flexed as he shampooed his hair. The white tiles highlighted the definition of his arms and biceps. Strong muscular legs curved in all the right places. He had a body to die for.

My pulse increased rapidly, and I quickly looked away. I turned the cold-water tap to full bore and gasped as the frigid water hit my body.

'Are you okay?'

'Yep. I'm done.' I turned off the taps.

Ben turned off his shower and grabbed a bath towel from the rail. He handed it to me and wrapped one around himself. Pulling on jocks, he finished drying himself.

Ben looked at Beans. 'Poor baby.' He bent up a leg and examined her paw. 'She's done some damage.' He opened the cupboard door under the vanity and took out a first aid kit. He looked up at me. 'Are you injured?'

'Apart from minor cuts and abrasions, incredibly itchy, burning eyes and a ton of moth dust in my lungs, I'm fine.' I placed my wet towel in the linen basket and looked around for clothes to put on. There were none.

I was stark naked. Ben was lucky — he had jocks on. Feeling self-conscious, I turned my back to him. As luck would have it, I turned to face a very large bathroom mirror. I had nowhere to hide. Ben laughed as he saw the look on my face.

'Here, I managed to bring something in.' He held out a beautiful black shirt. 'That's all though. I'm sorry.'

'Nice. Hugo Boss.' I slipped into the soft fabric.

Ben smiled and began to button me up. He started at the bottom of the shirt and worked his way up slowly and methodically. His beautiful hands took each button and carefully inserted it into the appropriate buttonhole. His body radiated heat, so close to mine, the scent of his hair, the touch of his bare legs against mine.

How could being buttoned up, as opposed to being unbuttoned, feel so incredibly erotic?

'How high shall I button you?'

'That'll do it. I don't think I could take anymore.'

We gazed into each other's eyes and simultaneously said, '*Jesus*, your eyes are red.'

'Moth dust,' I said. 'We should rinse them out.'

Ben found tubes of saline eyewash in the first aid kit, and we doused our eyes until they didn't feel itchy anymore. Ben bathed and bandaged Beans paws, leaving her front legs with a stylish white sock look. 'Don't try and chew them off, okay?' he warned her.

Beans looked at him gratefully and flopped onto the tiles. She was fast asleep in seconds.

Ben stroked her gently. 'Literally worn herself out to the bone.'

Beans groaned in appreciation. Ben then turned his attention to my cuts and abrasions, gently bathing and dressing them as required. I wasn't too bad, given the circumstances.

Ben had fared considerably worse. He was covered with impaled glass and cuts.

I refilled the basin with warm water. 'Come here, I'll do you now.'

He gave me a cheeky smile. 'Promise?'

'You have a one-track mind. Here, turn around. Crikey, there are bits of glass embedded in your back.' I rummaged in the first aid kit for a pair of tweezers. 'They're not shards, so I think I can extract them safely, but it might sting a bit.'

'Go for it.'

I methodically extracted the bits of glass from his back and dropped them into a little stainless-steel bowl. *Clink. Clink. Clink.*

There were thirty-three in all. Ben had taken the worst of it, and I'm sure the process wasn't erotic in the least.

'I feel like I'm in a Western,' I said. 'Me digging into your flesh and extracting bullets.'

'I wish I'd had a gun to take out those damn crows. My arse is killing me.'

'I forgot about that. You'd better let me take a look.' I tried to suppress the grin spreading across my face.

'Oh, I see. This is payback time. There's no way I'm going to let you poke around in my bum.'

'Well, it looked to me like the crow took out a fair chunk. If it gets infected, you won't be able to sit, or drive. Come on, bend over the vanity and let me have a look.'

He laughed and shook his head as he turned around and leant over the basin.

I hooked my fingers on each side of his jocks and slowly pulled them down to reveal his well-formed, gorgeous buttocks. As I suspected, the crow had bestowed him with a particularly nasty gash.

Ben's jocks were in the way, caught under his bum. I edged his legs apart with my foot and they fell to the floor around his ankles. A shiver ran through his body as they fell.

'Step,' I said. He lifted one foot and then the other so I could remove them from around his ankles. As I bent to retrieve them, my hair brushed against his legs.

'It's bleeding; there's blood everywhere. Are you all right with me cleaning you up?'

'Yeah, Maggie,' he said, somewhat hoarsely.

I took a clean face washer, dipped it in warm water and gently bathed the area until the blood was gone. The blood had trickled into some hard to reach places, but I managed to get it all. I flooded the cut with saline, patted it dry and applied Steri-strips to pull the wound together. Ben observed me in the mirror as I stood back to admire my handy work.

'Okay, you might as well say it.'

I grinned. 'That's a sight for sore eyes, if ever I've seen one.'

'Yep, I was waiting for that one.' He smiled. 'All done?'

'All done. You'll live. It's a nasty gash, but I don't think it needs stitches. See how you go.' I handed him his jocks.

Ben spoke to me in the mirror. 'Maggie, this may sound really weird, but that whole experience was incredibly erotic.'

'*What?* The whole cockroach, crow flapping, beak stabbing, moth laden, glass-shattering experience? You're crazy.'

'*No!* Not *that*. Of course not. The whole me bending over the sink, and you peeling off my jocks, having your eyes on me, feeling vulnerable and exposed, and the way you moved my legs apart with your feet so my jocks dropped. I felt every second against my skin as they fell. And bathing me with your gentle hands … I could feel your breath on my skin, down there. Jesus Christ …' he said trailing off.

He pushed himself off the vanity and turned around.

I took a step back. 'Oh, my God. That's obviously not a gun in your pocket, because you don't have a gun, or a pocket, for that matter.'

I covered Beans with a towel.

'What's that for?' Ben asked.

'You'll scare the dog. Now, where's my blanket? I looked around in the other direction. I needed to retreat into my blanket tent. Fast.

Ben laughed. 'It's okay, forget the blanket.'

I shielded my eyes as I turned from Beans towards him,

which sent Ben into a fit of laughter. He'd put his jocks back on and the fabric was straining at the seams.

'Do you think the material is gonna hold? I mean, really—'

We dissolved into gales of laughter. I laughed so much my sides hurt, and I could hardly breathe. I laughed so hard it turned into a nasty cough. Moth dust. Ben handed me a glass of water.

He wiped the tears from his eyes, sat on the closed toilet seat and tried to catch his breath. 'So, we're staying here all night?'

I nodded.

He beckoned to me. 'Come. Sit on my lap.'

'Is it safe?'

'Don't start.'

I sat and he held me and kissed my neck.

'Seriously, it's weird that what you did to me felt so erotic. Almost better than sex. Though God, it made me want to—'

'It's not weird. I felt the same when you buttoned my shirt.'

'Really?'

'Yep.'

He stroked the back of my neck. 'We're good together.'

'Very good.'

'Now, what the hell was that out there? I think you know more than you're letting on.'

'Maybe.'

'Then tell me.'

'You wouldn't believe me. No one would.'

'Try me.'

'No. I can't, so please don't ask.'

He hugged me and planted a kiss on my cheek. 'Forget it. It's fine. How are we going to sleep?'

'In the spa bath?'

I lined the spa bath with all the towels I could find. 'You get in first.'

Ben clambered in, and I positioned myself between his legs. I covered us with the blanket, popped a hand towel under the back of his neck, and somehow, after everything, we slept.

Chapter 12: Stake Out Make Out

After leaving Maggie at the café, I returned to the hotel room to sleep. I was bone tired and wrung out. I hadn't expected her to see through my disguise and confront me. She'd taken me by surprise all right. Great to see she still had fight left in her.

I lay on the bed fully clothed and stared at the ceiling. I felt lonely and desperate. I had plenty of friends but didn't want to see any of them. I just wanted Maggie and Jason back.

God, I wish she'd remembered ... when we touched. She could be lying next to me right now, tucked up in my arms.

I'd always carried a torch for her, but I'd had my chance and let her go. Dumb son of a bitch that I was. I'd thought she was too good for me, and had regretted that stupid decision ever since. In a shit twist of fate, she'd ended up with my best mate, Jason. Now, he was missing, probably dead, and I could've had a chance with Maggie. Except she couldn't remember me, and she was in love with the thing I hated most in the world. It was a cruel joke. Someone up there hated me.

Ben seemed like a top bloke. I was glad she'd found a friend. I wondered what the hell was going on with Tapakah? Perhaps she'd come to her senses, at least about him.

It was fantastic having Boo on the ground as a spy. I had to laugh at some of the vision she'd relayed back to us. The part where Maggie was searching high and low in the house for her. Boo had floated up on top of cupboards and bookshelves and even hovered behind her as she ran around the house searching. Anyone who said dogs didn't have a sense of humour didn't know dogs.

It was bloody hard seeing Maggie with Tapakah. Like torture. My heart pounded just thinking about it. Watching her want him. It was sick. And what was with him now? Trying to be the perfect gentleman, wanting to marry her? Fuck me.

I needed to focus on the positives. At least she was safe. She seemed healthier. It appeared Tapakah was looking after her well. And Billy seemed like an awesome kid. I wondered what his story was. He certainly loved Maggie. But that wasn't hard; everyone loved Maggie.

Drom was tapping inside my head, so I opened the link. It'd become second nature now.

'You okay, Ash? What's happening?'

'Yeah, I'm fine. Back at the hotel. Beans was upstairs in the café, so you wouldn't have seen this. Maggie rumbled me. Saw through my disguise and confronted me.'

'Jesus, how did that go?'

'Weird. She knew who I was from the WA mission, and when I saved her from being hit by a car, and from the photos, obviously. But she still doesn't remember. She was nice to me though. Thanked me. Perhaps it gave her something to reflect on. The whole thing sucks.'

'I know,' he said sadly. 'We've been watching Boo's relays.'

'What've you been up to, Drom? Still going back to Hanging Rock?'

'Yes,' he said, quietly.

'You really think Jasmine's still alive?' The image of Jasmine plunging to her death from the top of the rock still haunted me. I could only imagine how Drom felt, loving her as he did.

Silence.

'*Drom?*'

'Who knows. I'm drawn back there. I can't move on.'

'You're grieving. Don't be so hard on yourself. You'll just have to go with the flow.'

'When are you coming back? Everyone misses you.'

'Who knows.'

'Well, look after yourself. I'll let you get some shut-eye.'

'Roger that. Talk soon. Give everyone a hug from me.'

'I will, but maybe not Christos.' The tone in Drom's voice was grim.

'He's still causing trouble?' Bloody Christos. I was still angry at his shape shifting antics, tricking people into having sex with him. If it wasn't for Boo, I'd have believed he was Maggie and … well, I wasn't going there!

'Yep. He changed into Jasmine and rang the doorbell.'

'The sick bastard!'

'For a minute, I believed it was her. I wanted it to be true. I wanted to hold her, kiss her, but I knew it was a lie. You should've seen the Maestro. She went right off. I thought Christos was history. He was so ashamed and upset that I couldn't be angry with him for long. He's like a big, dumb, sex obsessed puppy.'

'Jesus, I would've punched his lights out. He'd better not try anything like that on me again.'

'Yeah, every time I talk to a nice girl, I wonder if it could be him.'

'I know. I considered making a few booty calls, but I won't until I'm sure Christos is under control.'

'Wise move, Ash. Night. Hope you sleep.'

'You too. Night, Drom.'

There was a sensation in my head, like a pressure valve shutting, as the link closed.

I thought about having a shower but couldn't be bothered. I

reached out for Maggie with my mind, but it was liking hitting a wall. Nothing. Whatever Tapakah had done to her had destroyed our ability to connect. *Bastard!*

I picked up the scotch bottle sitting on the bedside table and took a few slugs. And then a few more.

I lay back feeling the warmth in my gullet and the ease in my brain as the alcohol did its work.

Yesterday, I was so low, I came as close as damn to shooting up. I don't know how I did it, but at the last minute, I walked out of that shithole.

I did it for Maggie, I guess. I don't want to go back to that dark place. Just one taste and you're in heaven, and then you're trapped in hell. I deliberated about doing ice, but that's even worse. Plus, you don't know what the hell you're buying these days. I lost another mate to it last week. I'd stick to booze as my drug of choice.

The song *Bad to the Bone* blasted from my mobile phone. I looked at the screen. It was Melanie, a girl I'd met at the Hyatt.

I answered. 'What's up, Mel?'

'What're you up to?'

'In a hotel in the city, lying here doing nothing. I wish it was the Hyatt, but I'm on a stake out.'

'I've just finished my shift.'

'You're welcome to join me for a drink, but I'm probably not the best of company; I've already had a few.'

She said she was wired after a busy day and didn't want to go straight home. I gave her the address, and she said she'd see me in ten minutes. I hung up and thought I'd be sound asleep by then.

I woke to the sound of banging on the door and staggered out of bed. I nearly opened it without checking. *Shit.* I was losing my edge. I returned to the bed and retrieved my gun from under the pillow. I looked through the peephole. It was Melanie. Opening the door slightly, I confirmed she was alone, and shoved the gun down the back of my jeans.

'Come in, sweetheart.' I brushed my hair back and caught sight of myself in the mirror. Jesus, I looked wild.

'Hi, big fella.' She gave me a kiss. 'You stink.'

'Sorry 'bout that, luv. I haven't had a shower.'

'No, not BO, *booze.*'

'Want some?'

She nodded and ambled over to the minibar. Her buttocks, tightly encased in fabric, swayed gently as she walked.

Hooley Dooley. Talk about a hot babe in a tight dress. I'd forgotten how gorgeous she was.

It's your typical stereotype, Maggie would say. Long blonde hair, legs up to here. She wore a tight yellow knitted skirt, wide black belt, bare midriff, and a black boob tube covered her ample cleavage. Black high heels and black nail polish completed the picture.

Melanie bent over and took a bottle out of the minibar. I stood and admired the view. She turned and caught me looking. She had big brown eyes, a turned-up nose and the cutest smile. Her teeth were as white as snow.

Melanie poured herself a drink and sat in a tub chair. She crossed one long brown leg over the other and I caught a glimpse of — Holy *Moley.*

'What's with the Sharon Stone move?' I said, taken aback.

She smiled sweetly. 'Are you shocked?'

'Well, unbelievably, yes I am.'

She giggled. 'Can't be. Not big, tough, seen and done everything, Ashley.'

'I'm shocked because it's you. I've seen plenty of pussy in my life, sweetheart.'

'Want some of mine?' She uncrossed and parted her legs so I could see straight up her skirt.

'There's no beating around the bush with you, is there? What's gotten into you?'

'I want you to get into me.' She took a condom from her bag and placed it on the bedside table. Walking over to me, she put her arms around my neck and rubbed her body against mine.

She was bloody gorgeous. I could feel my heart pounding in my chest. I leaned to one side, surreptitiously took out my gun and tucked it under a nearby cushion.

Then I wondered if it was a trap. Maybe she'd been roached. No obvious signs, but.

Melanie ran her hands over my body, her nails dragging against my shirt. Making her way underneath my T-shirt, she ran them around my back and to the front again, where she undid my belt and the top button of my jeans. The zip went down and her hand was in my pants before I could stop her. I couldn't stop her. I didn't want to.

I groaned as she pulled down my pants. Pushing me onto the bed, she yanked off my boots and dispatched my jeans and jocks. I peeled off my T-shirt and she was on top of me. I could feel her warm, wet flesh on my stomach as she bent to lick my nipples. She removed her top, and I cradled her beautiful breasts as she undid her belt. She leant forward, allowing me to bury my face in her breasts and suck her nipples.

She was trying to mount me already. I held her off and grabbed the condom. I took it from the packet and she snatched it, rolling it on with her mouth. She mounted me, and I moaned with the heat of her. Her face flushed and her eyes shut tight as she rode me into oblivion.

Melanie had her eyes closed the whole time. I wondered who she was thinking of. My eyes were wide open, but all I could see and think of was Maggie.

Melanie lay quietly in my arms when she'd finished with me.

'What was that about, luv?'

'Revenge sex. Sorry.'

'Don't be. Anytime.'

'My boyfriend cheated on me.'

'Yeah, I figured. Thanks for choosing me.'

'You were handy.'

'Thanks.'

'No, that came out wrong. I knew you wouldn't mind. You're a good friend, Ash.'

'Glad to be of service.'

'I'd better go now.' She slipped on her gear and kissed me on the cheek. 'Later.'

'Yeah, see you later.'

In your dreams.

The door closed and sleep tugged at my brain. I reached over and turned out the light. Sex always worked better than any sleeping pill, I thought as sleep took me.

Shit! I sat bolt upright. Christos! It could've been bloody Christos. I felt my stomach turn.

Stuff it. I didn't care anymore.

I shook my head, flopped back on the bed and fell asleep.

* * * * *

I awoke with a start as Boo, Drom and Fox hammered in my brain for mind access. Opening the link, a visual stream from Boo flooded in — Maggie huddled up on a bed surrounded by cockroaches.

'Bloody hell! Where are you, Boo?'

Ben's café. Upstairs.

'I'm coming.' I leapt out of bed.

Stumbling to pull on my jeans, the vision stream showed Ben flying out of the bedroom with a baseball bat in his hand. He yanked Maggie out of there. Boo was way ahead of them and hightailed it into the bedroom.

'Bloody hell, Maggie. Just typical. No friggin' clothes.'

'Shall I shut the visual?' Boo asked.

'No!' Three instantaneous replies came back.

116

'We need to know what's going on,' Drom said.

'For intelligence and security purposes,' Fox agreed.

'Yeah, right, Fox,' I said.

We watched her run around as she took charge and sealed up the room. 'Jesus Christ, woman, put some friggin' clothes on. How could she not realise?'

Drom laughed. 'She does now.'

'What the hell is she doing under the blanket?'

'She's embarrassed, bless her,' I said. 'Boo! Why the hell were you pulling the blanket off her?'

'Ben told me to and it's fun. I love a good tug of war.'

'Ben seems to be a gentleman,' Fox said. 'See how he's turned his head away.'

'They're getting on like a house on fire,' Drom said.

'Yeah, that's the way. You go girl.'

Drom sounded confused. 'How can you say that? We know how you feel about her.'

'If she hooks up with him, it's a good thing as far as I'm concerned.'

'How so?' Fox asked.

'Well, duh. Because it would suggest things were not all rosy in the Tapakah camp. Anything which takes her out of his arms is a good thing. I don't care who she hooks up with, as long as it's not that piece of slime.'

'Ben just admitted he's got the hots for Maggie,' Drom said.

'So, who wouldn't?' I said.

'Now what's going on? She's picked up Beans and gone in the bathroom. She's making up a bed on the floor,' Fox said.

'Oh, Maggie, don't sleep in there. You're crazy, girl. So much for gentleman Ben,' I said.

'No, wait. She's gone back in the bedroom and closed the door on Boo. *Damn it!* Now we can't see,' Drom said. 'I wonder if we'll ever be able to access her mind again?'

'Ha! That's my girl!'

'What do you mean?' Fox asked.

'What I mean, and what's going on, is Maggie's gonna do Ben.'

'How the hell do you figure that?' Drom asked.

'Because, fellas, she's put the dog out. She used to do it with Jason all the time. Freaked her out if the dog was watching.'

'Is that true, Boo?' Drom asked.

'Indeed.'

'Bloody hell,' Fox said.

'Indeed. And I can't escape. There are no bathroom windows.'

'Oh well, she seems safe enough now, I guess,' Fox said.

'Can you hear anything, Boo?'

There was a loud crash and the sound of desperate barking as Boo went haywire. All we could see was a close-up of the door and two front paws scratching at it like a crazed machine.

We yelled, 'Boo! What's going on? Boo!'

'Bad things! Bad things! There's yelling. Screaming. Breaking glass. I smell feathers, and musty, dusty — moths! Phffft! They're in trouble, Ash.'

Got. *Scratch. Scratch. Scratch.*

To. *Scratch. Scratch. Scratch.*

Get. *Scratch. Scratch. Scratch.*

In. *Scratch. Scratch. Scratch.'*

Luca and Bella joined the mind meld. They must have sensed trouble.

'I'm on my way.' I slammed the hotel door behind me and flew down the stairs. I didn't wait for the lifts. Too slow. Ben's café was two blocks away. I charged up the hill and past that damn cathedral.

'I still get chills every time I see that place,' Luca said.

'Ditto,' Drom said.

I couldn't stop my mind going back there. Poor Luca must find it excruciating. He'd lost six of his brothers that night, and he had had to kill them. He'd had no choice. They were roached. So was he, but somehow, he managed to expel it from his body.

He's the only one to ever have done that. And talk about roaches. There were *millions* of them that day. Poor Maggie was tied up and covered in them from head to foot as they tried to crawl into her body. Beats me how we got through all that. No wonder Luca left the church and came out of the closet, thanks to Christos. That's one thing Christos did right.

'Um … Ash, I can hear your thoughts,' Luca said.

'Shit. Sorry. Thanks.' I compartmentalised my brain to keep my thoughts private. I could still receive the vision stream and communicate with the others.

Don't ask how we do it. I was still finding my feet and I had to be careful. It was like having a big screen TV in my head; I could have any number of channels on the screen at the same time. Took a bit of getting used to.

We'd got ourselves into a shit storm when we first started mind melding. We weren't skilled enough to tell when the link was open or closed. We encountered sound and vision that we shouldn't have seen or experienced. It was a bit like leaving a voice mail message, and fifteen minutes later you realised you hadn't hung up and it was still recording — *everything*. And by everything, I mean all the senses, not just sound. I think we'd pretty much mastered it now, except for my occasional cock up.

I cranked up the pace and my lungs burned. I had to stop the booze. My legs were lead. My guts were churning. My brain flicked through plans of attack. I'd have to smash the window to get in.

I ran past a tide of rubbish spilling out along a building wall and accidentally kicked a beer bottle. It spun into the gutter and smashed against a parking meter.

Someone shouted, 'Hey, watch it, arsehole!'

A pair of dirty feet stuck out of the refuse, wearing shredded socks that were more hole than sock. It wasn't rubbish. These were the homes of the homeless. People curled up between milk crates, dirty blankets, plastic bags, cardboard boxes, mattresses, towels and paper bags. Possessions caught my eye as I ran past. Cans of drink, peanut butter, crackers, a DVD, an umbrella, a thong, a guitar, a folding chair, a backpack, a dozen jumbo bottles of coke.

'Hurry, Ashley,' Boo said.

'ETA one minute.' I dug deep and picked up the pace again. In that last sixty seconds, my heart was ready to explode.

'Made it. I'm outside, Boo.'

The good thing about telepathy was you didn't have to use your vocal cords. I was breathing so hard speech was impossible. My chest rattled and my lungs wheezed, a legacy of too many fags. At least I'd kicked that habit.

I tried the handle on the café's humongous wooden door in case it happened to be open. It wasn't. All righty then.

I whipped out my Desert Eagle handgun, stood back, and took aim at the plate glass window. This would be spectacular. My finger tightened on the trigger.

'Wait! Stop! Ash, they're okay. They're in the bathroom.'

Thank bloody Christ. I sank to my knees as my body decided to take a well-earned rest.

In my head, a close-up view of the blood streaked bathroom door disappeared, and then reappeared, as the room whizzed around in dizzy circles. Boo was spinning around with joy.

'Boo! Keep still, for Christ's sake,' Fox grumbled. 'It's like watching a B grade movie made with a hand-held camera. Makes you feel sick.'

Boo stopped spinning and the vision showed floor tiles covered in bloody paw prints, and two people who appeared to have been rolled in flour and blood.

'Are you *sure* they're all right, Boo?' I said. 'They look like shit to me.'

'Minor cuts and abrasions and a coating of moth dust. They'll be fine.'

Maggie entered the shower, closely followed by Ben.

'I'm switching off the vision now,' Boo said. 'You voyeurs don't need to *see this. It's irrelevant.'*

'Oh, good one, Boo,' Fox and Drom said.

'I'll let you know if anything untoward happens.'

'And your definition of untoward is?'

'Probably different to yours. You can go now, Ashley.'

'Yeah, right, thanks for that. I busted a pooper valve trying to get here. What if everything turns to shit again? I can't keep running back and forth like a yo-yo. I'll break in and get them out.'

'Their plan is to sleep in the bathroom and wait it out 'til morning. The roaches, moths and birds should've gone by then. If you break in now, you'll be attacked. It's not worth it. Go back to the hotel and get some sleep.'

Boo could be an annoyingly bossy dog at times.

'That's easy for you to say, Boo, one who drops off at the drop of a hat. I'm not going anywhere. I'm staying right here, just in case.'

'I'll come by and keep you company,' Drom offered.

'Me too,' Fox said.

'Nah. Look, I appreciate the offer, but I'm fine. No point all of us sitting out here.'

'Okay. Yell if you need us.'

'Night all. Over and out.' I disconnected. A string of strange *thunks* reverberated in my head as the links snapped shut. It reminded me of yanking the hose from a ducted vacuum system while it's still on. *Ka-thunk! Ka-thunk! Ka-thunk!* It tickled deep in your ears too.

Cardboard boxes littered the adjacent alleyway. Perfect. Dragging them to the alcove in front of the café door, I spread some on the ground. I plonked myself down, leant my back against one side, put my feet on the other, and covered myself with the remaining cardboard. I took out the trusty Desert Eagle and laid it next to me, just in case.

I adjusted the cardboard to stop a draft and closed my eyes.

'Home sweet home.'

I'd joined the ranks of my mates down the road.

Where the hell was I? My brain ticked over slowly trying to make sense of my surroundings.

In the bath, of course. With Ben.

He was breathing into my ear, still fast asleep. My leg was numb. I think it had gone to sleep hours ago, and as I moved, it began to burn with pins and needles.

I peeked over the side of the bath and Beans was still asleep on the floor.

Everything seemed quiet. The remaining moths had arranged themselves into a neat pattern on the ceiling. Each row of moths interlocked with the other. Their heads tucked up underneath the wings of the moths in front of them. They must have been shading their eyes from the light. Tough luck for the front row of moths. I wondered if they rotated like penguins did.

I held onto the side of the bath and pushed myself up.

Beans lifted her head and opened a bleary eye.

I put my finger over my lips. 'Shhh, Beans.' She flopped back down and was instantly asleep.

I padded over to the washbasin and looked in the mirror. Not a pretty sight. My eyes were still red, though not as bad as last night, and my hair stuck out at weird angles from having slept on it while it dried.

The numerous cuts on my arms were crusty with blood. I stared at the ugly scars on the inside of my forearms. My arms were trashed. Oh well, at least I had arms. I forced myself to look on the bright side.

I tiptoed to the door and slowly turned the handle.

'What are you doing?' I jumped at the voice behind me.

'Seeing if the coast is clear.'

Ben hauled himself out of the bath. 'Let me look first.'

'How did you sleep?' I asked.

'Pretty good, considering what happened and where we were.'

I tried to rub the pins and needles from my leg. 'I don't think we moved all night.'

Ben opened the door a smidge and looked out. 'All clear.' He pushed it open and we stepped into the room.

Stuff was everywhere, and everything was obscured by a layer of dust. Broken glass littered the floor and sparkled in the morning sun. A blanket of black feathers, moth wings and dead moths decorated the room.

'Bloody hell, what a mess,' he said.

'I'm so sorry. Your beautiful room is ruined.'

'Don't worry about it. She'll buff.'

'I'll help you clean up.'

'I'll get professional cleaners in. They'll take care of everything.' He looked around in disgust. 'I don't want to spend another minute in this room.'

He returned to the bathroom. 'Come on, Beans, I'm getting you out of here. Up you hop.' He lifted her up, being careful of her bandaged paws.

Broken glass crunched under his shoes as he walked gingerly towards the lounge room door.

'Come on, Maggie, let's go.'

I followed and slowly opened the lounge room door. 'The

roaches are gone, and the room is fine.'

'Thank God for that.' Ben placed Beans gently on the floor. 'I've got clean clothes in the laundry basket.' He found jocks, jeans and T-shirt and relocated behind the kitchen bench to dress. I looked over and he grinned at me.

I laughed. 'What's with the false modesty?'

'Don't want to scare Beans. Or you. Are you hungry?'

'Starving.'

'I have to go downstairs and get things going in the café. Will you be all right on your own?'

'Fine. I'll have a shower and make myself presentable.'

'You look presentable to me.' He came over, kissed me, and slipping his hands inside the shirt he'd lent me, caressed my back and cradled my bum. 'Maggie, do you think we can pick up where we left off? I mean, not now, I have to go, but sometime?'

I kissed him back. 'I hope so.'

The kiss set us on fire, and it was hard to stop. Ben's phone eventually interrupted us. He checked the ID. 'Sorry, got to get this.'

It was torture to let him go. I fanned my flushed face with a magazine. He pulled his T-shirt in and out to get air.

Once he'd hung up, he looked at me and said, 'Damn it. Haley has a flat tire. I need to get cracking.'

'No worries.'

He blew a stray lock of hair back from his forehead. 'We're hot, you and I.'

I touched him with my finger. *Tssst!*

He kissed me on the forehead. 'Come downstairs when you're ready. We'll breakfast together. I'll get something ready for Beans too.'

I pulled on a pair of jeans. 'I'm coming to help. You can order me around and tell me what to do.'

He laughed. 'I like the sound of that.'

Beans was right behind us as we descended the stairs and

unlocked the door into the café. Ben pointed towards the window. 'Flick the light switches on and open the front door. The place needs airing.'

I snapped him out a salute. 'Aye aye, Captain!'

He smiled and looked me up and down. 'I could eat you, right here, right now.'

I giggled. 'I'm not on the menu.' I flicked on the lights, unlocked the door and tried to open it.

'Here, let me help you. It's a bugger to open, needs sanding. Stand clear.' He yanked hard on the door. It flew open, and a pile of rubbish cascaded in. On closer inspection, it wasn't rubbish. It was a nest of cardboard containing a derro with a gun.

I stepped back in fright. '*What the?*'

Beans barked wildly, flung herself at the man and tried to lick him to death.

'Beans, get back!' Ben dragged her away and pushed against the door, trying to shove the man out.

'Hey, take it easy!' the man said.

I recognised the voice immediately. 'Ben, it's Ashley! It's okay.'

'He's got a gun. It's not okay.'

I held out my hand to help him up. 'What the hell are you doing, Ashley?'

He poked the gun into the back of his jeans and stood in one fluid, easy movement without taking my hand. 'Sorry 'bout this, Ben. I'm harmless.' He collected the cardboard from the floor and moved it to one side.

'Doesn't look like it with that piece.'

Ashley stepped backwards holding his hands up. 'Don't worry, I'm leaving.'

'Were you sleeping there all night?' I asked.

He nodded.

'*Why?* Don't you have anywhere to stay?'

126

'Oh, I have places to stay, all right, places I'd much rather be than on the cold tiles out here.'

'So *why?*'

'I had a feeling you were in trouble, so I came by, but when I got here, I sensed everything was fine. I wasn't quite sure what the hell was going on, so I decided to sleep here in case you needed help.'

'Are you psychic?' Ben asked.

'You could say that. I get visual and auditory impressions.' He bent and patted Bean's head. She gazed up at him with loving eyes, one of which seemed to have developed a wink.

'What did you see to make you come by?' Ben asked.

'Bugs. Lots of 'em.'

'Jesus,' Ben said.

Ashley raised his eyebrows. 'I'm right, aren't I?'

Ben stepped back. 'You should come in. I'm gonna make us breakfast. And coffee, lots of coffee. I don't know what the hell is going on, but you obviously have Maggie's best interests at heart. Is that okay with you, Maggie?'

I nodded.

'I appreciate the offer, mate, but I'd better not. I need to go.'

'Why?' I asked.

'You know why, Maggie. Plus, I'm not in disguise.'

'You're scared of Tapakah.'

'I'm scared of losing my friends and family.'

'You're being ridiculous. Tapakah's not like that.'

'Well, this is the message we received from him after we found you in WA.' He flicked through his phone and showed me a text.

Listen up. This is a warning. You have heard what she said, and what she wants. There will be consequences for you and your loved ones if you try to find her, or come anywhere near her. No crystals. No contact. You have been warned.

'That's not his phone number, and it doesn't mention my

name.'

'I think he'd have more than one phone, and he's not silly enough to use names.'

'Well, as I said, he's not like that. I don't believe it. And anyway, he doesn't know where I am, so you'll be safe. Please, stay and have breakfast.'

'Yeah, come on, stay. I'll cook you up whatever you want, on the house.'

Ashley shook his head, moseyed out the front door, checked up and down the street, and came back in.

'Okay, thanks. It's a risk, but I'll stay. You might regret your offer, Ben. I'm so hungry I could eat the arse out of a low flying duck.'

Ben laughed. 'I'll order you the works. What about you, Maggie?'

Before I could reply, Ashley said, 'She'll have a poached egg, hash brown, bacon and a grilled tomato, oh, and a flat white coffee.'

'Good guess. Exactly right,' I said in surprise.

'It wasn't a guess. I know what you like. I know everything about you.'

As we headed towards a table, I realised Ben hadn't asked Ashley what type of coffee he wanted, so I dashed over and gave Ben the heads up.

When I returned to the table, Ashley sat tipped back in his chair, leaning against the wall, his long legs stretched out in front of him. Even though he looked supremely relaxed on the outside, I could sense he was on high alert.

Haley and the rest of the crew arrived, and they and Ben busied themselves getting things ready in the café and making us food and coffee.

Ben brought us our coffees, and Ashley looked out of the window. He was still avoiding eye contact with me. I couldn't communicate with people who did that. It was impossible to connect with them.

I shifted in my chair. 'Why won't you look at me?'

'I've told you why already.'

'Well, you're an idiot.'

He didn't respond and continued to stare out the window.

Frustration was rising, along with my blood pressure. 'You're being ridiculous. I don't know you, and I'm sorry, I can't help that. But I'd love to get to know you. If you won't make eye contact, you're shutting me out, not giving me the opportunity to get to know you. I can't change what's happened, neither can you. If you care for me like you say you do, then be willing to let me in. You'll always be a stranger to me unless you do. Is that what you want?'

Ashley brushed back his hair, crossed his arms over his chest and sighed. His T-shirt strained against his biceps. He stared at the ceiling and said, 'You're right. You're *always* right.' He finally shifted his gaze and looked me straight in the eyes.

The connection was instant and it gave me goose bumps. I found myself lost in his blue eyes as he held my gaze. There was a creak of metal. Ashley held a stainless-steel sugar bowl, and he was squeezing the life out of it.

'Um, Ashley, you're killing the sugar bowl.'

'Oh, shit. Sorry 'bout that.' He let go of the now deformed container. 'Are you cold?'

'No, why?'

'You've got goose bumps.'

I rubbed my arms. 'I know. It's from the eye contact. That wasn't so hard, was it?'

'It felt like coming home.'

'And now, even though I don't know you, I feel like I do.'

'Why don't you let me take you home?' he said softly. 'You don't have to stay. Just meet your dad, your sister, your friends. All the people in that photo album, well, except for Jason, who's still missing. Ben could come along, if you're scared … if you still don't trust me.'

Ben brought over our breakfast. 'What could I come along to?'

'I'm trying to convince Maggie to come and meet her family, and I said she should bring you along, as I know she still doesn't trust me.'

'I'd be happy to go. What have you decided, Maggie?'

'I haven't decided anything. I don't want to think about it. I just want to eat this delicious breakfast you made me.'

Ashley hoed into his bacon and eggs with the works. 'The ball's in your court. Mmmmm. This food is fair dinkum unbelievable, Ben. And the coffee is perfect. How'd you know I like it long, strong and hot?'

'Maggie told me.'

Ashley looked at me. 'I didn't tell you how I like my coffee.'

'Well, you must have. I wouldn't know a weird coffee preference like that.'

A huge grin lit Ashley's face. 'Exactly. You bloody well *remembered!*'

He leant across the table, grabbed my face and gave me a kiss. I sat back in shock.

'You little ripper!' He banged his fist on the table and laughed. 'You remembered!'

His enthusiasm was catching, and Ben laughed along with him. I felt confused. He must've told me. He *must* have.

Ben took my hand. 'He didn't tell you. I could hear everything you were saying. *You* came over and told me.'

'Crikey. I don't even remember doing that. I'm losing it.'

Ashley drummed his fingers on the table. 'No, you're not. You're *finding* it. Your memory's coming back.'

'One coffee preference is hardly my memory coming back,' I snapped. 'It was a lucky guess, is all.'

I was upset and annoyed. I liked to maintain status quo. I didn't like things out of left field. I think somewhere along the line I'd had too many things come out of left field. I just wanted simple. A simple life with Tapakah. Well, that's what I had wanted, until he and the floozy put a spanner in the works. And now there was Ben. I really liked Ben. And now there was Ashley, the mysterious, scary stalker who gave me goose bumps when I looked into his eyes. See, not good. Not simple. It was getting complicated.

I looked up and Ashley was staring at me. This time *I* looked away.

Ben shook his head. 'You're thinking too much, Maggie. I can tell. Let it go.'

'Yes, you're right. I need to concentrate on important things, like my breakfast!' I smiled at him.

'*That's my girl!*' Ben and Ashley said simultaneously, which sent me straight back into think mode.

The café was soon alive with customers and the buzz of conversation filled the room. The sun shone through the windows and painted the wooden walls with an amber glow. It was a warm and inviting space with a lovely ambience. No wonder it was popular.

As Ben cleared away the plates, the café plunged into darkness. The sun disappeared behind a cloud, and the colour was sucked from the room, leaving it grey and dismal. A shiver coursed along my spine.

A figure materialised in the doorway; a man wearing head to toe black leathers and a motorcycle helmet. He filled the space, shoulders squared, legs apart, hands at his sides. His fingers twitched as his hands opened and closed. The black visor on his helmet reflected the café as he scanned the room.

The café fell silent as he stepped through the door. His leathers creaked and the buckles on his boots clinked as he strode towards the counter. Partway, he stopped to pull off his black leather gloves one finger at a time. He tucked them into a pocket. The strap under his chin clicked loudly as he undid it. A nearby waitress started and a little girl dropped her spoon. The clatter as it hit the floor was amplified by the silence.

The whole room held its collective breath as he removed his helmet.

It was Tapakah.

Pushing his aviator sunglasses back on top of his head, he scanned the room with his black eyes. The tension in the room cranked into overdrive.

Ashley and I were out of his line of sight, concealed behind Ben and a waitress. I put my hand on Ashley's head and pushed him under the table.

Ben looked at me in surprise and I made wide eyes at him. He looked at the man in black and then back to me. I nodded. Ben gripped the waitress's arm so she'd stay put.

I didn't want to see Tapakah. I didn't want to talk to him. Not here. Not now. Later maybe. But not now.

A plate smashed in the kitchen breaking the silence and the spell. People began to talk, and Haley switched on music. Tapakah turned away, and I stood, ready to make a break for the stairs. It was a simple, quiet movement but he sensed it. Spinning around on his heel, he nailed me to the wall with his eyes.

Ben looked to me for instruction. I shook my head and shot him a look that said, *'Don't!"*

Tapakah strode towards me and I froze in terror. His expression was a blend of rage, relief, desperation and love. In that order.

'Maggie!' He grabbed my arm. 'Come home with me.' He moved in to kiss me and I turned away.

I shoved him. 'Let me go!'

'What's got into you? Talk to me. You're behaving like a crazy woman. I've been sick with worry.'

'Yes, we need to talk.' I jerked my arm free, pushed past him and made a beeline for the front door.

My intention was to lead him away from Ben and Ashley. I

132

didn't want them involved, and if Ashley was right, I didn't want to put him in danger. I felt sick about this happening in front of Ben. He'd be upset and concerned, and I hoped to God he wouldn't do anything stupid.

Tapakah was hot on my heels as I reached the pavement and headed off down the street.

'*Stop!*' He seized my arm and pushed me up against a hoarding. The back of my head cracked against the wood.

'Ow! Stop it. That *hurt.*'

'Sorry. You're trying my patience.'

He took my wrists and pinned me against the wall. His mouth twitched as his black eyes latched onto mine. The buckles on his jacket dug into my flesh as his body pressed up hard against me. He forced a kiss so passionate and intense my knees gave out completely. I slid down the wall out of his grasp and sat on the ground between his legs.

He squatted beside me. 'I bought you this.' He took out a small black velvet box from his pocket. 'You said you wanted to get engaged, but you left before I could give it to you.' He opened the box. I gasped.

It was the most exquisite object I'd ever seen. The design seemed modern yet mediaeval, contemporary yet ancient. Strands of gold, rose gold and silver intertwined around black stones. Intricate engravings moved and changed with the light. It seemed — *alive.*

'It's exquisite.' I marvelled at its chameleon like qualities. 'It's unpretentious, but stunning. Simple ... yet, yet so complex.'

'Just like you. I gather that means you like it?'

'It's divine.'

'It's made from precious metals, including Damascus steel, because you said you like that, and black diamonds. It's unique, bespoke, made especially for you. It's taken months to craft.'

'Months? But we'd only just discussed getting engaged.'

He smiled softly. 'I know. But I had hopes as soon as I laid eyes on you.'

'Well, you're obviously confused. You've presented it to the wrong woman.'

The smile left his face. 'What do you mean?'

'I think you're confused about who you actually love. You should've presented it to the blonde you were hanging all over at the Hyatt yesterday.'

Tapakah looked shocked.

I nodded. 'Yes, I was there. By happenstance, I saw you; I saw everything, you and her together. You lied to me. You said you were away working. And now, you want to give me a ring? You've got some nerve. Go back to your floozy. I don't want anything to do with you, ever again. To many lies, too much deceit. You can't start a relationship built on lies, and I'm up to my neck in them.'

'Maggie, you've got the wrong idea.'

'So, it wasn't you with that woman? You're denying it?'

'No, I'm not denying it, but it's not what you think. You're wrong about me. I love you. Only you.'

'Who is she? Why did you lie to me?'

'You wouldn't believe me if I told you, and it's nothing, she's just a friend.'

'Oh, here we go. Seriously? There was a whole lot more going on there. I'm not stupid.'

'Okay, it's true I do love her, but it's complicated.'

'Yeah, I know how that feels. Look, if you're not prepared to tell me the whole truth, it's all over, rover. Right here, right now.' I stood and glanced up the road. Two heads poked out of the café door. It was Ben and Ashley. They ducked back as soon as I saw them.

Tapakah pulled me to my feet. 'I don't want to stand in the street and discuss this. Come with me. I'll take you somewhere quiet. I'll tell you everything.'

'I don't know. I guess. Okay then.' I owed him that, and I

really wanted to hear what sort of cock and bull story he'd come up with. He took my hand as we headed back up the street and I snatched it away. He stopped at a parked motorcycle.

'You're kidding. Is this yours?'

'Yes.'

'I didn't know you rode a bike. It's stunning.' I admired the beautiful machine, finished wheels, stainless steel exhausts and muscular looking air intakes and tank. 'That's one sexy techno cruiser. A carbon black Ducati Diavel. Oh my God, I love it.'

'Have you ridden one of these?'

'I know how to ride, but I can't remember if I've ridden a Ducati. Probably not.' I ran my hand along its sexy curves. 'This bike is so hot, so evil looking, just like you.'

The look on Tapakah's face told me he didn't know whether to take that as a compliment or an insult. It was both.

'I can't ride; I have no gear.'

Tapakah unhooked a couple of bags hanging from the handlebars and handed them to me. 'Yes, you have.'

I caught sight of the buckles on a boot and discovered it was a pair of Icon 1000 Elsinore black boots with the classic five strap buckles and stamped metal heel plate. *Seriously* cool.

Next came an Alpinestars Vika Leather Jacket with matching pants and gloves, also in black. This gear, designed specifically for women, helped to make you look hotter than hot.

Finally, there was an AGC matt black helmet, so seriously badass, Darth Vader would have coveted it.

I couldn't wait. I slipped on the jacket, zipped it up, and pulled on the pants and boots. Everything fitted like a glove. Even the gloves.

I felt mega excited. I loved getting new gear I didn't have to go and hunt for myself. I hated shopping. I caught sight of myself in the shop window and I looked good, even if I said so myself. I loved the feel and smell of leather. I was in leather heaven.

Call me easily distracted, but I was elated. The boots were divine. I positioned my foot on the edge of a rubbish bin to better admire them.

I turned around to see Ben and Ashley peeking out from the café window. Ben's face was crinkled in an expression of concern, and Ashley's visage was one of unadulterated fury.

Tapakah had his back to the café, so wasn't aware of what was going on. I felt bad for them, but there was no way I could reassure them without Tapakah knowing.

'So, you like what I bought? Did I choose well?' he asked.

'You chose weller than well. This gear is divine. It's generated such a rush of joyful feelings that riding bikes must've been one of my passions. This gear must have cost you a fortune.'

'It's worth every penny to see you so delighted.' He appraised me with his black eyes. 'You look seriously hot.'

'I feel seriously hot. I just love leather.'

'Shall we go?'

'Let's.'

---

[14] *Maggie's Playlist: You Can Run But You Can't Hide — Solomun Burke*

Yeah, yeah. I was aware I'd been bought.

Bribed. Enticed. Cajoled and seduced by consumer goods. But at least I was aware. I was fully conscious I'd been lured and caught. I don't know if that made it any better, or right, but hell, I was a sucker for all that gear — and the *bike*. *Phew-whee*. I don't know why those things generated such happy feelings, but I felt starved of happy and I wasn't going to turn away from something that made me feel so intensely ecstatic.

I'd completely forgotten the ring. I'd take a pair of biker boots over a ring any day. Just get on bended knee, next to a motorcycle to die for — even though they could kill you in the end — and a pair of biker boots, and I was yours, baby.

Tapakah put on his helmet and swung a leg over the bike. He checked out the café window. I looked but couldn't see anyone.

Damn. *Beans!* I'd forgotten Beans. I'd have to come back tomorrow and get her. I had no doubt Ben would look after her in the meantime.

Tapakah tapped my arm. 'Get on.'

I swung my leg over. The passenger seat was well padded, and the pegs flipped over to just the right position. The engine rumbled into life, and Tapakah blasted off down the road. The acceleration dragged me back so much I had to fling my arms around him to stay on. He did that on purpose. Tapakah was an accomplished rider, but he went at it hard and fast. I had to make like a koala and hold on tight.

He sped past our street, so it appeared we weren't going home. Where the hell was he taking me?

I tapped the Bluetooth comms on the side of the helmet. 'Where are we going?'

'You'll see.'

'Obviously. But where?'

'Somewhere quiet so we can talk. It's an hour and a half ride. You okay with that?'

'Sure.' I was enjoying the prospect of a decent ride.

I settled in and relished the exhilaration as Tapakah weaved his way skillfully through the traffic. Once we hit the highway, Tapakah let the bike rip. It went like a dream, responsive, stable and gutsy. I hoped he'd let me have a go.

We drove though Macedon and the lovely township of Woodend. It seemed familiar to me, although I couldn't recall ever having been there. We rode past the Victoria Hotel, and a chill ran down my spine. I wanted to be sick.

'Tapakah, please pull over … at the milk bar. I need lemonade.'

He stopped at the kerb, and I jumped off feeling claustrophobic and in need of oxygen. I ripped off my helmet and sucked in lungfuls of the fresh mountain air.

Tapakah looked worried. 'What's wrong? You look like you've seen a ghost.'

I wiped sweat from my forehead. 'I feel ill. It hit me as we passed the hotel. Could you get me cold lemonade?'

'Sure.'

He stared at the hotel, his expression grim. Then he turned away and headed into the shop. I was sure he swore under his breath.

What on Earth would suddenly make me feel so crook? It didn't make sense. I was busting for a pee, so headed across the road to the hotel to use the ladies.

It was a classic old Australian pub with verandas and wrought iron lace work. I pushed open the front door and instantly a wave of nausea hit me. My stomach was somersaulting. Crikey, I was going to throw up. A sign pointed the way to the ladies' room, so I made a beeline towards it.

As I advanced, the sicker and dizzier I became. I stumbled in, focusing on the nearest cubicle. My head was spinning as I hit the floor. I remember thinking how nice the room looked with the sun streaming through the frosted windows. Then everything turned black.

* * * * *

I opened my eyes and stared up into the bluest of blue skies. My head bobbed as Tapakah carried me along the street.

'What happened?' I asked.

'You fainted in the women's toilets. How are you feeling now?'

'I'm fine. I remember feeling sick and … and terrified. It was weird, overwhelming. I can't explain it.'

Tapakah put down me on the grass under a shady tree and handed me a bottle of lemonade.

'Thanks.' I took a swig. The bubbly, lemony sweetness settled my stomach straight away.

Tapakah sat next to me. He seemed distant and lost in thought.

'Are you all right?' I asked.

'You should have waited for me to come back. I didn't know where you were.'

'Sorry, I had to pee. I figured I'd only be a minute.'

We both looked over to the hotel as the front door was flung open and a young man ran out and looked desperately up and down the street. When he saw us sitting across the road, he ran full pelt towards us.

'What's he want?' I wondered out loud.

He ran straight up to me and stopped, gasping for breath. 'Hey, I know you!'

'You do?'

'Yes, I helped you back there, in the ladies. You looked familiar, but I couldn't place you straight away, with the hair an' all, but now I remember! You're the woman abducted from here a few months ago. The cops were all over the place.'

'Really? I'm sorry, but I think you have the wrong person.'

He took out his phone. 'No, no it was definitely you. I got a copy of the CCTV footage from the shop next door.' He flicked through his phone and showed me a black and white still.

The grainy image depicted a man carrying a woman out of the pub. The woman seemed limp, her head lolling to one side.

He found another image. 'Here's the close-up of the woman.'

I felt the blood run from my face. There was no doubt. The woman had long black hair, but the pale, white face in the photo was no one else but me.

'See, it *is* you. A detective called Fox interviewed me, and I talked to another guy, a big bloke, um, what's his name? Ash, that's right. And someone else called Drom. So, obviously everything's okay, as you're back?'

The world spun around me. I heard myself mumble something about having lost my memory, but thank you, I was fine. The bike keys were sitting on the ground next to Tapakah's wallet. I curled my hand around them and stood up.

'Lovely to meet you, thanks for your help.' I sauntered over to the bike. The notion of fight or flight crossed my mind.

I wasn't really a fighter and I had the feeling this was a fight I couldn't win. I mean, who the hell was the enemy?

Flight was my preferred option, and I leapt onto the bike. It fired up in an instant, and I was gone. Naught to sixty in two point six seconds. Thank god for the curved seat or I would've slid right off the back.

I powered along the road aware I was on the run again, but this time I had the assistance of 1200 cc of Italian muscle between my legs. I laughed out loud at that fact because it made me think of Ben.

The bike had a gorgeous sound to it, and the brute force of a 162 horsepower engine was exactly what I needed to get me away from the hotel and the shock that addled my brain.

The bike weighed nearly three times more than my body weight, but it handled like a dream. All I had to do was push slightly harder on the bars to get around corners. It was so stable I could chuck it around a bit with no danger. Like so many things, I had no idea how I knew about bikes, but I did. My brain couldn't think of anything else other than staying on the thing, and that's exactly how I wanted it.

I turned a corner and saw the flash of a bright yellow car cruising down the road. It slowed and turned off into a side street. It reminded me of Ben's car, and I wished he were here with me now. He would love this bike and its distinctive Italian styling.

I slowed and enjoyed the ride. I had no idea where I would go. As I slowed, my brain came back online, and the ugly truth battered around in my brain.

Not only did I recognise myself in the CCTV snap, I recognised the man who was carrying me. It was Jason, the guy in the photo album. He was the one who had drugged and kidnapped me. Well, I assumed I was drugged. It sure looked like it. And somewhere along the line, Tapakah had stepped in to save me. So, Ashley was in on it too, and that Drom bloke. It was all a web of lies. And just as I was beginning to trust Ashley.

I wished I had a phone and money. I still didn't have anything other than the clothes I was wearing. I checked the petrol. It was low. I had no choice but to return. Not wanting to get stuck in the middle of nowhere, I dropped a u-ey and headed back from whence I came.

It was a magnificent day, the sun shone, the breeze was cool, and the ride made me feel better. A wedge tailed eagle hovered above me, its form silhouetted perfectly against the azure sky.

Flapping its wings, it gained speed before dropping into a dive bomb heading directly towards me. I knew eagles could dive at over 160 kilometers an hour, so I accelerated as it powered towards me, claws outstretched. I cranked up the speed to seventy kilometers, but the thing was still hot on my tail. This was Tapakah's doing. I powered up to eighty.

The eagle leveled out and flew alongside with ease. It fixed on me with its penetrating eyes. They were black. I cruised along with the magnificent bird at my side, marvelling at its power and majesty. I gave it the thumbs up as I hit Woodend, and it peeled off and headed skyward.

When I rumbled past the hotel, I had no reaction. Tapakah was still sitting on the grass where I'd left him, back against a tree, feet resting on his helmet.

I cruised up to him, turned off the engine and flipped up my visor.

His face was sombre. 'Have fun?'

'It was a blast. Sorry I ran off, but I was freaked out. Still am. I couldn't believe that guy. The photo … it was *me*.'

Tapakah stood. 'I'm so, so sorry. I'm sorry for everything. I said to you I was—'

I cut him off. 'Don't you be sorry. It's hardly your fault. It was the photo of me carried by that man Jason that sent me into a tailspin. It's obviously why I became sick and terrified passing the hotel. Unconscious memories. Now I *know* they're lying. They're the ones who did this to me.'

Tapakah smiled. 'So, there you have it, photographic proof.'

'It's hardly something to smile about.'

142

'Yes, it is. Because now you've found evidence. Proof as to the lengths they will go to, to destroy us.'

'But this happened before you found me, so I don't get it. They were after me *first*? Why? What was I to them before I met you? You said they wanted me to get to you.'

'That's what I always assumed, but now it appears it's you they want.'

'But I have nothing of value.'

'You obviously had something they wanted, or maybe it's you.'

'But for what?'

'I have no idea.'

'Jesus. I wish I knew what the hell was going on. Every day brings something that makes my life more confusing.'

Tapakah put his arm around me. 'Well, I plan to change that. I'll make it all go away. Don't give it another thought.'

'That's easy for you to say. What'll I think about then? Now, let me see, oh yes, what about you and that other woman and—'

Tapakah looked hurt and cut me off. 'I told you, we need to talk. Let's go.'

We climbed back on the bike and Tapakah blasted off at speed. I was ready for it and hung on tight.

Further up the road, he stopped to refuel. I sat on the bike, flipped up my visor, and watched him through the window as he paid the man at the counter. He certainly had presence — everyone seemed to defer to him as if he were royalty. Charisma. He had it in bucketloads, and people fell under his spell. Like I did, I guess. Like everyone. Creatures included.

When he'd paid, Tapakah strode towards me with his long-legged, fluid gait. He reminded me of a black leopard, relaxed but ready to strike at any moment. However, unlike the green eyes of a leopard holding me spellbound, these were black and fixed on mine. I suddenly knew what it felt like to be prey. I hoped I wasn't going to be preyed upon.

143

He strode up to me still holding my gaze. 'Your beautiful eyes, looking out from a full-face helmet. Green and mesmerising. So. Goddamn. Sexy. I could look at you all day.'

I felt myself blush and flicked down my visor. Beetroot and sexy were incompatible. Tapakah laughed and his voice sounded in my helmet. 'What's wrong? Did I embarrass you?'

My face was still burning. 'No. I assumed you were ready to go.'

He gave a gritty chuckle. 'Oh, I'm ready to go all right. What about you? You'd better hold on tight.'

'Yeah, yeah. Just go already will you.' I was annoyed he could make me feel so aroused when really, I was furious with him.

Tapakah laughed and that annoyed me too. He knew the effect he had on me, and he knew I was annoyed about it. That was *doubly* annoying.

Tapakah hummed to himself and began singing a Matt Nathanson song. '*So come on, get higher, loosen my lips. Faith and desire and the swing of your hips. Just pull me down hard, and drown me in love…*' He reached back and squeezed my leg as he sang the last line. I held on tighter as my knees gave up the ghost.

Tapakah's throaty voice came through the microphone. 'I want you and I will have you.'

Oh, crikey. Bluetooth helmet sex.

'I'm looking forward to peeling off your tight leathers and making you more comfortable.'

'I'm perfectly comfortable, thank you,' I said, primly. 'There will be no peeling off of leathers by anyone but myself.'

'That's perfectly fine. I'll be more than happy to watch.'

'Hmmph!'

'It's not long until we reach our destination. Oh, and by the way, I think you've been quite rude and sarcastic today. Feisty and non-compliant. And you stole my bike. That can't go unpunished. After I watch you remove your clothes, and you're standing naked before me, I'm going to bend you over my knee and spank you.'

'Yeah? You and whose army?' An involuntary quiver ran through my body.

'Keep talking like that and I may have to tie you up and—'

I switched off my headset and pulled down the zip of my jacket to let in cold air. I would not be distracted from the job at hand. Wherever we were going, it was so he could explain himself.

He reached back and knocked on my helmet.

I switched the comms back on. 'What?'

'As I was saying, Maggie, I'm going to get your gorgeous—'

I switched it off and his shoulders shook as he laughed.

Oh, ha ha. I wriggled in my seat to get comfortable, straightened my back, and held onto the pillion grab bar behind me. There would be no more physical contact or I'd go insane.

Tapakah throttled up hard, and just as he intended, I had to wrap my arms around him to stay on. The pillion grab bar was way too small to hold onto at speed. Damn him.

---

[15] *Maggie's Playlist: Memory Lane — Adeaze, Come on Get Higher — Matt Nathanson*

"For nothing is hidden that will be made manifest; nor is anything secret except to come to light." — Mark 4:22

We rode for another half hour before reaching the town of Daylesford.

'We're two minutes away,' he said. 'This place has Australia's largest concentration of natural mineral springs. Have you ever been here?'

'I don't remember.'

'One positive thing about losing your memory is everything's new again.'

'True. I hope my memories stick this time round, or it'll be like having Alzheimer's.'

Once we'd passed through the town, Tapakah turned left along an unsealed road and pulled up in front of a gorgeous, contemporary style house.

'This is it.' He turned off the bike and dismounted.

Tapakah held out his hand and helped me off the bike. He took my helmet and grabbed the pannier bags.

I hurried towards the house. 'This looks beautiful.'

The home was a simple, modern design. The façade consisted of midnight blue panels interspersed with stainless steel rain heads and soft down lights. A rusted steel fascia framed the entryway, and a path made of polished boards led up under a covered walkway to the front door.

We entered the house and to the left was a large bedroom with ensuite. To the right was a private deck with a Jacuzzi. The tub bubbled and steamed invitingly, illuminated by an ethereal blue light.

I walked along the corridor to steps leading down to the living area and kitchen. Softly lit, the tastefully furnished lounge room sported a state-of-the-art fireplace, with a fire flickering warmly within. A wrap around deck encircled the space, with views overlooking the forest.

Set out on the table was an ice bucket with champagne, crystal glasses and assorted canapés.

Tapakah followed me out onto the deck. I leaned on the railing and took in the view as the late afternoon sun ignited the treetops with gold and amber.

'It's wonderful!' I also wanted to say, "Has she been here too?" but I bit my lip and shut my mouth. It *was* bothering me, so instead I asked, 'Is this the first time you've been here?'

'Yes.' He looked at me knowingly. 'I've never been here before.'

He returned to the lounge and I heard the pop of a champagne cork. He'd set this up as a romantic interlude rather than an opportunity to explain his actions. He returned, champagne glasses in hand.

'For you.' He handed me a glass and held up his for a toast. 'To us.'

'Listen, this is all very nice, but there is no us, not until you explain yourself. I mean that is why you brought me here, isn't it? Or did you think I might forget, swept away with the beauty an' all?'

He sighed. 'I wouldn't imagine you would forget, and yes, that's the reason I brought you here, amongst others. Have a seat and we'll start. So much for the niceties.'

'There'll be plenty of time for niceties later, if there is a later.

It all depends on you.'

Gosh, if everything turned to shit, I wouldn't want to ride back on the bike with him. He'd have to give me money for the train, or I could hitch hike, I guessed.

Tapakah unzipped his jacket, took it off and threw it over the back of a chair. Underneath he wore a simple black T-shirt that set off his muscular arms. The tattoos on his right arm seemed different each time I saw them. Today, they were stronger, blacker and more angular.

'Can I take your jacket?' he asked.

'No thanks, I've got it.' I unzipped and struggled to peel the bloody thing off. The corner of his mouth twitched as he watched me, but he wouldn't dare laugh.

'Let's sit at the table. You can eat while I talk.' He put his hand on my back and guided me inside.

I stepped aside from his touch. 'I know the way.'

I sat on the chair opposite him and made myself comfortable. The champagne was delicious, so I finished it off. Tapakah raised his eyebrows and poured me another.

'Thirsty,' I said, by way of explanation. 'Fire away.'

He took a deep breath. 'The reason I didn't tell you about my meeting with Rachael — the floozy — as you call her, is because it's hard to explain, and you wouldn't have believed me.'

'Yes, we've established that already. Get to the point. Who is she and what is she to you?'

He spoke quietly. 'Her name, as I said, is Rachael, and she's my mother.' He searched my face for a reaction.

'Your *mother*? That's impossible. She's half your age. Pull the other one.'

'She *is* my mother. I've told you before; I developed from infant to maturity in a short space of time. I've outgrown her, so to speak.'

I took a breath.

'Maggie, listen, don't interrupt. You can ask questions when

I'm finished. Okay?'

I nodded.

'The other thing that's complicated is she doesn't know I'm her son.' Tapakah raised his hand as I began to speak. 'She gave birth to me, and everything was fine, everything seemed normal. I was a normal baby. But once I reached three months of age, I metamorphosed, and my brain switched on. I had the mental capacity of a teenager, an extraordinarily intelligent teenager.

'One night, driven by instinct, I climbed from my cot, crawled out of the house and into the garden. I made my way into the bush nearby and discovered a warm and dark place to hide. I dug into the soil until it covered me. That's where I remained for two weeks undertaking a transformation every few days. My growth and development were exponential.

'I had absorbed the knowledge, intelligence and experience of my parents. With that as my base, I set out into the world. I assimilated more learning and experience with every human contact. Just a touch would do it. It was like walking through a living library. I sought out the best and brightest people in universities, at symposiums, in corporations, wherever I could get close to the highest levels of intelligence and experience.

'So, you see, my mother and father lost their baby boy. Gone missing, maybe kidnapped, maybe dead. They would never know what happened to their child.

'I couldn't go back; they wouldn't recognise me. And if I tried to explain? They would think I was a lunatic.

'With my superior intelligence, it didn't take long for me to find my feet, set up various ventures and generate enormous amounts of capital. Aside from that, I established a foundation for missing people. It provides resources and support for individuals and families who have a missing loved one.

'I reached out to Rachael in my capacity as CEO and offered her and her husband counselling and support services. With the stress and grief of their loss, their marriage failed, and her husband left her. Not only had she lost her beloved child, she'd lost her husband too. She was isolated and bereft. I offered her a position at the foundation, and she threw herself into it, forgetting her own grief by assisting others.

'Rachael invited me out to lunch, saying she had news she wanted to share and as a thank you to me for my assistance. The news instigating the body contact and kissing you witnessed, was that her husband had come back to her and she was pregnant again. That was it. No affair. No floozy. Simply joy, joy to see my mother happy again.'

I sat there stunned, as if someone had dropped a grenade in my lap. How bad did I feel? Lower than whale's poo.

I should've known not to take anything at face value with Tapakah. My stomach churned, and the lovely canapés rose in my gullet. How bad a person was I? Jesus Christ. I didn't know what to say. Sorry wouldn't cut it after the way I'd behaved. Ben was right.

The devastation I felt regarding my behaviour was overwhelming.

'*Maggie?* You can talk now if you want to.'

I stood and mumbled, 'I'm irredeemable. Totally and utterly beyond redemption. I won't insult you with a *sorry*.' I dashed up the stairs to the front door and hightailed it outside. I would do a Forest Gump. That's what I'd do. Run into the forest and keep on going. I now knew what mortified felt like. I was so mortified; I didn't think I'd ever recover.

The gravel crunched under my boots, and there was a nip in the air. A pair of boots crunched behind me, and a hand grabbed my arm.

'Maggie, what are you doing? Come back inside.'

I was betting he'd be loving this. Tapakah's revenge. Maggie's humiliation.

'Let me go. Please. I'm doing a Forest Gump. I'm going to walk to the end of the Earth and then some. It'll take that long for me to stop feeling so ashamed of myself. If ever.' I picked up the pace.

'Stop being so dramatic. It's okay. You saw what you saw, and it looked, for all intents and purposes, like a lover's tryst. If I'd been in your shoes, I would've assumed the same thing. Don't be so hard on yourself.'

'I feel so awful. And you're making it worse by trying to make me feel better. I'm the bad guy here. It's appalling how badly I've misjudged you. If I were you, I'd be telling me where to go.'

'I *am* telling you where to go. I'm telling you to go back inside. If you want to make it up to me, then do that. Don't leave. Don't run away on me again.'

'Okay.' I stared at my feet and kicked at the gravel with my boot.

He took my hand and we walked silently back to the house. I sat on the couch in front of the fire and stared into the flames. Staring into a fire always made me feel better, but in this case, it didn't seem to help.

So Tapakah was innocent. All he'd ever been was kind to me, and how did I repay his kindness? With an atrocious lack of trust. He wasn't unfaithful or deceitful, but now I was. I'd let things happen with Ben before I'd given Tapakah the chance to explain. Now *I* was the one who needed to explain herself. Jesus, what a mess.

Tapakah sat at the table watching me. I couldn't bring myself to look at him. This was going to be a long and awkward night. If we were going to move forward, I'd have to lay my cards on the table and tell him about Ben. I didn't really want to do that. It wasn't serious, but it could have been, if circumstances hadn't intervened.

Tapakah sat next to me. 'You haven't said a word. Are you going to sit here all night in silence? You want to run away, don't you?'

I nodded. 'I like that option. Running away gives me a chance to clear my head, and once that happens, I can return and deal with whatever it is I must deal with.'

'But there's nothing here you must deal with.'

'You're kidding, after the way I misjudged you.'

'I told you, it doesn't matter. I would've thought the same. Don't hold onto this, let's move on. I love you. The question is, do you love me?'

'Yes, I do love you. Very much.'

He smiled and a look of relief flashed across his face.

'That's all that matters to me.' He kissed me gently on the lips. 'Do you have any questions to ask me, after everything I've told you?'

'Um, yes, I do, actually. You could've had a DNA test to prove to Rachael you were her son. Then she might have believed your story. Why didn't you do that?'

'Because the DNA test would have revealed what I was, and I didn't want that, for me or my parents.'

'Yes, of course, that makes sense. So how did you survive with no food for two weeks while you were changing?'

'I had plenty of food. I was fed.'

'By whom?'

'You don't need to hear this. It will gross you out.'

'I need to know.'

'I was covered by a cocoon of thousands of cockroaches. They fed me. Do you want more detail?'

'No, that'll do me, thanks.'

I had one more question to ask. It was a question I had wanted to ask since the day Tapakah told me what he really was. I'd never had the courage to ask the question because I feared the answer. Perhaps now was as good a time as any.

'I have one more question. How did you become a hybrid? How can a human being give birth to something half human, half insect? I mean, both of your parents are human. So how is it

152

possible? And how much of you is insect compared to human? I mean you look human.'

This time it was Tapakah's turn to go quiet.

Finally, he said, 'That's four questions right there, and I'm not sure I want to answer them.'

'Why?'

His black eyes locked on to mine. 'Because I don't think you'll be able to hack the truth of it.'

'I'll try my best. Don't you think I should know?'

He broke the connection, looked down at his hands and sighed. 'Okay, here goes. I became a hybrid by merging with a human fetus. My mother gave birth to me like a normal human child. I can't give you an exact percentage of human to insect because it varies each time I change. Sometimes more, sometimes less.'

'So, when you say you became a hybrid by merging with a human fetus, what was it that initiated the merging?'

'Me. I did. The genetically modified insect I was. It was instinct that drove me to kidnap a human fetus. It was an evolutionary imperative enabling me to evolve into the creature sitting here today. I had no choice.'

'Holy, holy hell. Can other roaches do what you did? And how on earth did you merge?'

'To the best of my knowledge, no other roach can do what I did. I am unique. I merged by gaining access to her body while she was asleep. I dissolved into DNA, which locked onto and amalgamated with the fetus. At least that's our best guess at the lab, as to what happened.'

My body flushed hot and cold. I couldn't catch my breath. Someone had sucked the air from the room. I couldn't process what I was hearing. It was an abomination. Something from a horror story.

My boyfriend used to be a cockroach. *All* cockroach. All creepy, scuttling cockroach like the ones I freak out about now, and try to kill with baits and poisons, and suck up with the vacuum cleaner because there's no way I could step on one, or smash it with a shoe. Too big, too crunchy, too messy, too … too … *disgusting.*

'The look on your face tells me everything I need to know.' Tapakah stood and hurled his champagne glass against the wall. The glass shattered into a million pieces. The shards glittered in the firelight as they fell to the floor, a shower of red and orange sparks.

He took the five stairs in a single bound and the front door slammed so hard it vibrated in my chest. I sat stunned until something smashed in the hallway. I started and raced up the stairs. A picture had fallen off the wall and shattered glass filled the hall.

Outside, the Diavel fired up with a throaty rumble. The motor roared as Tapakah sped off like the proverbial bat out of hell. I stood and listened until the engine noise faded into the night.

---

[16] *Maggie's Playlist: The Ugly Truth —Matthew Sweet*

"Never assume the obvious is true." — *William Safire*

I found a dustpan and brush and swept up the broken glass. After looking in the cupboards, I discovered a vacuum cleaner, so I cleaned the floors again. Then, I entered the ensuite and looked at myself in the mirror. There was something I needed to do.

I closed my eyes. I was going to put myself back in the moment when Tapakah told me he was a cockroach. I wanted to see my expression. My face generally was an open book, reflecting my thoughts. Breathing in, I took myself back. I opened my eyes and there it was. The expression that had sent him packing.

The downturned mouth, the wrinkled nose and forehead, the lowered eyebrows and lids, the puckered chin. It was an expression of pure *disgust*. A perfect portrayal of revulsion and loathing. Good one, Maggie.

Oh well, considering the cock up I'd made of everything to date, him leaving was probably for the best. I put on music, stoked up the fire and poured myself another glass of champagne.

I sat on the couch and stared into the flames for I don't know how long. How long does it take to drink four glasses of champagne? It was getting dark. I found another bottle in the fridge. It was mega stocked, so I could get myself well and truly sloshed if the mood took me. And it did.

I poured myself another drink and wandered out onto the deck. Maybe I could sit in the Jacuzzi. The night was beautiful, and it would be relaxing. The plan appealed, so I headed into the bedroom.

The bedroom was a loft. I could look over the low wall to the lounge downstairs. It was a gorgeous room and the bed looked inviting. I stripped off my clothes and found a robe in the bathroom. I'd have a spa and then go to bed. I was buggered. Maybe when I woke up, things would magically be better.

The champagne had gone to my head. I shuffled somewhat unsteadily out to the Jacuzzi. It was the Rolls Royce of spas, so I knew I was in for a treat.

The deck was completely private with a slatted fence on one side, and at the front, a steel strung fence obscured by bushes. Trees surrounded the whole place, so it felt safe and secluded.

I slipped off my robe and stepped into the spa. I hit the button for air and slid into the hot, bubbling water. The scent of lemon and lavender filled my nostrils. The tub was spiked with essential oils. I closed my eyes and felt my body relax under the Jacuzzi's care.

It would've been nice to have someone to share the moment with. Oh, well.

I picked up my champagne glass intent on drowning my sorrows. The lights from the spa illuminated the glass and transformed it into a glowing flute of unearthly colours. I was drinking alien wine. I held up the glass to admire its effervescent hues.

A noise cracked through the night, and the glass exploded in my hand. Fragments of glass sprayed outwards, stinging as they hit my face.

I screamed and dropped the remains of the glass on the deck.

156

What the?

Another crack and a *zzzzffhpht* sound as an angry bee whizzed past my ear. I turned to see a hole in the windowpane behind me. The bee had flown straight through the plate glass window.

That wasn't a friggin' bee. I was under bloody gunfire!

Crack!

I ducked and heard the pop of a bullet as it flew over my head. I dipped under the water. My heart thumped in my ears. My mind raced. Whoever was taking pot shots at me must be high up in one of the trees. It was the only vantage point they could take a bead on me. The wind had sprung up. It would be blowy up there. Hard to aim true from a swaying tree. That was in my favour. What about the Jacuzzi — was it bulletproof? It had plenty of mechanical bits. Surely they would deflect a bullet? I knew water slowed bullets. There was plenty of water in the tub. That was in my favour too.

Crack! Ping.

I screamed as a bullet hit the tub and blew out a light. I came up for air. One less light. Another good thing. How did I turn out the rest of them? I was a sitting duck in an illuminated box. They were refining their aim, allowing for the sway of the tree and the spin of the earth. I'd have to make a run for it. It was only a matter of time. They would get me.

It was about ten feet to the door. I'd go straight after the next shot. Flop out over the side. Stay low, duck and weave. Throw myself through the doorway. Lucky I'd left it open. I could run right in.

Crack! Fhooot!

The bullet passed straight through the side of the tub and into the water. The side of my ankle stung with pain. A cloud of rust swirled upwards. I pushed my feet against the tub and shot out of the Jacuzzi. The deck was unforgiving as I slammed into it and gasped for breath. Like a drunken crab, I scampered on all fours towards the door.

On my haunches, I launched into a flying swan dive. I hit the deck inside the door and rolled to one side as another bullet hit the floor. Just missed me. Talk about lucky.

I curled up in the corner as bullets flew in thick and fast. Someone was pissed off. It had to have been Ashley. Or one of his thugs.

A window shattered over my head. Glass rained down. The whole place was windows. Blood was running from my ankle, my face stung. I wiped at my face and blood covered my hand.

There was a landline in the kitchen. I had to call for help.

Silence. Probably reloading.

I made a run for it, over the broken glass, keeping close to the wall. Along the hallway and down the stairs. I took a dive, crawling on all fours behind the couch. Then a commando crawl to the back of the kitchen bench.

I reached for the phone. An avalanche of bullets exploded around me. I screamed again. I couldn't help myself. The noise was terrifying, as was the prospect of death by firing squad.

The phone was on the wall. Damn it. I opened a draw — pots and pans. Not good. I rummaged through another draw and took out a wooden spoon. I poked the spoon at the phone trying to dislodge the handset. It fell short and I stretched up a bit further. Another volley of bullets raged around me. There was a sting as one grazed my wrist, but with a final prod the phone fell into my lap. I shook uncontrollably as I dialed triple 0. Engaged! How could that be? I dialled again. Same outcome.

Silence. The bullets stopped.

Where the hell was Tapakah?

I had discovered I had an excellent memory for numbers, and that I liked to count things. With only a handful of friends, I knew all their numbers by heart.

Thank God for small mercies, I thought as I dialled Tapakah's number. A phone rang on the lounge room table. *Shit.*

There was no one else to call — except for Ben. I dialled his number. I started to hyperventilate. He picked up straight away.

'Maggie?'

'Ben! I need help. Someone's shooting at me. I'm trapped. I've tried the police; I can't get through. Tapakah's not here. He's gone. I'm in Daylesford. *Shit*, I don't even know the address.'

I screamed as another barrage of bullets filled the room. I curled into a tiny ball as all hell erupted around me.

Silence. Reload.

The frantic sound of Ben's voice in the phone. I put it to my ear and sobbed. 'I'm dead. I can't tell you where I am.'

'I know where you are. Sit tight. Don't do anything silly. I'll be there in two minutes. We're in town. We followed you.'

What? Oh hell. This was a trap! It must've been Ben. *He* was the one sitting in a tree trying to take me out. Crikey. I'd have to play along and make a run for it before he got here.

'*Maggie?* Maggie! Are you there?'

'Yeh ... yes, I'm still here. They've stopped shooting for a minute. Who's *we* Ben?'

'I'm with Ashley. We're coming to get you. Stay on the line.'

'Okay,' I squeaked.

Jesus. I'd already considered the possibility they could be in cahoots. I was right. I had to move.

I abandoned the phone on the floor and commando crawled towards the stairs. I was fully exposed. I had to go *now*!

I ran, and a volley of bullets ripped up the stairs behind me sending splinters flying into the air. The sting of bullets and wooden slivers bit at my heels as I bolted up the hall. I opened the front door and slammed it shut behind me.

My breath came in ragged gasps. I turned and held onto the door frame for a moment to hold myself up. A barrage of bullets hit the back of the door and the wood vibrated under the palms of my hands. My ears buzzed with the sound of a thousand angry bees. It was so loud I could barely hear myself think, let alone hear. The gunfire had trashed my ears.

Even though they had a clear shot along the hallway, they couldn't get to me now. I was safe. By the time they climbed out of the tree, I'd be long gone.

I turned towards the path, ready to run for my life. Two men with guns blocked my exit. Ashley and Ben. I involuntarily stepped backwards, hitting the door. My hand fumbled for the doorknob behind me. I had to get back inside. I jiggled the handle. The door had locked.

Time slowed to a crawl as they approached. The light above the door illuminated my naked, blood-streaked body. One foot wore a scarlet sock. My right hand had a matching red glove. Bright red droplets splashed from my face onto my breasts.

I screamed as they grabbed me. How had they got out of the tree so fast?

A gun flashed silver in Ashley's hand. Ben had one too. The cold steel brushed against my skin as he tried to hold me down. I punched, kicked, screamed and bit. They yelled at me. My knee connected somewhere, and Ashley crumpled. He let go of my arm.

Crack! Ping. The light over the front door blew out.

Now who was shooting?

I paused to look around. Ben seized the opportunity, picked me up and flung me over his shoulder. Ashley staggered up and held my ankles to stop me kicking. They ran like fury along the pathway making a beeline for Ben's Monaro parked out front. Ben threw me in the back of the car and Ashley followed. Ben leapt in the front and took off. He dropped a massive wheelie and spun the car around. The side of my head slammed against the window.

A bullet bounced off the rim of the car door right near my head. I screamed and tried to open the door.

'No, you don't, luv.' Ashley reached across and grabbed my arm. He yelled. 'Floor it, Ben!'

'What the hell do you think I'm doing?'

Another bullet ricocheted off the car.

I needed to get the hell away from these maniacs. I was safer on my own. I didn't know what I was dealing with here — what they had in store for me.

I swung my legs around and kicked Ashley fair in the guts, slamming his head into the side of the car. The cool night air rushed in as I opened the car door, and the gravel road flew past at 150 kilometers an hour. If I jumped, it wasn't going to be pretty. I hesitated for a split second too long. Ashley snatched my arm and dragged me across to the other side of the car. He reached out and tried to pull the door shut. Seizing the moment, I stuck my feet against his back and using the side of the car for leverage, tried to shove him out the door.

I nearly had him — he was hanging out of the car. He grappled for the seat belt, hauled himself back in and slammed the door shut.

'Fair fuckin' dinkum,' he screamed into my face. 'I've had enough of you! *Stop it for Christ's sake!* We're not the fucking enemy here. We're trying to help you for fuck's sake. Stop trying to kill me.' He fumbled around under the back seat.

'Ah, ha. Here it is.' He held up a jumbo roll of duct tape. 'I'm sorry, but this is the last straw. This is *your* fault.' He grabbed my wrists and attempted to tape them together.

I fought, wriggled and kicked.

Ben yelled, 'Mama Mia! Can you two stop it back there!'

Ashley growled. 'Jesus, I've had enough of this!' He plonked his body weight on top of me. He bound my wrists and ankles with way more tape than necessary. Finally, he heaved himself off me and fell back in the seat, exhausted.

I wound down the window with my bound hands and started to scream.

'Help! *Heeeeelp!* Help!

'Oh, for *fuck's* sake!' Ashley ripped off another strip of tape and plastered it across my mouth. 'You leave me no choice.' He wound the window shut. 'Why can't you get it through your thick head? We. Want. To. Help. You. I don't want to do this to you, Maggie. It's fuckin' doing my head in, okay? And no, Boo, I won't stop swearing. Get out of my head. A bloke's entitled to fucking swear in this sort of situation. You put me under too much pressure not to swear, and it builds up inside, and this is what you get. Butt out dog and mind your own fucking beeswax.'

Oh dear. The man was seriously deranged. A bloody nutter. A psycho. He was talking to someone else — in his head. There was no telling what he'd do to me. I'd better settle. Not aggravate him.

'And another thing, while I'm at it. Why the *fuck* is it, whenever I find you, you're always *naked*. Always. And blood. You're always covered in the stuff. Don't you *have* any clothes? *What is it with you?* Jesus Christ.' He pulled a blanket off the front seat and covered me with it. He tucked it under my legs and around my body until I resembled a mummy.

'Mmmm. Mmmmm. Mmmm,' I tried to speak through the tape.

'*What?*'

'Mmmmmm.'

'If I remove the tape from your mouth, do you promise not to scream?'

I nodded, and he gently peeled back a portion of the tape.

'The blanket's itchy.'

'Tsk.' He rolled his eyes and stuck the tape back over my mouth. 'Suck it up, kiddo. Hey, Ben, do you have any handy wipes in the car?'

Ben reached across and took a pack from the glove box. He tossed them to Ashley.

I didn't think big tough men went in for handy wipes.

Ashley ripped out a handful and turned towards me. 'I'm

going to clean the blood off your face.' He dabbed at my forehead, nose and cheeks. 'That's better.' He sat back and appraised me. 'When we stop, I'll take a look at your feet and that wrist. I've got clothes, but they're in the boot.

'We're *not* the enemy. One more fucking time, just so's you're clear. We are not going to hurt you. Okay? Nod if you understand.'

I nodded. There was no way I was going to antagonise him. He'd calmed somewhat, which was good, and he was reassuring. I wasn't feeling so scared. But that was the thing with psychos — they could go off willy-nilly. I couldn't drop my guard.

I sat quietly, my mind at maximum warp speed. Ben and Ashley had guns, so I assumed they'd shot at me. But someone was shooting at *them*, or maybe, that someone was still trying to take me out, and they'd got in the way.

Surely it couldn't be Tapakah? Maybe he was the shooter. Perhaps his bug brain took over when he became upset and he returned to annihilate me. He could scale a tree in seconds flat and run around to the front of the house in a flash. Jesus. Of course. It made perfect sense.

I nodded my head. 'Mmmmm. Mmmmm.'

'No screaming?' Ashley said.

I nodded, and he gently peeled off the tape.

'I know who it was! I've worked it out. It was Tapakah doing the shooting. Not you.'

Ashley looked at me like I was an imbecile. 'No shit, Sherlock.'

'We had a disagreement and he took off in a huff. Shortly after he left, the shooting started. And he'd be the only one who could scale a tree so fast and get around to the front of the house. He's the one who wants me dead.'

'I'm pleased you've finally come to your senses, but I wish you'd done so sooner. It would've saved us both a lot of grief and trauma.' Ashley rubbed his groin. 'But listen, even though I know the evil Tapakah is capable of, I don't think he wants to kill you. And if he did, it wouldn't be by shooting, he'd think up something way dastardlier than that.'

'If it wasn't Tapakah, you or Ben, who the hell was it?'

Ashley scratched his head. 'Stuffed if I know, luv.' He reached into his jeans, took out a Swiss army knife and extended the blade. 'Now you've come to your senses, let's get the duct tape off you.'

I extended my arms and legs and he cut me free. My head hurt and my body ached. My face, wrist and ankles stung like a bastard, and the itchy blanket was making everything feel worse. I tried to ignore my physical body by staring out the window into the darkness. Up ahead, something moved out onto the road. I screamed, 'Watch it, Ben!'

The headlights homed in on a man standing in the middle of the road. Ben swerved the car and missed him by a whisker. We hit the gravel at the side of the road, skidded, recovered and returned to the bitumen.

Ashley leaned forward and held onto the front seat. 'Jesus Christ, Ben, top notch driving, mate. Look out, there's another one!'

'There's two!' I said.

A man and woman stood next to each other in the middle of the road, arms outstretched. The man wore blue striped pajamas, and the woman's pink nightie fluttered in the breeze. They were motionless, with expressionless faces and dead eyes.

'What the hell's going on?' Ben yelled over the engine's roar. He spun the steering wheel and swerved off the road.

Luckily for us, there was a large expanse of grass to swerve onto. We bumped and skidded along it, and Ben handled the steering wheel like a grand prix driver. The car fishtailed as we hit the gravel, but he recovered, and we were back on the highway still in one piece.

Ben brushed his hair back off his face. 'Fuck me.' His eyes

met mine in the rearview mirror. 'Apologies for the language.' His face was shiny with sweat.

'That was some seriously awesome driving,' I said. 'But what's with all the locals on the highway for God's sake?'

'Tapakah's kamikaze cronies sent to stop us,' Ashley said.

The familiar note of an engine came from behind us, and I turned around to check. It was a Ducati Diavel.

'Ashley, it's Tapakah. He's found me.'

'This day just gets better and better, Ashley mumbled. He looked out the back window. 'Ben, pass me the sawn-off, mate. It's under the front seat.'

'It *is?*'

I noticed Ben's horrified expression in the rearview.

'Bloody hell, what else is in the car I don't know about?' He leant over and pulled a gun from under the seat.

Ashley leaned across and took it. 'Don't ask.' He knelt on the back seat and wound down the window.

'What are you doing?' I asked.

'I'm going to take him out.'

'Don't do that! We don't know for sure it was him.'

'Even if he wasn't the shooter, he still needs to die.'

'No. Please don't, Ashley.'

'I'll go for the tyres then.' He leant out the window with the gun, but after a couple of seconds, he jerked his body back in. 'Hit it, Ben! The arsehole's got six more cronies on bikes coming up from behind.'

'*What?*' I turned around to look.

Sure enough, six motorbikes spread across the road, coming up behind Tapakah. The riders rode right handed. They had to, because their left hands held guns. Big guns.

'Holy crap,' Ashley said. 'Go faster, Ben.'

'For Christ's sake, I haven't slowed down! I've had the pedal to the metal the whole way, man.'

I turned to look out the front window. A string of people

were dotted along the highway in front of him. *'Ben!'*

'I've got this!' He swerved in and out and around the people. The tyres smoked and screeched in protest. It was just as well Ashley had buckled me up as the G-force whipped me back and forth. When the car steadied, I looked out the back window. People were running off the road to avoid the bikes.

Ashley observed the same thing. 'Yep, it's Tapakah all right.'

I rubbed the side of my head. I'd lost count how many times my head had hit the side window. My neck was stiff from trying to turn my head around and see out the back. I unclipped my seat belt, spun around and knelt on the seat.

Tapakah was gaining on us, and the bikes behind were catching up to him. Bright flashes of light lit up the darkness around the riders. The crack of gunshots filled the air. Tapakah powered up and started swerving back and forth across the road.

'What the *hell*? They're trying to take him out!' Ashley yelled.

'So, they're after *him* not us?' Ben said.

Ashley grinned. 'Sure looks like it.'

'It's not funny. You have to help him. Please!' I screamed, watching Tapakah dodge and weave over the road.

A bullet thunked off the rim of the car and I ducked.

'For you, Maggie, but it's against my better judgment.' Ashley leant out of the window.

The bike roared as Tapakah accelerated away from his pursuers. His body was flat against the bike, and he reached into a pannier with one hand. Rounding a corner, he slammed on the brakes and slid the bike around to face his pursuers. His gun flashed twice, and two riders hit the road. Their bikes spun off into the bush.

'Nice work,' Ashley said begrudgingly.

The Diavel roared as Tapakah took off again. The other bikes had gained ground. One of the riders was shooting at Tapakah, keeping him busy, while the other two blasted past him and were right up our hammer.

166

'Get down!' Ashley said. He pushed me off the seat and onto the floor.

The roar of engines flanked us, and the car swerved as Ben tried to side swipe them. A bullet exploded through the window spraying us with a deluge of glass. I screamed and Ben yelled. 'Anyone hit?'

Ashley looked down at himself. 'Nearly. Ruined my shirt, the mother fucker.'

Chk. Chk. BOOM!

Ashley's shotgun blasted, hurting my eardrums. There was the shriek of steel on steel and Ashley yelled, 'Got 'im!'

I stuck my head up. A rider looked back at me. I ducked as a bullet exploded through the window. I swear it parted my hair.

'*Cocksucker!*' Ashley screamed.

I attempted to look up without lifting my head. My eyeballs strained in their sockets. Blood covered the front of Ashley's shirt.

'Ashley's been hit!'

'Don't stop,' Ashley instructed. He pressed against his ribs and blood seeped through his fingers.

'Get your shirt off!' I yelled to him.

He winked at me. 'Now's not the time.'

I wiggled over and yanked at his buttons. 'Just do it!'

'You, ripping off my shirt. That's my fantasy, Maggie. But it doesn't go quite like this.' He stared at his blood-soaked hands.

I ripped his shirt off and bundled the material into a thick pad, which I pressed against the wound.

'Hold it there.'

'Down, Maggie.' He shoved me on the floor again.

The rider was back at the window with his gun pointed straight at Ashley.

Ashley pressed against his stomach, holding the pad in place. Dropping the shotgun into the crease of his elbow, he squeezed his arm together and pulled back on the gun with his other hand.

That's a novel way to cock a shotgun, I thought as the rider's head exploded. But Ashley hadn't fired. Tapakah had taken him out.

I was betting the rider wished he'd worn a helmet. Safety comes first, plus, he was breaking the law. I think he'd broken quite a few laws. But who were we to talk?

The dead rider's bike careered into the side of the Monaro. Metal shrieked on metal as the bike slid along the car and the remnants of the dead man's head caught on the window frame.

The bike slid out, but he stayed put, hanging by his neck from the window, his bloodied face squashed into an insane grin and one eyeball dangling on his cheek. The other one looked straight at me.

I was too shocked to scream. I sat on the seat and kicked with my bare feet until the head came loose. It was warm against my feet, which was kind of nice in a sick way, as my feet were freezing. They felt much warmer after that.

I stuck my head out the window and watched the body roll along the road and into a ditch. Tapakah swerved to avoid it. He saw me and raised his gun in salute.

Another rider came up on the left of the car, level with the front window.

'Watch out,' Ashley yelled to Ben. 'He's after you.'

'Hold on!'

The rider had his gun leveled at Ben's head as we hit the bridge. With perfect timing Ben swerved into the bike. The familiar sound of screaming metal on metal shredded our ears as he jammed the bike and rider against the side of the bridge.

Four down. Two to go.

Another rider flew past Tapakah and took out the back window of the car.

Ben's expression in the rearview was shocked. 'Holy Mother Mary.'

Tapakah took a shot at the rider, while ducking and weaving

to dodge the other guy.

'Give me the gun, Ashley. I have to help him.'

'It's all right, luv. I'll do it. Get your head down.' He leant out the window and blew the guy away. 'One to go!' he shouted to Ben.

I poked my head up again just as Tapakah took out the other bike. The rider slumped over the handlebars and the bike tipped over as he slid off and hit the road. Tapakah's back wheel clipped the skidding bike, sending him spinning off into the bush.

'He's down; we have to go back,' I shrieked.

'No, he'll survive. We've got to get out of here. More could be coming.'

A string of Italian expletives erupted from Ben's mouth. In the distance, something appeared to cover the whole road. Ben dropped back the speed. 'Hundreds of people!'

'Drive through them for fuck's sake,' Ashley shouted. 'They're roached. *Just keep going!*'

'*Roached?*' Ben yelled, as he put his foot down. The faces of the people came into view. Shoulder to shoulder, they covered the road and the verge. There was nowhere to go but straight through.

'Don't do it!' I screamed.

Ben slammed on the breaks. 'I can't. I can't do it!'

Smoke and the stink of burning tyres filled the cabin as the car spun. It stopped with a jerk. I opened my eyes.

Hundreds of blank eyes stared back, illuminated by the headlights of the car. A young child reached across the two-inch gap and touched the bonnet.

No one moved. The people stood and stared, and we stared back, caught in their spell.

Ben shook his head, put the clutch into reverse and slowly motored backwards. The crowd remained still.

Ben turned the car around and took off. 'We have to go

back. Find another way.'

'Stop and find Tapakah. *Please*. We can't leave him. He helped us for heaven's sake.'

'I have to defer to Ashley. I don't know what the hell is going on.'

'Ashley? *Please?*'

'Yeah, yeah. *Okay*. For once, it appears Tapakah may not be public enemy number one.' He shook his head and grimaced as he moved.

I looked down and saw that the wad was soggy with his blood. 'Jesus, we have to get you to hospital.'

'Nah, it's just a flesh wound. I'll be fine.'

'Here's a towel,' Ben said, flinging one over the back seat.

'Sit up, and I'll tie it around your waist.'

He groaned as I threaded the towel around him and knotted it tightly over the pad.

'Press against it. You're losing too much blood.'

'There's his bike!' Ben yelled. He slammed on the brakes and leapt out of the car.

'I'd better go too,' Ashley said.

'No! You can't. I'll go.' I attempted to open the door, but it was jammed. I kicked at it with both feet and winced with pain. It flew open, and I leapt out with the sound of Ashley yelling in my ears not to go. I ignored him and ran after Ben. He had disappeared into a ditch. Tapakah was lying on the ground. Ben was leaning over him. I flew across the rocks and gravel in my bare feet, oblivious to the pain. As I ran, my brain rattled over and over. *Please don't be dead. Please don't be dead. Please don't be dead.*

He looked dead.

Ben checked his pulse and breathing. 'His vital signs are strong. I think he's going to be fine.'

'Thank God.'

Tapakah's eyelids fluttered and his eyes opened. They were pitch black. Even the white bits were black. Ben gave a shout and jumped back.

'It's okay. His eyes do that sometimes.'

He muttered and crossed himself. 'He's the devil on a Diavel.'

Tapakah's eyes closed, and when they opened again, they were normal. He looked at me. 'Maggie, why are you naked?' Tapakah noticed Ben and gave him the stink eye.

Ben stepped backwards, crossed himself again, and took off his jacket. He moved to put it on me and thought better of it. Instead, he held it out at a distance.

I put it on and zipped it up. 'Th … th … thanks, Ben. Huh … he won't bite you.' The jacket was warm and soft and long enough to cover my nether regions. My teeth chattered uncontrollably.

I held out a hand to help Tapakah, but he was already up.

'S … so … so, j … just … to … be … clear, y … you weren't trying to kkk … kill me?' My body began to shiver violently.

Tapakah rolled his eyes. 'No, as if.'

The crunch of gravel sounded at the top of the ditch and the silhouette of Ashley appeared, doubled over and holding his side.

Ben yelled. 'Don't come down! Everything's fine.'

Tapakah put his arm around me as we made our way back to the road. He noticed my bloodied feet and hands and appeared distraught. 'I should never have left you.'

'Yeah, you can say that again, arsehole,' Ben muttered under his breath.

'I heard that,' Tapakah said.

We reached the top of the ditch and Ashley and Tapakah came face-to-face. Ashley straightened as best he could, and they stared each other down.

Ashley spoke quietly. 'I guess I'd better say sayonara to my friends and family, but not just yet.' He brought a shotgun from behind his back and cocked it with a flick of his arm. 'First, it's time for *you* to say sayonara, you alien scumbag. All you've brought Maggie is misery and pain. You've ruined her life, plus the lives of countless others, including my own. Any last words before I blow you away?'

'Yes. You saved my life. I wanted to thank you. But now you want to kill me? It doesn't make sense.'

'It makes perfect sense to me. I wanted the satisfaction of staring straight into your black eyes as I killed you.'

'I saved your life too, Ashley. Why would I do that?'

'So you could do to me what I'm going to do to you, right now.'

'Not at all. I'm grateful to you, Ashley. And to you, Ben. I'm in your debt. You rescued, Maggie. If it hadn't been for your tenaciousness and courage, your total and almost stupid, disregard for your own safety ... your ... your love, Maggie would be dead. If it weren't for you, I would be sitting outside that house holding her corpse. You saved her life, and for that I'm eternally grateful.'

No one said a word. Ashley looked stunned. Ben looked taken aback, and I teared up as I realised how badly I'd misjudged this man.

Ashley shook his head. 'Unbefuckinglievable. You twist everything around to suit yourself. You're the cause of this, related and unrelated. Do you think we saved her for you? Get real. We're trying to save her *from* you.'

Ashley pointed the shotgun at Tapakah's chest. Illuminated by the car headlights, Ashley's naked torso gleamed with sweat. The towel tied around his waist was dark with blood. His chest muscles and biceps rippled as a spasm of pain racked his body. He staggered slightly and in that instant Tapakah struck. The movement was so fast I barely registered it. One minute, Ashley had the gun; a split second later it was Tapakah's.

Tapakah pushed Ashley in the leg with his boot. Ashley fell to his knees holding his side. Ben made a move. Tapakah warned him off with a wave of the gun.

Ashley swayed on his knees, his head hanging forward, nearly unconscious.

'You look ready to be executed, Ashley.' Tapakah grabbed Ashley's hair and yanked his head back. He rested the shotgun on Ashley's chest. 'I can help you with that. It appears you have a death wish and are immune to seeing reason. I find that annoying.'

'Go on then, arsehole. Do it. Show Maggie what you're made of, you piece of shit,' Ashley hissed at him.

I croaked in protest. 'Tapakah, p ... p ... please, stop this.'

I could hardly speak for shivering. I'd gone into shock. 'He's dying ... so much blood loss. Help him.' My knees buckled and thudded into the gravel. I knelt for a moment, mimicking Ashley, before face planting into the dirt.

'Maggie!' Ben yelled.

The gravel crunched as Ben approached. The sound seemed a million miles away. He gently rolled me over and pulled me to my feet.

I mumbled. 'I'm o ... okay.' At least I think it was me.

'No, you're not.' I sensed my body leave the ground, the gentle motion as he walked, the strength of his arms as he held me tight.

Tapakah snapped, 'Ben! Where are you going? Leave her. I'll take care of her.'

'Yeah, like you did before? Besides, you're a bit busy. You've got an injured man to kill. I'm taking her to hospital.'

The voices came from far away. Was Ben really speaking to Tapakah that way? He was crazy.

'Ben, stop! Tapakah shouted. 'I'm warning you.'

Ben turned. 'Yeah, what? You're going to kill me too? Shall I put her down so you've got a clear shot, or would you prefer a two for one and save yourself a bullet?'

I expected Tapakah to go right off, but there was no answer, just silence.

Ben turned away and kept walking. He was either extremely brave, or extremely stupid.

The measured crunch of the gravel under Ben's feet was soothing to my ears.

Crunch. Crunch. Crunch. BANG!

The crack of a shotgun ripped through the silence and echoed into the night.

Ben froze.

I waited for him to fall.

Then, the soft thud of a body hitting the dirt.

It wasn't Ben's.

---

[17] *Maggie's Playlist: Fire Your Guns — ACDC*

"The only whole heart is a broken one because it lets the light in." — *David J. Wolpe*

I was screaming. I swear it. But I couldn't hear a thing. I must've been screaming on the inside, too weak to let it out.

My head rested on Ben's chest; his heart thumped in my ear. I don't think I'd ever heard a heart go that fast before. It worried me.

Ben hoisted me up and started walking again. 'He shot Ashley. We're next. I know it,' he whispered.

What? No. I couldn't believe it. Tapakah a murderer?

Ben picked up the pace until he was almost running.

Chk. Chk.

The sound of a shotgun cocking. Ben broke into a run.

BOOM!

Ben stopped dead in his tracks.

I waited for him to fall. To drop me. But he did neither.

'Maggie, wake up, wake up. I need you to wake up!' He squeezed my body as he tried to nudge me back to awareness.

'I'm here, but I don't know for how long.' I figured it was me talking, but I couldn't be sure. I was so far removed from myself.

'I'm going to put you down, and you have to run for the car. Get out of here. Drive to my parent's farm. Remember? I told you where it was, in Woodend. I'm going to create a distraction,

175

keep Tapakah away from you. Okay?' He shook me. '*Okay, Maggie?*'

I nodded.

'Ready? On three. One … two … *three!*' He threw me from his arms.

Chk. Chk. BOOM! My feet hit the ground to the sound of gunfire and the clatter of gravel as it exploded around us.

'Do I have your attention now, Ben?' Tapakah shouted. 'Must I shoot you to get you to stop?'

'Go, Maggie!' Ben ran flat out towards Tapakah, arms outstretched and screaming like a crazed samurai warrior. Perhaps it was an Italian war cry. I wasn't sure if Italians had such a thing. Ben the kamikaze coffee maker was on a suicide mission. He must be; he was no match for Tapakah.

'Wait, Maggie!' Tapakah yelled. The words had just left his mouth and he was next to me, gripping my arm. In the ditch, Ben leant over Ashley's lifeless body.

Tapakah's face flashed with anger. 'Why won't any of you listen to reason?'

'Maybe because nothing seems reasonable?'

'Don't run off again. We need to take care of him. I can do it.'

'Take care of him? Bury the body?'

'What body?'

I tilted my head in the direction of the ditch. 'His body.'

'Ashley's?'

'Yes.'

'But he's not dead.'

'You shot him. I heard it.'

'I didn't shoot him, for Christ's sake. I was attempting to stop Ben running off with you. They were warning shots, that's all.'

'Are you sure you didn't shoot him?'

Tapakah stared at me like I was severely lacking in

intelligence. Which, at this point in time, was probably the case. I was cold and exhausted, and I could barely function.

'While the two of you were off on your little jaunt, I was trying to stem his bleeding.'

I wobbled on my feet. 'So, you're not going to kill Ben, or me?'

Tapakah gripped my other arm to support me. 'I'm not going to kill anyone, but you might yet drive me to it.'

Scooping me up, he strode to the car and placed me in the back seat. Leaning in, he bundled me up tight in the itchy bloody blanket. He pointed a warning finger. 'Stay!'

He disappeared into the ditch, and I half expected to hear gunshots again.

Minutes passed in silence before Tapakah and Ben appeared carrying Ashley. He looked dead. They laid him on the back seat next to me. I put his head in my lap and touched his face. It was pale, cold and sweaty.

Tapakah tapped quickly on his phone. 'Ben, I've texted you the co-ordinates of the Daylesford footy oval, but follow me, it's not far.'

'You sure we shouldn't go to hospital?'

'I'm sure. And I'm also sure Ashley would be pissed if we did take him there.'

Ben fired up the Monaro. 'Okay, your call.'

'Everything all right?' I asked Ben.

He sighed. 'I guess.'

'What's happening?'

'Tapakah's very convincing. He has a place we can go to, not far from here. He said he can fix Ashley and look after you. I have to trust him. I can't beat him on my own. I don't want to put you both in danger either. I'm going with the plan and see what happens. There's not much else I can do at this point.' His tone was despondent.

'I'm so sorry you've been dragged into this. And your poor

car—'

'Don't worry about the car. She'll buff. I just want to see you safe.' He put his hand back between the seats and squeezed my leg.

'Ow.'

'Sorry.'

'Thanks for everything, Ben. You're incredible. I love you.'

'I love you too, Maggie.'

The Monaro rattled, shook and groaned as we headed back along the highway. It sounded like we felt. I cradled Ashley's head and tried to find his pulse. A faint pulse quivered under my fingertips. He was breathing, but it was shallow.

I studied the face in my lap. It was rugged, with a well-defined nose and a strong jaw and chin. At least it appeared to be, under that beard. He was heavy, solid muscle, and my legs were going numb.

He looked so peaceful and didn't appear to be in pain. When he wasn't raging and swearing, his expression was kind, almost placid. I gently kissed his forehead, eyelids, and traced my finger across his eyebrows. I held him close until I was too tired to take the weight anymore, and carefully laid his head back in my lap. I felt a strange surge of tenderness towards this person. Who the hell was he?

His eyelids fluttered open and I gazed into two kindly, but somewhat bloodshot, blue orbs.

'See what I've got to go through to get a cuddle from you?' he croaked. A slow grin spread across his face. 'And the bonus was the kisses, and having you hold my head against your breasts. I thought I'd died and gone to heaven. But no, it was heaven right here in your arms.'

'You were *conscious?*'

He smiled. 'Yes, and I thank my lucky stars.'

I felt my face go red hot. 'I should throw you out of the car right now.'

'Well, it's not as if you haven't tried *that* before.' He chuckled, and then groaned with the pain of it. His breath rattled in his chest.

'Don't talk. Conserve your strength.'

He lifted a hand and stroked my cheek. His fingers were rough and smelt of iron, petrol and sulphur.

'I'm glad you convinced me to look in your eyes, Maggie. I can die a happy man.'

'You're not going to die, Ashley.'

He fumbled for my hand and linked his little finger with mine. A rush of energy flooded my body and his hand dropped. His head rolled to the side.

'Ashley? *Ashley!*' I tapped his cheek. There was no response.

I felt for a pulse. I couldn't find one. I tried his neck. I tried his wrist. I prodded and pushed to locate the flutter of a pulse under his skin. I listened for a breath. No movement. There was nothing. Everything was still. His body was motionless. He wasn't there anymore. He was gone.

'Ben!' I screamed. 'Ashley's *dead!*'

---

[18] *Maggie's Playlist: Died and Gone to Heaven — Tommy Castro*

"Revenge is sweet and not fattening." — Alfred Hitchcock

'Frank, we've a medical emergency. Gunshot wound to the abdomen. I need the Eurocopter ASAP. Daylesford footy oval.'

'Shit, Tapakah. How bad are you?'

'Not me, Frank. Ashley Beringer. You have his stats, send them. I need his blood group. How long for the chopper?'

'One minute, I reckon. It's in the area. I sent Tony in as back up, for your protection. Lucky for you. I've sent out an alert as we speak.'

'Is the chopper stocked with blood?'

'It has everything you need for a medical emergency. Except me.'

'I don't need you, Frank, I'll do this myself.'

'Yeah, right, Tapakah. You've always wanted to kill him. I don't get it.'

'I'm going to save his life. I've absorbed an entire library of medical books. I can do this.'

'Why the hell would you want to? Are you insane?'

'If I save him, I'll be a hero to Maggie, and Ashley will be forever in my debt.'

'You need to keep your focus on the plan, not her.'

'So you keep telling me, Frank. It's wearing thin. Where's the nearest airport that can land the hospital jet?'

'You need 1500m of runway, so that'd be Tullamarine.'

'Get the jet and yourself there now. I'll stabilise him until then. How far to Tulla from here?'

'A hundred k's.'

'The copter can go up to 472 km per hour, so that's twelve minutes, forty-two seconds. Get moving, Frank.' I clicked off my helmet Bluetooth.

I wanted nothing more than to see Ashley die, after what he'd done to me in the past. But saving him would serve a greater purpose.

Ben was right behind me as I rocketed up the road to the oval. He was flashing his headlights. I skidded to a stop at the oval and he slid the car in next to me, spraying me with gravel.

You'll keep, Ben.

He leapt out. 'Ashley's dead!'

I ran to the car and opened the back door. Maggie was cradling Ashley's head, her face streaked with blood. It appeared both were swathed in a blanket of red.

Her tone was stony and robotic. 'It's too late. He's dead.' Her eyes were unfocused.

Shit. She could be heading into catatonia.

A loud whining noise, combined with a deep chugging rumble filled the air. Dust whipped up around us as the Eurocopter came into land.

I yelled over the racket, 'Maggie, he'll be fine. Ben, help me get him out of the car.'

Tony and two men ran towards us with a gurney. We were in the copter and airborne in under a minute. I barked out orders to Ben as to how to care for Maggie, while I attended to Ashley. Ashley looked dead, but I detected a faint pulse that fluttered erratically. He needed blood and an IV as a priority. Maggie had done a sterling job with first aid.

I worked quickly to connect blood and IV tubes. 'There's still a pulse,' I told her.

Ashley began to twitch and convulse. Maggie screamed as his arm spasmed and flicked backwards sending implements flying. Then he was still. All vital signs ceased. He'd gone.

Maggie grabbed his hand. Her eyes were unseeing as she interlocked her little finger with his. A flash of blue energy sparked with the contact, her head flipped back, and she collapsed into the aisle.

I shouted over the roar of the engines. 'Ben! Help Maggie!'

He leapt to his feet and collected her limp body. Ashley twitched violently under my hands and then lay quiet. I reached for a defibrillator, and the monitor beeped. His heart rate and breathing came back online. The heartbeat was slow and steady, his breathing regular.

Ben held Maggie like a sleeping child. He kissed the side of her face.

You're pushing it, Ben.

I glared at him. He glared back. I turned my attention to Ashley. His eyes were open, and he was staring at me.

'Welcome back.'

'Check Maggie,' he whispered hoarsely. '*Check her!*'

I didn't want to argue with the urgency in his voice.

I moved Ben aside and knelt to check her pulse. She barely had one. Her breathing was almost non-existent. It was as though she'd taken on Ashley's physiology. Her heart faltered and stopped.

'I've lost her! What the *hell?*'

Ashley slid off the gurney, pushed me into the cockpit, and seized her hand. There was a flash of blue light, not as strong as before, and Ashley sank to the floor. Maggie started in Ben's arms and her eyes opened. 'Ashley! She cried. 'Are you okay?'

He struggled to speak. 'Now you are, I am.'

I had to nip this in the bud. 'Let me get you back on the gurney to reattach your IVs. We have to keep the blood up to you. You're not out of the woods yet, Ashley.'

'Where are you taking us?'

'My private medi jet is waiting at Tullamarine. Frank, my surgeon, will look after the rest of your treatment there. You'll be well cared for.'

'You're going to make me better so you can kill me? Or lock me up in a dungeon somewhere and leave me to rot?'

'Stop being melodramatic. We'll care for you until you're well enough to leave. It's up to you.'

I turned my attention to Maggie. She sat on Ben's knee watching me with wide eyes. She was shivering. I took out a blanket and held it open. She stood up, squeezed past Ashley, and fell into the blanket and my arms. I bundled her up, sat her on my knee and held her tightly. 'Are you okay?'

Ben replied. 'Um ... well, a bit shaken, but I'm—'

I glared at him. 'Not you, idiot — Maggie.'

She nodded. 'I'm all right. Thank you for saving Ashley. He'd be dead if it wasn't for you.'

'Maggie had more to do with saving me than you,' Ashley growled.

Maggie looked surprised. 'I didn't do a thing. It was Tapakah who saved you.'

'Whatever.' His fists clenched and he looked ready to hit someone. Probably me.

Ashley was right. Something had happened between them. They'd saved each other. I wondered what that mechanism could be. I didn't like it one little bit.

I checked Maggie's pulse. It was strong and her face had life in it. Thank God I hadn't lost her. I stroked her hair, loving the feel of the brush cut. She looked at me and I dissolved into the depths of those green eyes. The roar of the engines faded. Nothing existed but her. I kissed her, and she kissed me back. It was a kiss of gratitude and passion, and her body undulated with it. I would have her right here, right now, if it weren't for the audience.

Well, I wouldn't care. But Maggie would. In fact, I'd like nothing better than to take her in front of them both. It would be the ultimate revenge. Maggie was mine, and I relished throwing the fact in their faces.

The sound of vomiting interrupted our kiss. It was Ashley, throwing up over my shoes.

"We cannot live only for ourselves. A thousand fibers connect us with our fellow men; and among those fibers, as sympathetic threads, our actions run as causes, and they come back to us as effects." — Herman Melville

Bella brought a plate of freshly made scones to the table. 'How are you feeling, Drom?'

'Hanging in there.'

'Like all of us, I guess. Bring your coffee and join us.' Bella settled herself next to Christos.

It was our regular Sunday breakfast meeting at Maggie and Jason's. The Maestro was there, along with the Prof and Fox.

The sensation hit us simultaneously. My cup dropped to the floor and smashed, sending a slow-motion wave of coffee up over my shoes. It felt as though someone had punched me in the gut, ripped out my heart and smashed the top of my skull with a hammer.

Bella screamed and clutched at her head. Luca, Fox and the Prof hunched over the table and groaned, while the Maestro and Christos gasped and held their hearts.

'Ashley's dead!' I held on to the back of a chair to steady myself as shock rattled through my body.

Bella sobbed while the rest of us sat in shocked silence.

An anguished cry from the Prof broke the stillness. The pitch made my hair stand on end. That's until a second wave of sensation hit me too.

The Prof's face was a twisted mask of emotion. 'Maggie's dead!'

Fox clutched his chest and yelled. 'No. *No!*'

The Maestro leapt to her feet. 'Wait! She's back! She's alive. They're both alive!'

A warm feeling flooded my gut, like a belly full of joy. My heart filled, bursting with love, and my head hummed with the presence of Maggie and Ashley.

Fox wiped tears off his cheeks. 'What in *God's* name just happened?'

Luca wiped sweat from his brow. 'Ashley and Maggie died and were resurrected. We're etherically bound, so we experienced the separation and the reunion.'

'So, they're alive?' Fox asked.

'What do you feel?' I asked him.

'I feel like … like … they're warm and alive in my heart. So, yes, they're okay.'

'You nailed it. Exactly right.'

Fox put his forehead on the table with a clunk. 'I prefer the days when you got a telegram with important news. This is seriously taking years off my life.'

Everyone nodded tiredly in agreement, except for Christos, who wanted to know what a telegram was.

---

[20] *Maggie's Playlist: Never Tear Us Apart — INXS*

Maggie Chapter 20: Escapee

"Sex is as important as eating or drinking and we ought to allow the one appetite to be satisfied with as little restraint or false modesty as the other." — Marquis de Sade

I tucked another blanket around Ashley. Frank had worked on him for three hours and he'd just regained consciousness. He lay quietly, looking at me. 'What did he do to me, Maggie?'

'He fixed you. He operated and saved your life. You're going to be fine.'

'He put a bloody roach in me, didn't he?'

'Ashley, I witnessed the whole procedure. There was nothing untoward. You're being paranoid.'

'I have every reason to be paranoid.'

'You trust me? I'm saying everything is fine.'

'Okay.'

I turned to Tapakah. 'Who do you think was shooting at me?'

'I don't know, but I'll find out. I promise. And when I do, I'd hate to be in their shoes.' He looked directly at Frank.

Frank sat back in one of the leather chairs, feet up on the table, cradling a tumbler of Wild Turkey and ice. He downed the drink. 'Don't look at me. I'm on your side.'

'Why were you in the area?'

'I told you. I sent a chopper as back up, for your protection. And just as well I did. Not that I get any thanks.'

Tapakah grunted in response.

The medi jet was parked in a hanger, and it felt safe and cozy inside the plane. Ben was fast asleep on one of the beds. His tussled black curls spilled across the pillow, and a five o'clock shadow highlighted his strong jaw and sensuous mouth. His eyebrows arched even in sleep, and he radiated an air of strength and innocence. I tucked the sheet over his bare chest and felt a strong urge to climb in and lie beside him.

Poor Ben. He didn't need this crap in his life. And all of it was thanks to me. He must be cursing the day I walked into his café. And his poor Monaro, absolutely trashed. He was a brave man to stand up to Tapakah like he had. Brave or foolhardy.

His eyelids flickered open and he fixed me with his gaze. It was green eyes meeting green eyes. He mouthed the words, 'Be careful.' His eyes closed.

'What are you doing?' Tapakah asked.

'Just checking on Ben.' I returned to Tapakah's side.

'Someone is trying to kill me, and I need to know who and why. You left me, and the shooting started. I believed it was you. Then I thought it was Ashley and Ben, but someone was still trying to take me out while they were with me. Then, people were trying to kill all of us. What the hell is going on? Nothing makes sense. It's freaking me out. And maybe when you were shot in WA, 'they' were really after me there as well.' Trouble seems to follow me wherever I go, and I don't know why.' A hysterical edge had crept into my voice.

Ashley stirred on the gurney. 'The trouble is Tapakah. With a Capital "T". He's behind everything.'

'But why would Tapakah hire people to kill me, and him, plus you two? It doesn't make sense.'

Tapakah put his feet up on the gurney. 'You have to admit it, Ashley. It doesn't make sense. And I've asked Maggie to marry me, so why would I want her dead? You're an idiot.'

'Maybe they weren't really trying to kill Tapakah. It was a clever ploy to exonerate him in your mind. I'll bet you haven't accepted his proposal. Have you?'

Tapakah glared at Ashley. 'The attack felt pretty goddamn real to me.'

I put my face in my hands. 'It felt real to me too.'

I couldn't take much more of this. Too much intrigue and confusion for my liking. My head hurt, my body ached, and I wanted out. This wasn't what I signed up for. Something wasn't right. Well, nothing was right, and the worst thing was, I didn't know who to trust. I suspected everyone in the room — except for Frank — for trying to kill me. It was insane. I should probably add Frank to the list.

I loved Tapakah, felt a growing respect and connection with Ashley, and a warm affection for Ben, yet I didn't trust them. In fact, I didn't trust anyone, except maybe Billy. My hands were shaking. There was a constant, annoying twitch in my eyelid, and a background headache that never seemed to leave, except when I drank Champagne. I knew sex would alleviate my overactive brain, but *that* certainly wasn't a happening thing at the moment. Looked like Champagne was still the drug of choice.

Frank sat next to me. 'Are you okay? You're shaking.'

'No, Frank, I'm not okay, but thanks for asking.'

Frank shot Tapakah a look and Tapakah nodded.

'What say I give you a sedative? It will chill things out, settle the nerves.'

'Thanks, but no thanks. I want my wits about me.' A knot of anxiety twisted in my gut. 'By the way, who's looking after Billy?'

'Lilith,' Tapakah said.

The name Lilith sent my pulse racing and my mouth went dry. 'Oh, the lovely Lilith. He'll love that. Not.'

Tapakah frowned. 'Why do you say that?'

'I ... I don't know. I don't even know a Lilith.' I gasped as the shock wave of an ice-cold water jet blasted my body. An image of a woman's bitter face appeared in front of me. The sensation and image lasted a fraction of a second, but it took my breath away. I staggered, groping blindly for support. Ashley's arm whipped up, gripped my shoulder and held me steady.

Tapakah quickly pulled me from Ashley's grasp. 'What's wrong?' You're as white as a ghost.'

Ashley scowled at him. 'That's because she's probably seen one, you arsehole. One of your making.'

Tapakah snarled and raised his hand to Ashley. 'Shut the fuck up! I've had enough of your accusations and insolence.'

'Stop it! Stop it both of you. Enough already! I can't take this anymore!'

I pushed open the folding door to the ensuite, stepped inside and locked the door. The scent of fresh gardenias filled my nostrils. I sat on the toilet and examined the stylish design and gold fittings. It was a nice space. Nicer than out there, even though it was a toilet. I stared at my bandaged hand and foot and the blue bruises covering my legs. I dreaded the thought of looking at myself in the mirror. I wouldn't. I'd sit here in peace, on the toilet, until the next person tried to shoot me. Dead set. I so needed to run away.

I realised running was my default option. I ran, not because I was scared, or cowardly, but because I needed space and time to think, to allow answers to come. Solutions could never find their way into a crowded, frenzied mind. You had to run to the silence, let it enfold you, and answers would come. If I couldn't get peace, get some time out, it would drive me to destruction. Maybe that's what had happened to me before. I tried to kill myself to get peace.

Yet anytime you told people you needed space they'd always say, "what for?" And then not let you have any. Like they felt threatened and insecure by your need for it. That's why I needed to run.

I thought again about the fleeting image of the water jet that had rocked me. What did it mean? I was seriously starting to lose it.

Conversation mumbled outside. I put my ear to the door and heard Tapakah's deep, distinct voice.

'Stop going on, Ashley. Shut up and listen to me for one minute. Whatever you think of me, I swear to you, it was not me who was the shooter, or who orchestrated the shooters. I'm in debt to you and Ben for saving Maggie's life. I know you don't believe a word of it, but things are different with me now. I will never hurt Maggie. I *swear* to you. You have my word.'

'Your word doesn't carry any bloody weight with me,' Ashley snarled back. 'The damage is done. You've hurt her beyond words.'

'I didn't expect anything other than pig headedness from you. I didn't expect you would believe me. I've said what I wanted to say.'

There was silence for a while, then Ashley said, 'Listen, as much as it pains me to say this, I think I believe you. I've seen my share of action, and I don't reckon you orchestrated the attack. Someone else was out to get Maggie and you. Ben and I were caught in the crossfire. So, no matter how powerful or shit hot you think you are, you obviously can't protect Maggie. She'd be dead if it wasn't for us.'

'I'm aware of that. As I said to you, I'm grateful, and I *will* protect her.'

Ashley's voice cracked. 'You have to keep her safe. 'She's...'

His voice dropped to a whisper, and I couldn't make out the words. Tapakah said something back, and then there was silence.

I pulled a handful of tissues from the gold-plated tissue box and blew my nose. I tried to do it quietly, but that was an impossibility for me.

I still had Ben's jacket on. I found a wallet in one of the pockets. It was a stylish, Italian Tom Ford, leather bifold with gold trim. Typical Ben.

Please let there be cash. I flipped it open. Bingo! Four big ones nestled in the money clip, along with smaller notes. Enough to get me away and find a bolt hole.

The jet door was open. I could sneak down the stairs into the hanger. There were plenty of places to hide.

When we'd taxied in, I'd noticed old cars, vintage fire trucks and other assorted automobiles around the outside of the hanger. There appeared to be workshops at the back and several exits. My plan was to pick up Billy and head to Ben's parent's farm.

I really had nowhere else to go, and if they were as nice as Ben, I'm sure they wouldn't mind. He'd said I could go there. The only bad thing about the plan was it dragged Ben further into the mire, and then perhaps his parents. Maybe it wasn't such a good idea. But where else could I go? I could find temporary lodging at a Salvos refuge. Blend in with the homeless folk. Who knew? I'd have to go with the flow.

I carefully and quietly opened the bathroom door and peeked around the corner. No one was in eyeshot. The open door of the jet beckoned me. I tiptoed across the aisle and flew down the steps to the hanger floor. The coast was clear. The hanger was open, the night air smelt fresh, and lights twinkled in the distance. I was going to make a break for the open space. I looked back to ensure no one had followed me. Then I turned and ran straight into Tapakah.

'Going somewhere?'

'Um ... ah ... just needed some air, is all.'

'Is that right? You're lying to me. You're running away, aren't you?'

'Nuh ... no ... I just needed air.'

'Don't lie. Ashley told me you'd run. I didn't believe him, but wonders never cease, you did.'

'Ashley said that?'

Tapakah nodded, locking onto me with those damn blasted black eyes.

How the hell had Ashley known? Was he psychic? And why

the hell had he dobbed me in? He'd said he was my friend, but he was just a dirty, stinking dibber dobber. See why I couldn't trust anyone? No wonder I was friggin' paranoid. I. Couldn't. Trust. Anyone.

Tapakah gripped my arm. 'Come back inside. It's freezing out here.'

I shook myself free. 'I don't want to.'

'You want to stay out here and freeze?'

'I want to leave.'

A wave of emotion swept across Tapakah's face. 'You want to leave *me*?'

'Not just you. Everyone and everything. I've had enough.'

'Maggie, you need to talk to me. If you need space, you can have it. You don't need to run away to get it. You can go anywhere you want. Tell me and I'll make it happen. It's too dangerous for you out there. Where were you running to anyway?'

'No idea. Just away. Running is good; it makes me feel better. Things happen when I run. Things change.'

'I'll give you space.'

'I know you will, but it's not the same as running.'

'For Christ's sake, come back inside. You're shivering. It's dark and it's cold, and you were going to run with nothing on except Ben's jacket? Seriously? It barely covers your arse. You wouldn't last five minutes.'

'I would've got by.'

'If you want to run, run tomorrow. For now, come back inside.'

'Okay.' I was too tired to argue, so I reluctantly climbed the metal stairs. The steel was icy on my bare feet, but I burned with anger at Ashley's betrayal. I'd reached the top step when Tapakah spoke. 'Stop!'

'What?'

He attempted to speak but his words caught. He cleared his

throat and spoke in a hoarse whisper. 'Watching you climb the stairs. Christ, Maggie.'

In a millisecond he was up the stairs holding me in in his arms. His mouth found mine, and his hand slipped inside Ben's jacket to fondle my breasts. The steel of the banister dug into my back as he pressed himself against me. His other hand moved between my thighs. His passion ignited mine, and my troubled world slipped away as I gave in to his lust.

'I can't bear the thought of you leaving, of being so unhappy. I'll make it up to you.' His breath was hot in my ear and his deep voice stole the power from my legs.

'I couldn't run if I wanted to.' I gasped as his fingers entered me.

'Christ, you're wet. That can't go to waste.' He dropped to his knees in front of me, held my buttocks, and drew me to his mouth. He devoured me with his tongue, his lips, his mouth, his … I'm not sure what the hell it was, that probed, sucked, licked and consumed me. I held the head of a ravenous creature between my legs, and its appetite was insatiable.

I entered a world of exquisite pleasure almost too intense to bear, as wave after wave of orgasm engulfed me. I cried out with the pleasure and pain of it.

Time ceased. I didn't know if minutes or hours had passed when finally, he stopped.

I sat spent and comatose on the cold steel step, feeling the metal edge dig into my back. There was no thought, no worry, no fear or concern, just an abiding sense of peace that saturated every atom of my being.

When Tapakah drew back there was an odd sensation of withdrawal. It was as if six feet of rubber chord were being extracted from my body, or my innards were being removed by suction. There was no pain, but I groaned from the intense strangeness of it.

'Relax, it's okay, Tapakah whispered.' He picked me up and

carried me inside. 'Do you still want to run?' His dark eyes blazed into mine.

I croaked, trying to find my voice. 'I … I don't need to. Can't. Ever. Legs … cactus.' I closed my eyes and sank back into the peace pervading my body, and the most welcome hush that saturated my mind.

He laughed softly. 'You'll feel like running in a day or so. I'm putting you to bed.'

Non compos mentis, I simply nodded in response.

Tapakah marched into the cabin and Ashley's panicked voice yelled, 'What the hell have you done to her?'

Tapakah wiped his mouth on the back of his sleeve. 'I convinced her to come, not go.'

---

[21] *Maggie's Playlist: Take Me Away — Avril Lavigne*

"Ever has it been that love knows not its own depth until the hour of separation." — *Kahlil Gibran*

The conversation came from a million miles away. I wasn't asleep, but not far from it.

Frank checked Ashley's blood pressure. 'He needs to rest for the next few hours. He shouldn't be moved.'

'Then we'll wait out the night here,' Tapakah said. 'Send the pilots home. No point in everyone hanging around. I'll arrange transport for Ashley and Ben tomorrow.'

'Transport to where?' Ashley said. 'Roach central to get an implant?'

'I'm sure that can be arranged, Ashley, if you really want one. But no, I'll arrange transport to wherever you want. You need to take it easy for the next few weeks and get yourself checked out by a doctor.'

'And what happens to Maggie?'

'Maggie stays.'

'Does she have any say in that?'

'Of course she does. I'm not having that conversation again. It's tedious. Are you hungry?'

'I could eat the arse out of a low flying duck.'

'Charming. Our chef is on board. What would you like?'

'Ham and cheese toastie.'

'And Ben, what about you?'

'Same will be fine, thanks.'

'I'll go to the galley and get things underway.'

Silence for a few seconds, and then Ashley whispered. 'Well, this is a turn up. Tapakah making us ham and cheese toasties. Who would've thought?'

'I don't know what to think,' Ben said. 'I'm just glad you two are okay.'

'Maggie's zonked,' Ashley whispered. 'Have a look at her. Bruised, scratched, bandaged, *Mad Max* hair, yet she still looks bloody gorgeous. At least we've built a connection, a friendship, hopefully, and trust.'

The word *trust* propelled me to consciousness. Ashley started as I opened my eyes.

'Friends don't betray each other, and you betrayed me. There can be no friendship without trust, and I don't trust you.'

Ashley looked shocked. 'What are you talking about? How on earth did I betray you? I would never—'

'You told Tapakah I was going to run. I would've been long gone if it wasn't for you.'

'Oh, that.'

'Yes, *that*. And how the hell did you know? Are you psychic?'

'I didn't think Tapakah would tell you, but obviously, any chance to make me look bad.'

'You've made yourself look bad. And you haven't answered my question. How did you know?'

'I'm not psychic. I knew, because I know you. Inside out, and back to front. It comes from years of friendship. More than friendship. We have a connection. I could see it in your face. You were overwhelmed, and when that happens your default mechanism for recovery is to run.'

'So why didn't you let me run?'

'Because if you did, I couldn't keep you safe. Unbelievably, I would rather see you with Tapakah than have you out there on your own. I'm not in a fit state to protect you, so I had to make a call. You may see it as betrayal, but I had your best interests at heart. That's why I gave him the heads up.'

'He's right,' Ben said. 'It's too dangerous for you on your own. Particularly now, when no one knows who the real enemy is.'

'Well, it feels pretty damn dangerous right here,' I said.

'True, but at least you've got backup,' Ashley said.

'S'pose so.'

'So, do you forgive me?'

'S'pose so.'

I didn't want to admit it, but he was right. He probably had done me a favour. I felt totally fine now, without having to run. My chances of survival were better here.

'You're right. I am safer here. Thank you.'

'Jesus Christ.' Ashley cleaned out an ear with his finger. 'Did I just hear you say I was right?'

'Yes, what's the big deal?'

'Say it again.'

'Why?'

He grinned. 'Because I never thought I'd ever hear those words come out of your mouth.'

Feeling happy and magnanimous, I said it again. 'You were right, Ashley. I'm better off here.'

There was a sequence of sharp popping noises, and I ducked instinctively. A series of holes appeared in the side of the plane just above my head, and then another row underneath. More holes appeared on the opposite wall.

'Famous last words!' Ashley yelled. He grabbed my arm and dragged me onto the floor.

Ben hit the deck and crawled up the aisle. He collapsed a nearby gurney and pushed it along the aisle on its side. 'Maggie! Get behind this and stay low. I need to get Ash off the trolley.'

'It's okay, mate.' Ashley ripped the IV from his arm, slid off the gurney and tipped it onto its side.

'Get in between the gurneys,' Ashley shouted at me. 'They'll give us protection. Keep your heads down!' He pushed our craniums into the carpet.

Rapid pops and thunks filled the air as the jet was sprayed with bullets. The aircraft walls began to resemble an aboriginal dot painting.

Tapakah and Frank were at the front of the plane. 'Is Maggie okay?' Tapakah yelled.

Ashley gave him the thumbs up.

Tapakah slid a machine gun, and two semi-automatic pistols along the aisle into Ashley's hand. 'I'm taking the plane out. We don't stand a chance stuck in here. The guns are just in case. In the meantime, keep your heads down.'

'You can fly a jet?' I yelled.

'I know the theory. It shouldn't be too hard.' He disappeared into the cockpit.

Frank stood there looking stunned. Tapakah's arm appeared and grabbed him by the collar, pulling him backwards into the cockpit. Frank's face resembled an emoji — the one screaming in fear.

'Oh Jesus. We're screwed,' Ashley said. He ducked as bullets pinged off the gurney.

This was a cream between. A gurney sandwich. Me in the middle, Ben on one side, Ashley on the other, and a gurney on each side of us. It was squeezy.

'This is cozy,' Ben said from his position pressed up hard against my back.

'It's a triple spoon,' I said.

'Maggie, put your arms around me,' Ashley said. 'It'll give us more room.'

'Yeah, I could do the same,' Ben said.

'I don't know about that.'

'Rest your head on my arm,' Ben suggested.

'Okay, that's better.' Ben's arm was under my head and I

could feel his breath on my neck.

The engines rumbled into life and the floor shuddered beneath us as the plane began to move.

'I'm going to cover Tapakah,' Ashley yelled. 'If he's our only hope, he needs protection. Frank won't cut it. If they take Tapakah out, we've got Buckley's.'

Ashley slid out from between the gurneys, which then tipped together and formed a little tent over Ben and me. We watched him commando crawl up the aisle with machine gun in hand, and a gun tucked in the back of his jeans. Bullets flew everywhere and our gurneys had developed a serious case of pockmarks.

The engines were building speed. Frank fell out of the cockpit clutching his arm. Ashley yanked him to safety, took cover behind the toilet, and shot out of a window. The engines screamed, and so did Ashley as he let rip with the machine gun. A bullet grazed his cheek, but he stood his ground and kept firing. He only stopped when the plane left the ground.

Ashley grinned and pumped his fist. 'The fucker did it!'

Ben pushed the gurneys aside and helped me up, as the plane leveled out. Ben looked at me with wide eyes. 'He's flying the thing.'

'Amazing!' I said, feeling that my eyes were equally as big.

Ashley helped Frank up off the floor and sat him in a chair. He took off his shirt and examined his arm.

'Just a flesh wound. You'll live. I'll look at it when we land.' He tied the shirt around Frank's arm and then wrapped him in a blanket.

Frank looked pale. '*If* we land.'

The speakers crackled into life. 'Ladies and gentlemen, this is your captain speaking. Our flight will shortly arrive at Essendon Airport at precisely 3.23 am. Weather is fine, and we expect a smooth landing. I do suggest, however, that you fasten your seatbelts.'

I laughed. 'He's *enjoying* himself.'

Ben looked worried. 'Not at our expense, I hope.'

The speaker crackled again. 'Did you know in Australian aviation, they measure flight in *nautical* miles, take off in metres, climb rate in feet, fuel in litres, fuel burn in pounds and passenger weight in either pounds or kilos? The conversions must do pilots' heads in.'

'I hope it hasn't done this pilot's head in,' I said.

'Ladies and Gentlemen, prepare for landing. Place your trays in the upright position and fasten your seatbelts.'

'And kiss your arse goodbye,' Ashley said, dragging Frank up the aisle behind him. He herded us along to the end of the plane. 'Safer at the back.'

'You have the window seat, Ben, Maggie in the middle, then me and Frank.'

Ashley pulled my seat belt in so tight it hurt. He held my hand. 'If we die, at least we'll go out together.' Ben took my other hand as the plane descended.

'What about Tapakah? He's there by himself. It's not right. I'm going to help.' I unbuckled my belt. 'The rest of the crew, where are they?'

Ashley shook his head then growled, 'Sit!' He buckled me back up.

'Ladies and Gentlemen, four minutes to landing. Maggie, do as you're told. Stay put.'

Ashley nodded and gave me an "I told you so" look.

The plane dropped suddenly, and my stomach travelled to my mouth.

Ben closed his eyes and whispered, 'Holy Mother Mary.'

Ashley squeezed my hand. The engines roared, and the air made eerie shrieking noises inside the cabin. The shrill howling gave me a feeling of déjà vu. It was as if a thousand ghosts wailed around us. Frank squeezed his eyes shut and gripped the armrest. Ashley sat calmly flipping through the in-flight magazine. Blood trickled down his face from the bullet graze on his cheek.

He closed the magazine. 'Well, you guys, I'm leaving the link open, along with my eyes, but be warned, it could get ugly. Love you all.'

I was puzzled. 'Are you talking to me?'

'No, to the men and women in my head.'

'Oh, right, of course.'

Oh, dear. The man had finally cracked.

The engine noise reverberated through the chassis. 'You're too low, Tapakah, too low,' Frank muttered. The plane sounded as if it was on its last legs.

BANG!

The wheels slammed into the tarmac; the engines screamed their guts out. Another bump and a bounce to the side.

Frank gripped the armrest even harder. 'Too fast, Tapakah, too fast.'

I had faith in Tapakah, but as the G-Force pushed us back in our seats I closed my eyes and prayed. No one had the guts to look out the window, not even Ashley. If it was coming, none of us wanted to see it.

The scream of engines softened as the speed reduced.

Tapakah spoke through the comms with a slight breathless stutter. 'Ladies and Gentlemen, wuh … welcome to Essendon Airport. I h … hope you enjoyed the flight because I sure as hell did.'

The four of us broke into spontaneous applause, followed by hoots and high fives.

The wailing of approaching sirens reached our ears.

'Attention, Ladies and Gentlemen. Every man, woman and their dog is going to be here to greet us, along with the police, Feds, fire crews, emergency services, TV news and possibly amongst them, more bad guys. Maggie, I suggest you find clothes to put on. There's a wardrobe at the back. You too,

Ashley.

Ashley flicked open my seatbelt and gave me a kiss on the cheek, as he helped me up.

I opened the wardrobe and found some clothes. I slipped off Ben's jacket not realising I had an audience.

Ashley pushed me behind the wardrobe door. 'Turn around, fellas,'

'That goes for you too,' I said to him.

'Oh, yeah, sorry, Mags.'

Then it hit me. 'Well, really, we needn't bother. Everyone here has already seen everything there is to see of me.'

'True,' everyone said, nodding.

We dressed quickly and raced to see Tapakah. The cockpit door was open, and he'd taxied to a stop. He looked very happy with himself, leaning back in his chair, captain's hat pushed back on his head.

He caught sight of Ashley and leapt up. 'Thanks for stepping up and covering me. I couldn't have made it without you.' He offered his hand. Ashley extended his, they locked arms, and pulled in for a man hug, garnished with enthusiastic slaps on the back.

Bloody hell. I stared in shock at the two of them. I wasn't sure who'd pulled whom in first for the hug, but this was the last thing I'd ever expected to see.

Ashley grinned and gave Tapakah one more slap on the shoulder for good luck. 'Friggin' awesome job flying this thing and getting us landed. Best thing ever, man.'

I caught Tapakah's cap as it slipped off his head. 'Ashley had the utmost confidence in your flying abilities. He was casually reading the in-flight magazine, while we were white knuckle flying with our eyes closed.'

Tapakah pointed at the mass of flashing lights heading our way. 'I've called in reinforcements, folks, so when they arrive, go straight to the black Audi. It will take you to safety. I'll deal with the onslaught and meet up with you later.'

'What reinforcements?' Ashley asked.

'You'll know when they arrive.'

Ashley looked sceptical. 'What's plan B if plan A turns to shit? What do we say?'

'It will work. Trust me.'

I waited for a smart-arse response, but Ashley said nothing.

Tapakah took my hand. 'How are you?'

'Fine now I'm not dodging bullets and we're back safely on terra firma. All thanks to you.'

'I've booked the penthouse at the Sheraton. The car will take you there. Ashley, Ben and Frank will go with you. Ashley needs to rest. If you need medical attention Frank can arrange it. Looks like he needs some himself. I'll join you once this is sorted. You'll have everything you need on tap. Is that all right with you, Maggie?'

'God yes. I can't wait to have a hot shower and go to sleep.'

'No food?'

'Of course, food first!'

Tapakah smiled. 'You had me worried there. And are you planning to run?'

'No, I'm not planning to run.'

'Promise me you'll talk to me next time. I want you to be happy.'

I put my arms around his neck and kissed him. 'Promise.'

I wasn't totally sure it was a promise I could keep, but I'd do my best. That's all a girl could do.

Ashley cleared his throat. 'Um, hate to interrupt you two lovebirds, but there's a shitstorm outside that needs dealing with.'

Emergency vehicles surrounded the plane, and heavily armed police moved into place.

Tapakah nodded. 'I'll go out alone. When the reinforcements arrive, go straight to the car. You'll be totally safe. Look after

Maggie, Ashley.'

'Always.'

Tapakah gave me a kiss. 'See you soon. All of you, keep out of sight.' He opened the plane door to the sound of a cascade of guns cocking. Tapakah descended the stairs and called out, 'I'm unarmed. Don't shoot. No one else is on board. I'm coming down.'

We peered out of bullet holes to watch the unfolding scene. The moon shone brightly in a cloudless sky, highlighting a strange black cloud that swelled and fluxed on the horizon. It travelled at speed and headed our way. Within seconds the sky outside was black, and the air vibrated with a screeching cacophony which shredded our ears. It appeared the gates of hell had released a million winged demons which moved as one to encircle their foes.

Ben looked horrified. 'What in God's name are they?'

'Tapakah's reinforcements,' I said.

'You're kidding me?' Ashley said.

'Nope. Looks like he's called in the fruit bat brigade.'

'Christ Almighty,' Ashley said. 'I thought he meant men with guns. Holy flying fox, Batman!'

The police, TV crews and emergency services disappeared. Everything vanished inside the tornado of bats that encircled them in a shrieking, cackling frenzy. Enclosed in a bat tempest, they had no hope of escape.

'Time to get the hell out of here.' I descended the steps and a black Audi was waiting, just as Tapakah had said. The driver alighted and opened the door for me. 'Good evening, Maggie. Please take a seat, and we'll be on our way,' he shouted over the din.

I blocked my ears. The sound of the bats was overwhelming. The leather like flap of their wings, the smell of earth and musk, the air whipping around in a maelstrom of movement, the hellish squeals and cackles. And that was on the *outside* of the bat tornado. God only knows how it was on the inside.

The noise receded as we sank into the luxurious leather seats and the driver whisked us into the night.

* * * * *

I barely registered the magnificence of the penthouse suite; I was so tired. I couldn't face food, or even muster the energy to have a shower. Ashley looked like death on a stick. Frank didn't look much better. Exhausted, Ben had sunk into brooding mode. I noted it was a mode in which he looked seriously gorgeous.

He took my hand. 'You're swaying on your feet.'

'I need to lie down. For at least a week.'

He put his arm around my shoulder. 'Come with me. I'll put you to bed. The master bedroom's this way.'

Ashley glared at Ben. 'You'll do no such thing.'

Ben rolled his eyes. 'Keep your knickers on. I didn't say bed her, just *put* her to bed.'

A knock on the door made us jump. Ashley grabbed a pistol and tucked it in the back of his pants.

Frank staggered across to answer it. 'It'll be your blood delivery, Ashley.'

'Back up. Let me go first. Who is it?' Ashley shouted.

'Medical delivery for Frank Ashmore.'

Frank pushed past Ashley and opened the door. He seized the Esky from the man and slammed the door. 'Get into bed, Ashley. I'm going to hook you up before you die, and then I'm going to bed before I die. Ben, see Maggie goes to bed, and then take the pills I've put on the coffee table for you. It'll settle you and help you sleep.'

The guys saluted Frank who had suddenly shifted into Alpha dog mode.

Ben steered me into the bedroom, and I flopped onto the huge bed. Someone had lit the scented candles on the bedside table, and the room smelt divine.

'I can't get you into bed with you lying on top of the blankets.'

I groaned, nearly asleep already. 'Can't move.'

Ben held my ankles and dragged me to one side. He tossed back the covers and rolled me under the sheets. 'You've still got your clothes on.'

I held out my arms and muttered. 'Take 'em off. I hate sleeping with clothes.'

'I'd love to, but there's no way. Ashley would kill me.'

'S'all right. Night, Ben, thank you. I love you.'

'I love you too.' He kissed me on the forehead, and the door closed softly as he left the room.

I found the energy to drag off my clothes and throw them on the floor. I loved the feel of expensive sheets on my body. They felt sensuous and feeling sensuous reminded me of Tapakah. My body was tired, but my brain buzzed with thoughts of him.

He truly was a remarkable man. Well, man creature. I didn't know how to describe him. I guess no one did. The events of the last few hours had convinced me he was not my enemy. Someone else was. I knew in my heart it couldn't be Ben, and I was pretty sure it wasn't Ashley. The only other people I knew well were Frank, Hugh, Elizabeth, Billy and Beans, if you could include a dog. It couldn't be Billy or Beans; I couldn't see it being Elizabeth and Hugh. That left Frank. I couldn't see it being him either. I didn't like having enemies. I couldn't remember much, but I knew stuff, and I knew I wasn't a bad person. Why would someone want to kill me?

I needed Tapakah. Not only needed him, I wanted him. I knew he wanted to possess me and, if I was honest with myself, I wanted that. In fact, I wanted to possess him too. Was it love? In a way, but a whole lot more. It was desire, passion, obsession, excitement and madness. He was a drug. I wanted to break free of him but being with him was like nothing I'd experienced. Well, I couldn't remember anything of my past life, but I knew in my heart this was unique.

I kept the ring he'd given me on a chain around my neck. I undid the chain and held the ring in my hand. It appeared to pulse with energy, and its woven metals shimmered with life, seeming to writhe in the soft light of the candles.

He'd made a commitment to me, but I'd resisted, been scared. I refused to be afraid anymore. No more fence sitting. I needed certainty in my life; I couldn't keep going on this way. I would make a commitment to him and damn the consequences.

I picked up the ring and spoke aloud. 'I, Maggie McLaine, take you Tapakah ... um ... hell ... I don't even know your last name. Oh, well, I take you, Tapakah Hell, to be officially engaged to be married to me, at some stage in the future. Not now, but soon, well, at some point in time, down the track.' I slid the ring onto my finger.

I cried out as the ring blazed with firelight and tightened around my finger. It dug into my skin and appeared to be melding with my flesh. I tried to pull it off, but surges of energy zapped my fingers. I gritted my teeth and tried again to remove it.

'Ow!' The energy zapped me hard. My hand jumped back and knocked a glass off the bedside table.

The door burst open and Ashley flew in, gun in hand. He was wearing only jocks and bandages. His eyes darted around the room. 'Who's here? What's wrong?'

'S ... sorry, Ashley. I knocked a glass off the bedside. False alarm.' I slid my hand under the sheets. The ring seemed to have returned to normal, and I didn't want to create more worry for Ashley.

He sat on the edge of the bed, holding his side. 'Would it be okay if I leave your door open? That way I can hear if anything's going on, or you can call out for me.' He looked at me intently. 'Something wrong?'

I buckled under his gaze and looked away.

208

'*What*, Maggie?'

'You're making me nervous is all. You rattled me, bursting in like that.'

'Right. Whatever you say. You can't lie to me, you know. And please don't. It's insulting.' He stomped out, slamming the door behind him. I jumped with the ferocity of it.

I examined the ring again. It looked stunning on my hand and seemed to have returned to its original state.

I was going to take it off.

I grimaced with the expectation of pain as I moved my fingers towards it.

No, no. I'd do it in the morning.

I was way too tired to handle anything else untoward, and Ashley's reaction had upset me.

I blew out the candles and snuggled under the blankets. I lay staring into the darkness, unable to shake the feeling something had broken.

* * * * *

My eyelids felt so heavy, I struggled to open them. When I did, I found myself staring into the black eyes of Tapakah.

I gasped with fright. 'You scared me! You're like a creeping Jesus. How long have you been there?'

'A while. Sorry. I didn't mean to scare you. You looked so peaceful; it made me feel peaceful watching you.' He bent over and kissed my forehead.

'What time is it?'

'Seven in the morning. They didn't keep me as long as I anticipated.'

'Is everything okay?'

'Fine. Nothing for you to concern yourself with.'

'The fruit bats were amazing, as were you. You saved us.'

'I had help. I couldn't have done it without Ashley.'

'Yes, he's amazing too.'

'Changing the subject now. You've made me a very happy man.' He picked up my hand. The ring seemed to ignite at his touch, sparkling with a light of its own.

'What do you mean?'

'You accepted my proposal.'

'You *know? How?*'

'Of course I know. Your intention activated the ring when you put it on.' He showed me the ring on his hand. 'It's linked to mine.'

'It scared the bloody life out of me. I was having my own personal engagement ceremony and it ruined the moment.'

'I should have warned you, and I would have, but I didn't think you'd ever accept.'

I examined it suspiciously. 'I'm too scared to try and take it off.'

'Don't be, it won't react now. Thank you, Maggie. I still can't believe it.' He leant over and kissed me gently on the lips.

'Well, you're the perfect man, I reckon, so I had to bite the bullet and make a decision. And really, you're not a man, entirely, so that's probably what makes you perfect. You're one of a kind.'

'As are you.' He kissed me again, this time with urgency and passion.

I came up for air. 'Phew. You're making me hot and bothered.'

He smiled and slid his hand under the sheets. 'Just the way I like it.'

'Have you had anything to eat?'

'A sandwich and a coffee. Fox was there, the detective inspector. He organised it for me. But that's it, nothing else. I'm so hungry, I could eat the arse out of a low flying duck, as Ashley so crudely puts it.'

Tapakah explored my body, and I closed my eyes enjoying his gentle touch.

210

I made a move to get out of bed. 'Better get you something to eat then.'

He pushed me back on the bed. 'I have all I need right here.' His words made me gasp and my body involuntarily quivered with desire.

Tapakah tossed back the blankets and swung me around by my ankles to face him. He knelt on the floor between my legs and pulled me towards him. I knew what was coming next.

Well, obviously I didn't. The door flew open and in blasted Ashley, bag of blood in one hand, gun in the other.

He grabbed Tapakah by his jacket and hurled him against the wall. The panel cracked as Tapakah's head buried itself into the plaster in the corner of the room. His legs gave way and he slid to the floor.

'What the hell are you doing? It's *Tapakah!* I yelled.

Disoriented and confused, Ashley looked across at Tapakah's crumpled body. 'Oh, bugger me dead, I thought it was an intruder. Jesus, I'm sorry.'

Tapakah groaned and rubbed his head. 'I didn't want to wake anyone, so I snuck in. Not much escapes you, Ashley. You should join my team.'

Ashley stared at me. The expression on his face was intense. His voice was a bare whisper. 'That ring. I've never seen you wear it before. Maggie, please tell me you … you haven't?'

'Um, I'm engaged to be married. To Tapakah.'

Ashley clutched the pistol so hard the veins in his arm and bicep stood out. The colour not only drained from his face, but his entire body. He resembled the walking dead.

I leapt out of bed and took his arm. 'Ashley! Sit. You look like you're going to die.' Panic pummelled in my chest.

He shook free from my grasp. 'This is insane. Don't you realise what you've done? Not only are you sleeping with the enemy, you're marrying the fucking enemy. You're marrying an abomination.'

'That's not true. He's not what you think. You've got it wrong.'

Ben appeared at the doorway, machine gun in hand. Tapakah waved him to stand down, then leapt to his feet, fists clenched, body tense. I surmised he would take Ashley out, but he simply stood and stared.

Ashley looked incredulous. 'I've got it wrong?' He paused for a moment, swaying slightly on his feet. 'You know what? You're right. I have got it wrong. I can't do this anymore. You've made your choice. I'm making mine. You're on your own. I'm done.' He turned on his heel and walked out the door.

'Ashley, wait! Don't go!'

I chased after him as he strode along the marble tiled hallway. He yanked the IV tube from his arm, pulled on a pair of jeans, T-shirt, boots and headed for the front door.

A pinprick of pain stabbed in my chest and I gasped. An awful sensation arose in my heart, as if someone had plucked at a loose thread and my heart was unravelling.

'Ashley, you're not well. How can you go?'

He turned to face me and said mockingly, 'Maggie, you're not well. How can you stay?' He glared at me. 'I told you. I'm done. I'm done with you. I'm done with Tapakah, the crystals, the musketeers, the dark fucking force, everything. The world can go to hell for all I care. It's over. I'm out of here and I'm not coming back.'

'Don't leave! You're overreacting. Where will you go?'

'I'm going to the Hyatt to find Melanie. It's my turn for revenge sex.' He slammed the door in my face.

---

[22] *Maggie's Playlist: It's All Over Now — Rod Stewart*

The six of us were sitting around the kitchen table at Maggie and Jason's place, staring into space. The scene that played out in our heads was riveting and disturbing.

A familiar *thunk* reverberated in our heads as Ashley slammed the link shut.

Bella winced, rubbed her temples and looked at me. 'Did you feel that?'

'Sure did.'

Bella stood and rubbed the small of her back. 'He's closed the door on Maggie, and, by the looks of it, on us too. No wonder. Poor Ash, after what he's been through for Maggie, and then this happens. It's horrible.'

Fox ran his hands through his hair. 'This is bad.'

'This is so much more than bad,' I said.

Bella's expression was bleak. 'He's on the road to oblivion.'

'Way more than oblivion. I'm going after him. He's heading to the Hyatt.'

'What do we do about Maggie?' Luca asked.

The Prof looked up from scribbling in his brown notebook. 'I think she'll be fine where she is, for now. As much as we don't like it, it appears Tapakah cares for her, and she for him. Ashley's the one who needs rescuing.'

The Maestro caressed Christo's bald head with her long fingers. Her expression was the saddest I'd ever seen it. 'Poor Ashley. This planet, the dramas. It's like watching one of your soap operas. I should go after him. I could fix him. Forget Melanie. Give me a few minutes with him, and he'd forget Maggie or Melanie ever existed.'

The Professor nodded his head in agreement. 'Indeed, he would. It's a good idea, Maestro, but perhaps we should save that as a last resort. It might make him angrier.'

Christos looked hopeful. 'I could go?'

The Maestro quickly canned his idea with a look and a raised eyebrow.

'True. He is an angry man,' Christos said.

Bella shook her head. 'No, he's not. He's a gorgeous man. He's had a massive kick in the guts. To tell you the truth, I feel the same. I can't believe Maggie. It's insane. Everything's going to hell. Tapakah's winning, for God's sake. How on earth do we continue? No Maggie, no Jason, no Jasmine, no Ashley? Who the hell is next?'

Bella was ready to dissolve into tears or erupt into anger.

Fox put his arm around her. 'We'll get through this. We're Musketeers. If Jason, Maggie, Ashley and Jasmine were here, and in their right minds, they'd want us to keep fighting for them. We can't let this beat us. We must do it for them. We have to be tougher, smarter, more resilient than our enemies, even if we don't know who the bloody hell they are half the time.' He shook his head. 'Don't give up. We're still here, and we're here for each other, and we're here for you, Bella.'

Bella gave him a weak smile. 'Is that how you inspire the troops? You're very good.'

He stroked her cheek. 'Well, at least I got a smile, and a beautiful one at that.'

'I'm not thinking of giving up, no way. I'm in shock, that's all.'

Fox picked up her hand and held it. 'Yeah, we all are. Drom, do you want me to go with you to see Ash?'

'Thanks, Fox, but I'll go solo. I'll let you know if I need backup.'

Fox nodded.

He knew me. I preferred to work alone. Be nimble like a ninja. Unencumbered, I got more done. Fox was great to work with, but I didn't want the responsibility of another person. My heart tightened at the thought of losing someone else.

Jasmine was it for me. Never again. The pain was still too much to bear. Her red raincoat swirling to the ground, the sound as she hit the rocks, continued to play over and over in my mind. I'd have to get some of Ashley's combat nightmare drugs. If I wasn't careful, I could end up like him. It sucked. He'd had his lion heart ripped from his chest and torn to shreds in the worst possible way.

'Drom?'

'Yep, just thinking. I'm outta here.' I tapped my head. 'Keep connected folks. At least we're saving a heap on mobile phone calls.'

---

[23] *Maggie's Playlist: Get Out of My Head — Firewater*

Tapakah Chapter 23: Parting is
Such Sweet Sorrow

It had taken all my will power not to run to Maggie, cover her, and drag her away from Ashley's blazing eyes. But I hadn't. I'd let Ashley gaze upon Maggie in her naked glory. I'd let him gaze upon the woman he could never have. The woman he fought for so desperately, the woman he'd lost. I'd found the whole scene strangely erotic, if I was honest.

The front door slammed, which I assumed signaled Ashley's departure. Ben and I headed into the lounge.

Maggie stood frozen, staring at the back of the door. Her hand pressed hard against her chest, her face was a twisted mask of pain. She wore nothing other than my ring, and her naked body appeared ghost like against the white marble and tiles. She looked beautiful and I wanted her. But now was not the time. I was learning.

'Ben, get a bathrobe for Maggie.'

'Sure, Tapakah.'

I drew Maggie into my arms and held her close. 'Ashley's a survivor. He'll be fine.'

She trembled, clutched at her chest and sobbed. She looked at me with those green eyes I loved so much. 'My heart's unravelling.'

I swaddled her in the bathrobe Ben offered. 'I think mine is too. Either that or I'm going insane.'

The sensations of victory I'd relished five minutes ago had vanished, replaced with something that felt weak. What the hell was happening to me? I must've been developing a human mental illness. These sensations, emotions, were too erratic to be normal.

I was jubilant, ecstatic, filled with joy at Ashley's humiliation and departure. I was victorious. Ashley was a broken man and Maggie was mine.

Now, reflecting on their expressions — the indescribable pain on Ashley's face, and the sorrow and torment on Maggie's — it gave me no pleasure. I couldn't understand it, and I didn't like it.

I sat Maggie on my knee and held her tight as she cried. I buried my face against her neck, inhaling the scent of her skin. She looked up in surprise and concern. 'Are those tears?'

I wiped away the salty fluid. 'I guess.'

'Excuse me,' Ben interrupted, 'but I'm going to find Ashley. I want to check he's okay.'

Maggie stood and gave him a hug. 'Oh, Ben, thank you. Thank you for everything. And I'm so sorry — for everything.'

He gazed into her face. 'Don't be sorry, it's not your fault.'

'I feel everything is,' she said sadly.

'It's not. Promise me you won't go down that path.'

They seemed lost in each other's eyes. Finally, I felt something other than despair. A spike of jealousy flared in my heart. I pulled Maggie aside. 'I have something for you, Ben.' I reached into my pocket.

They flinched and stepped back. Christ, she still didn't trust me.

I took out a set of keys and dangled them in front of him. 'Your car.' I threw him the keys. 'I took the liberty of having it repaired. I hope you don't mind. Original parts. It's as good as new, if not better. It's parked out front.'

Ben seemed surprised. 'I didn't except that. Thanks, I appreciate it. I love that car.'

'I hope it meets your expectations. It's the least I can do. Goodbye, Ben.' I shook his hand. 'Thank you for looking out for Maggie.'

'Bye. And congratulations on your engagement. Stay safe and be happy.' He kissed Maggie's cheek.

She wiped the tears from her face. 'Bye, Ben. Thanks for everything.'

He turned and walked down the hallway without looking back.

* * * * *

Maggie

Tapakah looked as flat as I felt.

'I want to go home,' I told him. 'I need to see Billy.'

My heart felt raw and empty.

'Yes, let's do that.'

Frank staggered out of the bedroom looking tired and dishevelled. His thinning hair stuck to his scalp and his face looked squashed on one side.

'Morning all. I hit the bed and didn't move all night.'

'Sure looks like it,' Tapakah said.

Frank noticed the discarded bag of blood on the floor. 'What happened to the other two?'

'They left,' I said.

Frank looked shocked. 'Ashley shouldn't be going anywhere in his condition.'

My eyes filled with tears again.

Tapakah gave Frank a look. 'He'll be fine. He's tough. My friends will keep an eye on him. Now, I want to have breakfast

218

before we leave. We need to eat. We'll function better with food in our bellies. What do you say, Maggie?'

'Yes, okay, you're right.'

Frank examined his injured arm. 'You won't get an argument from me.'

'And then I intend to find out who's behind this.'

'How do you plan to do that?' Frank asked.

'I have my ways. You know that.'

Frank scratched the palm of his hand. 'Indeed, I do.'

Tapakah snatched hold of Frank's hand. 'What the hell is that?'

'Don't know. Must have injured myself on the plane. It's like a burn.'

'Let me see.' I took Frank's hand. 'It's a weird looking burn.' I ran my thumb over the ridges. There was an imprint of a small square in the middle of his palm, out of which ran a thin line, which folded around itself six times to make the shape of a square.

Tapakah frowned. 'The pattern resembles an RFID tag.'

'What's that?'

'Radio Frequency Identification. It's used for automated identification in everything from library books to train tickets.'

Frank wiggled his fingers and scratched at the mark. 'I'll get one of team to examine it when we get back to the lab. It's really itchy.'

'Let me know the results. I'd hate for it to be anything untoward. We wouldn't want you to lose your hand, would we?'

---

[24] *Maggie's Playlist: Basket Case — Green Day*

Chapter 24: Time is of the Essence

Melanie was at reception when I'd arrived at the Hyatt. Being a tall, leggy blonde, I assumed it was Ashley's Melanie.

'Hi, my name's Drom. I'm looking for a friend, Ashley Beringer?'

'You just missed him. He's gone. He called in to see me, but I'm on duty all night.'

'Do you know where he went?'

She screwed up her nose. 'Victoria Street, Richmond.'

'Shit.'

'Yep, that's what he's gone there for. He's not himself. I've never seen him like that before. There's something cold about him. What's happened? Is he okay?'

'It's a long story. No time. Thanks, Mel. I'll try and track him down before he tracks down drugs.'

A deep voice spoke from behind. 'Excuse me. My name's Ben. I'm looking for Ashley Beringer. Big bloke, six four, built like a ... I mean, well built with—'

Melanie cut him off. 'Yes, I know Ashley. He's popular today. Drom's looking for him too.' She nodded towards me.

'Hey, I know you! You're in the photo book Ashley made for Maggie. Why are you looking for him?'

'He's in a fragile state of mind. I need to get to him before he does something stupid.'

'I was just with him and I was worried about him too. I'm a friend of Maggie's. How did you know he was upset? Did he call you?'

'No. He didn't. I … I just know things.'

'I'll help you find him,' Ben offered.

'Listen, Ben, I need to find Boo, or Beans, as Maggie calls her. She'd find Ashley quicker than we could.'

'Beans is at my café. It's only around the corner.'

'I'll follow you. I'm on a Ninja.'

* * * * *

Boo flew into my arms, put her front legs around my neck, and gave my face and ears a thorough going over with her pink tongue. I laughed and pushed her away. 'Ew, Boo! Enough already!'

I can't tell you how good it is to see you, Drom. I'm up to speed with everything through the mind meld. I was hoping you'd turn up soon. I've been beside myself in here, out of the action. We have to find Ashley.

That's why we're here. I reckon with your nose, we can sniff him out, no worries.

Boo spun around in circles and jumped up and down with excitement. *Let's go!*

No flying, Boo. Ben doesn't know you're a super dog.

Roger that. But he does think I'm super though. He loves me and he gives me lemon tarts, and makes me the best steak and—

'Chill, Boo.'

If Boo got on a roll you could never shut her up and I needed to focus.

Got it. Ten four. Over and out.

'Ben, is it okay if Boo — Beans — rides shotgun with you? If you let her stick her head out the window, she'll pick up Ashley's

221

scent. I'll follow on the bike.

'Okay. But how will I know where to go? Does she bark once for left and twice for right?'

'That's exactly what she does. Once for left, twice for right, three times to stop. I've got a Bluetooth helmet. Call me on my mobile.'

'Okay, this'll be interesting. Come on, Beans, let's go!'

That's an excellent idea, isn't it, Drom? The left right barking thing, given we can't mind meld with Ben.

'Sure is, Boo. Get your nose into gear. Time's running out.'[25]

---

[25] *Maggie's Playlist: Time is Running Out — Muse*

Chapter 25: Search for Oblivion

"Time is an illusion." — Albert Einstein

I'd slammed the door on Maggie and walked out. I was walking out on everything. Who would've thought it would end like this?

Anger burnt in my gut, and a sense of devastation enveloped me as I traipsed the backstreets of Richmond. I'd failed. Failed Maggie, myself and everyone. I'd always hung on to hope, but hope was gone, faith had evaporated, and I was left numb and gutted.

The pain of losing her, our connection, was bad enough, but losing her to *him* — that was the ultimate cruelty. I could put up with anything whilst I figured there was a chance, but now? I couldn't do it anymore.

I'd go fight somewhere, sell my services. With my life on the line there was no time to think. I was in the moment. Kitted up, it was me, my crew and the enemy. I couldn't fight here anymore. What I was fighting for was gone. Being here was torture. Seeing her with him. Worse than any torture I'd faced in the field. My heart had been ripped from my chest.

Pressure points inside my head prodded and poked at me — the individual psychic efforts of the Musketeers trying to reach me. Fuck off. I couldn't bloody wait to get wasted.

Could they get in my head when I was stoned? If they did,

it'd be a damn scary place to hang out, that would be for sure.

A couple of shady looking characters turned into Victoria Place. I waited for a minute and followed them into the laneway. I'd been here years before, and always got lucky. Or unlucky, depending on how good or bad the stuff was.

I stumbled, catching my toe on the uneven cobblestones. Funny, I couldn't remember cobbles here before. What had happened to the friggin' lights? If it wasn't for the moon, I wouldn't be able to see a bloody thing. Lightheadedness descended, and my eyes wouldn't focus. Everything seemed hazy. It was the injury. I was sick. I rubbed my eyes and shook my head.

On my left, a crooked picket fence enclosed a ramshackle, two-storey wooden house. If you could call it a house. It appeared as though a couple of kids had built it. Wooden planks, nailed roughly together, ran in crooked lines across the front. Upstairs, the sad eyes of tiny crooked windows gazed out surveying the roof below, which was no more than a wave of rusty corrugated iron plonked haphazardly on top of a timber frame.

Jesus Christ, I didn't remember this place. Everything was crooked, warped or bowed.

A nursery rhyme rattled around in my brain. "*There was a crooked man, and he walked a crooked mile. He found a crooked sixpence upon a crooked stile. He bought a crooked cat, which caught a crooked mouse, and they all lived together in a little crooked house.*"

This was the goddamn crooked house. My head spun. I stepped back to lean on the brick wall behind me and fell straight onto my arse on the cobblestones. There was no wall. *Christ, was I stoned already?* The temperature dropped, and a shiver rattled through my body.

'Watcha doin', Mister? You want grog? We can getcha some. Looks like yer've had a skin full already, but.'

Two barefooted youths wearing baggy shorts and peaked

caps looked down at me. Tattered jackets and fingerless gloves hung off their bony bodies. Even in the poor light I could see they were filthy. I figured them to be around fourteen or younger, but they appeared old before their time. They reminded me of a couple of seasoned midget sailors with faces straight out of old sepia photos.

I staggered to my feet and brushed the dirt from my pants. 'I'm after ice.' I started as a handful of cockroaches fell from my jeans and scuttled off into the night. *'Shit!'*

The taller boy stepped back from me. 'Strike! You're one big bloke. Don't know 'bout no ice, Mister, but we can get snow.'

Maybe I'd been out of the game for so long, something new had come onto the market. 'What the hell's snow?'

'Snow's like snow, Mister. A white powder. Makes you feel a million quid for only two shillings a packet. We got some 'ere if you want.' He prized the lid off a small battered tin. 'Stick your finger in that, mate.'

I dipped a finger in the shiny white powder and sniffed it. It smelt like a mixture of nail polish and petrol. I stuck my finger in my mouth and rubbed it across the top of my gums. A bitter metallic taste exploded across my tongue, and a tingling numbness spread through my gums.

'This is cocaine, boys, and bloody good stuff too.'

'Yeah, that's the fancy name, Mister. We call it snow.'

'How much did you say?'

'Two shillings a packet, Mister. That'll give yer three good sniffs.'

I laughed. 'Shillings? They went out in 1966. I still remember the jingle my Dad used to sing.' I sang it to them. *"In come the dollars and in come the cents to replace the pounds and the shillings and the pence. Be prepared folks when the coins begin to mix on the 14th of February 1966."* I wasn't in bad voice, considering I felt like crap.

'That's *Click Go the Shears*, and you're pissed, mate.' They giggled. 'Gotta long way ta go 'til 1966.'

'What do you mean? What year do you think it is?'

'Strike, you *are* pissed Mister. Everyone knows what bloody year it is.'

'Tell me.'

I stepped back to the road and looked along the main street. Rows of drunken wooden sheds leant up against one another on each side of the street, and the odour of shit and piss flooded my nostrils. A clanking, putt putt noise echoed through the night as a vintage car swerved around the corner and zigzagged down the road. A horse and cart clip clopped slowly into the night, whilst a man threw up over a nearby picket fence, falling in a crumpled heap on top of it. The crack of gunshots sounded in the distance.

The ground shifted and fluxed under my feet. *What year?'* I yelled.

'It's 1935, Mister.'

* * * * *

Drom

I can smell Ashley!' Boo said in my head. *'Drom! Get ready to stop!'*

We caught the red light and I sat at the intersection waiting to turn. A steady stream of traffic flowed past like an angry river. Floating amongst the speeding machines was a piece of diaphanous white plastic. The size of a small tablecloth, it hovered on the currents of air created by the vehicles. It floated over and under cars, folding in and out and over itself in a graceful dance, reminiscent of a jellyfish.

I was mesmerised by its flowing contractions. For a second, it was as if water, rather than air, surrounded me. It appeared to be alive, moving with intelligence and skill amongst the onslaught of cars. In fact, it seemed to be enjoying the interaction — a surfer at one with a wave.

---

[26] *Maggie's Playlist: Out of Control — Rolling Stones*

The plastic whipped upwards and hovered in the air above me. I shook my head, freeing myself from the hypnotic trance. The light turned green and I accelerated. The plastic whipped across my face. It cloaked my body, and flapped loudly with a rapid and angry, *rat a tat tat.*

The plastic tightened around me. I was riding blind. I had to stop. Release the accelerator. Jesus, I couldn't. The plastic wound tight around my hand and pulled it backwards, making me accelerate.

Drom, where are you going? Slow down! Keep the handlebars straight. Turn slightly to the right.

Following Boo's instructions, I hit the kill switch on my bike. The engine died.

I felt rather than heard the rumble of the Monaro nearby. I coasted to a stop amidst the blasting of horns and the sound of Ben's voice shouting at passing cars. I tore at the plastic wound tight around my neck. I could barely breathe.

Someone ripped and tore at it until it became limp, falling away to lie in tatters, inert and still across my bike.

Ben's face stared into my visor. 'Bloody hell. That's a friggin' hazard. You were nearly skittled.'

'Tell me about it. Never had that happen before. It was like the bloody thing was alive.' I rolled the plastic into a tight ball and shoved it into my pannier. 'Don't want that happening to anyone else. Thank God for the kill switch and you two. Come on, let's get going.'

We took off and a minute later Ben pulled the Monaro into Victoria Place. Boo jumped from the window and hightailed it up the lane. I parked nearby and raced over to Ben who looked around nervously. He whispered, 'Perfect place to get mugged, I reckon.'

'All seems pretty quiet.'

Boo ran around in circles, her nose to the ground, huffing and puffing like a canine vacuum cleaner.

I've found him, I've found him. He's right here, Drom. Right here!

But there's no one here, Boo, the place is deserted.

But he's here, right under my nose!

'You're losing it, Boo, there's no one around.'

'Oh, yes there is.' Ben pointed to two figures emerging from the gloom at the end of the laneway.

As they headed towards us, I whispered, 'On your guard, folks.'

The first guy was short and stocky. His muscles bulged through his T-shirt. He had close-cropped hair highlighting a wide, ugly face with a broad nose and cruel mouth. The other guy was Asian, slim build, with slicked back hair, high cheek bones and a cocky expression on his face that seemed to say, '*What,* arsehole?'

'You guys looking for something?' the stocky man asked.

'We're looking for a bloke, big build, six foot four. He was down this way trying to score.'

'And who might you be?' Asian dude asked.

'He's our mate. He's been clean for years, and we're trying to keep him on the straight and narrow.'

The two considered us for a couple of seconds before the stocky man replied, 'A bloke like that followed us into the lane a couple of minutes ago. We watched him walk towards us and he disappeared.'

'What do you mean *disappeared?*' Ben asked.

'Just that, dipshit. He fucking vanished right before our eyes.'

The Asian man looked pale. 'I reckon he was a ghost. Trust me, there's no one in the lane, only us, and we're getting the hell out of here.'

'I reckon you should piss off too,' the stocky man said, as they pushed past Ben and strode quickly away.

Ben watched them go. 'That's weird.'

Ashley is here, Drom. We might not be able to see him, but he's here. His scent is as strong as a possum on a hot night.

Ashley

'*Say again?* I shouted at the two boys. 'What year is it?'

'It's 1935, Mister.'

Christ. I'd downed a few beers at the Hyatt, but not enough to get legless, let alone hallucinate. I checked around the corner and the scene was the same. I shook my head, rubbed my eyes, and looked again. Still the same.

Bloody hell. I wanted to run from everything, but not this far. Friggin' 1935 of all times. I knew a bit about Australian history, and I reckoned 1935 was pretty much around the time of the Great Depression. I remembered my grandparent's stories of poverty and desperation.

'Are you all right, Mister?'

I sat back down in the gutter. 'Not really. I don't belong here.'

'Thought you weren't from round here, with your clothes an' all, and your funny talk.'

'I'm well and truly lost. I've got money, but it won't get me far here.'

'Come back to me mum's place, Mister. I reckon she'd fancy a bloke like you. You could stay 'til you get sorted.'

'Where's your father?'

'He took off a few years back. Went on the track to get work. A mate said he jumped the rattler. We never 'eard from him since. Mum gets in boarders. One just left, so I reckon she'd be chuffed if we brought you home.'

'Well, lads, lead the way. I have nowhere else to go.'

'Not far, Mister, just round the corner.'

'What are your names?'

'I'm Jack and that's Harry,' Jack said, pointing to the younger of the two.

'My names Ashley, or Ash for short.'

'Done never heard a name like that before,' Harry said.

'Me neither,' Jack said. 'You're a strange un all right.'

'Yeah, that's what everyone says.'

We walked a block or two past rows of ramshackle houses. The air reeked of destitution and misery, along with an array of other disgusting odours. Turning into another narrow laneway, we stopped in front of what looked like an old outhouse.

Jack pushed on a narrow gate with his shoulder. 'We're going in the back. That's the dunny, if you need to go.' The gate squeaked and groaned under his weight, and the whole laneway of palings and corrugated iron shuddered with each push.

'Here, let me,' I said, 'before you send the whole 'hood crashing down.' I lifted, pushed, and the gate opened.

The boys guided me through a small yard hung with washing, into a tiny flagstone floored room containing a hearth, rough bench, table, chair, shelves and a kerosene lamp fixed to the wall.

A woman with short bobbed curly hair sat on the chair and stoked the fire. Like her boys, she was young but looked old at the same time. She was attractive, despite having a world-weary look and a coating of grime.

'Well, bugger me, boys, who in God's name have you brought home with yer this time?' She leapt out of the chair and backed up against a wall.

'Don't be scared, Mum, he's 'armless, we reckon. Lost is all. Needs a place to kip.'

She eyed me up and down. 'Crikey, he's too big for a place like this.'

The roof was so low I couldn't stand up straight. I had to tilt my head to one side to look her in the eye. Either that or get on my knees.

'Sorry to intrude, Ma'am.' I tried to figure out what the polite mode of address would have been in the day. 'My name's Ashley, Ashley Beringer. Your boys said it might be okay to stay the night. But I can see that's probably not a good idea.'

She pushed the chair across with her foot. 'Ere, sit. You're giving me a stiff neck just lookin' at you, Mister Beringer.'

I gratefully sat, but still felt I took up more than my fair share of real estate. The boys sat on the bench and stared at me from across the table.

She held out her hand. 'My names Rosie, Rosie Steele.'

'Pleased to make your acquaintance, Miss Steele.' I smiled and shook her hand.

She smiled back. 'Well, ain't you a right one with the manners and all.'

I'd expected to see a mouthful of bad teeth, so it surprised me to see a pretty smile light up her face.

She stared into my face. 'You've got the nicest, whitest teeth I've ever seen.'

'I was thinking the same about you.'

'Oh, you're a right charmer, you are. Mine are nowhere near as white.'

'Listen, I have money, but it's not from around here, so it'll be of no value.' I took out my wallet and emptied my pockets. I had three hundred in cash, and a handful of loose change.

The boys pounced on the coins and peered at them in the dim light.

'Look at this — big silver one with edges, got a kangaroo and an emu.'

'That's a fifty-cent coin. You need about six of them to buy a loaf of bread,' I said.

'Fifty cent? Is that like a shilling? We need sixpence to buy a loaf of bread. It says 1979 on this coin. That can't be right. And this gold one, with an abo's head says 2004. And this one with kangaroos says one dollar on it and 1995.' Jack stared at me incredulously.

'This gold one's real shiny,' Harry said. 'Says one dollar and 2016. It's got written on it *100 years of ANZAC*. I reckoned they'd be Yankee coins, but it says Australia on all of 'em.'

Rosie quietly turned over the coins and examined the notes. She held a five-dollar note to the light and gasped.

'It's beautiful; you can see right through it! Look how it sparkles in the light like rainbows. It's got a spinebill bird and wattles, and a lady on the front. Never seen anything like it. That's gotta be worth something, even if it ain't from here. But it says *Australia*?' She looked at me with a puzzled expression.

I figured I had nothing to lose, so I decided to tell the truth.

'It's Australian legal tender, but not from this time. It's from the twenty-first century. That's where I'm from. I was standing in a laneway in Victoria Place, Richmond, in the year 2017, when suddenly I found myself in the same laneway but in 1935.'

Jack began drawing in the dust on the floor. 'That's, that's—'

'That's eighty-two years in the future,' Rosie said, interrupting his calculations.

I spoke to myself more than anything. 'I can't believe how much things have changed in only eighty-two years.'

Rosie stared at me. 'It can't be.'

'I can't believe it myself.'

A smile exploded across Harry's face. 'Well, if it's true what you say, then that means you know what's gonna happen, and you can make us rich! You would know who wins what race and everything, wouldn't you?'

'Sorry to disappoint you, Harry, but I could hardly know the outcome of a horse race eighty-two years ago.'

Jack looked at me hopefully. 'But you know things no one else would know. You must be able to make money outta something, couldn't you?'

'I'm sure there would be something. I'm just not sure what that'd be right now. I'm still trying to get my head around what's happened to me.'

'How can we believe such a tale?' Rosie said. 'Surely you must be demented?'

232

'Well, look at the money, and this watch, and here's a pen, and then there's this.' I took out my phone. 'This is what you call a telephone. We call it a mobile phone. In 2017 even kids have them and they can ring anyone, at any time, wherever they are. It takes photos, you can play games on it, and even send messages and letters to anyone you want. Here, let me show you. I'll take a photo. Smile, Rosie.' I took a shot and showed her the photo. 'Here you go. That's you.'

Rosie's jaw dropped and her eyes were as wide as the fifty-cent pieces on the table.

'Holy Mother of God.' She grabbed the phone and examined the photo closely.

The boys whipped the phone from her hands. 'Let me see! Let me see!'

'Hey, gentle, don't break it,' I said.

'It's you, Mum!' they said in amazement.

'Take one of us, take one of us!' They shouted in unison.

So, I did. 'I could send that picture to someone else, anywhere in the world.'

'Can you do it now?' Jack asked. 'It's amazing! Look at us!'

'That part doesn't work in 1935. I'd have to be back in 2017 to make it happen.'

'You could take this to a scientist, show 'em. They could make one just like it. Then we'd be rich,' Harry said. 'Richer than rich.'

'I wish it was that simple, Harry.'

Jack removed the credit cards from my wallet. 'What are these?'

Rosie picked one up. 'This says driver's licence. It's got Ashley's photo on it. Look boys.' She pushed it across the table.

'What does it mean?' Jack asked. 'What can you drive?'

'It means I'm licensed to drive a car, and this one means I'm allowed to ride a motorbike.'

'What? A motor car with an engine?'

'Yes, in the future most people have cars. In fact, there are so many cars, they block the roads and it takes ages to get anywhere. I reckon you could get through Richmond faster now by horse and cart, than we can with our fancy cars. Look, here's a photo of me on my bike.'

Jack and Harry stared at the photo with eyes as big as saucers. 'Strike, look at you, and the cars too!'

'If you want to look at more photos, you flick your finger across the screen, like this, see?'

Rosie moved around the bench to watch as Harry flicked through the images. 'Oh, my goodness.'

'Do you have someone … someone special in the future?' Rosie asked.

'That's who I was running from.'

'Why?'

'She's in love with someone else. Look, that's a picture of her. Maggie. Her hair's normally long, but it was shaved off by the creep she's in love with.'

Rosie looked horrified. 'That's terrible.'

'I know.'

Harry squinted at the photo. 'She still looks beautiful though.'

'So, you don't love her anymore?' Rosie asked.

'I love her more than anything.'

'Why would you run from her?'

'Because there's no hope. I can't torture myself any longer.'

'You may as well be from another planet,' Rosie said. 'I daren't believe you, but … but I do.'

'It feels like I'm from another planet. I'm glad you believe me. That helps. My head's spinning. What the hell am I going to do?'

Rosie reached across and tentatively touched my hand. 'We'll be your friends. We'll help you, and you can help us. Would you have grandparents alive here?'

234

'Jesus Christ, I didn't even think of that. Probably. But there'd be no point searching for them, they wouldn't know who I was. I'd just be some madman to them.'

'Oh dear, that's true. How's you being here an all, how's that going to affect the future? You're from the future, not even born yet, but you're here. Taint right,' she said.

'You're telling me, luv.'

* * * * *

Drom

Come on, Drom! Follow me. Ashley's on the move!

Boo shot off around the corner and trotted up the street.

'Hey, where's she going?' Ben asked.

'She's following the invisible Ashley, apparently. Come on, she won't stop. We'd better take our wheels. Not safe to leave them here.'

We motored slowly along the road following Boo's little tan bum as she trotted determinedly along the footpath. After two blocks, she turned into Princess Street and stopped outside a house halfway down. Boo sat up in her meerkat beg position.

Ashley's here, in this house.

Ben grinned. 'Beans ... I mean, Boo, sits up like that for lemon tarts.

'She thinks Ashley's in there.'

'Should we knock on the door?'

'At this late hour? No one will let us in. They'll think it's a home invasion or something. I reckon we come back in the morning.'

No. I'll go in and scout around. I can try and float down the chimney, or maybe there's a window open somewhere. Distract Ben for me.

'Ben, is that those two blokes at the end of the street?'

He turned to look. 'Where? I can't see anything.'

---

27 *Maggie's Playlist: Long Time Traveller — Wailin' Jennys*

Boo took off as fast as a rocket and landed softly on the roof.

I'm not leaving. I'll sleep here in case Ashley makes a move. I don't mind camping out for the night. I'll sleep on the roof. It's safe and warm up here.

Okay, Boo. I know I won't be able to convince you otherwise. Keep the mind meld open. We'll revisit our options tomorrow.

Roger that. Can you bring me something to eat when you come back? I'll be hungry by then. Maybe some of Ben's fillet steak and a lemon tart? That would be nice.

Jeepers, you don't ask for much do you?

Don't ask, don't get, Drom.

Cheeky dog.

'Where's Boo gone?' Ben asked.

'Doing a recky. She won't leave until she locates Ashley. Let's go. I'll come back in the morning. She'll still be here. Thanks for your help, Ben.'

'No worries. Ring me. I could meet you if you want. I'll bring fillet steak and a lemon tart for Beans.'

See, Drom? What did I say?

* * * * *

Ashley

I slept on the chair at Rosie's place for the rest of the night, leaning my head on the table. She offered me her bed, but I wouldn't hear of it. She slept in a small bed with one of the boys, while the other had a narrow cot nearby.

I'd rather sleep under the stars, but until I got the lay of the land it was too risky.

A rooster crowed nearby, and I figured it must be morning. You wouldn't hear that sound in Richmond 2017, that was for sure. I guessed a long, strong, hot coffee was out of the question, as well as a long, hot shower. Damn it.

I couldn't stand straight to stretch my body, so I stood out in the little yard amongst the washing. A pair of rabbits were hanging on the back-door handle. Their brown-grey fur and bright amber eyes stood out in stark relief against the greyness of the timber and corrugated iron. The carcasses radiated more life than the drab surrounds.

The fur was soft and the bodies still warm. Somebody had left Rosie a present. The rabbits reminded me of my grandparents. When we left their house, they always said, as a joke, 'Thank your Mum for the rabbits. Ask her if she wants the skins back.' I remember Grandpa saying, in his day, the rabbit industry was the largest employer of labor in Australia. Old Gramps made a fair living out of rabbits, and a few possums and foxes too.

I'd skin and gut these for Rosie, save her a job. I found a couple of knives in a drawer and set about the process. Snapped off the legs at the joints, cut off the head, separated the skin at the belly and yanked it back on both sides to form a rabbit handbag. I put a leg bone on the floor and peeled off the skin. Repeat on other leg. Yanked the skin up and over the neck and front legs. Perfect. Fully intact skin. You could use it for a glove. I thought of Jason and Maggie. Jason used to say, "skin a rabbit" to her, when he pulled a jumper off over her head.

I carefully slit the rabbit along the belly and removed the stomach contents, reached up and pinched out the kidneys, heart and lungs. I knew in this day they wasted nothing. I wasn't sure how Rosie was going to use the rabbits, but I butchered it cutting across the haunches, saddle, shoulders, and cut two nice pieces of loin. It was good to have something to do. I repeated the process with the other bunny and returned inside to look for a pot.

Rosie came out of the other room and shrieked. 'Holy Mother of God! What's happened? You're hurt!' She took my wrists and stared at my blood-soaked hands.

'No, it's okay, relax. I skinned a pair of rabbits for you. Someone left them on the back door.'

She clutched her chest. 'Oh, you scared the bejesus out of me. That'd be from Eric. He's a friend, always drops me off a pair of rabbits when he comes down from Kyneton.'

'I took the liberty of skinning and gutting them for you. I hope you don't mind.'

She smiled. 'God love you, certainly not. I hate that job. Best present ever, I reckon.'

'Well, good. I've made myself useful. The meat's outside butchered and ready to use. I've stoked the fire as well.'

Jack and Harry's tousled heads appeared in the doorway and stared at my bloodied hands.

'You done killed someone?' Jack asked.

'Don't be stupid,' Rosie snapped. 'You two boys should take a leaf outta Ashley's book. He's skun and butchered two rabbits and stoked the fire, all afore breakfast.'

'That's women's work,' Harry said scornfully.

I shook my head. 'That's rubbish. If you want to be a real man you can turn your hand to anything. It's about what's fair and right, and it's not right to let Rosie do everything. In 2017 men and women do all sorts of things. Women are in the police and the army; some men stay home as house husbands and look after the kids. Men who can cook are admired, and celebrity chefs earn more than the prime minister.'

Jack sniffed. 'Can't be. Don't believe it.'

'Really?' Rosie asked.

'Yep, things have changed heaps. However, women still don't get equal pay, even after all those years.'

Rosie shook her head in disbelief. 'Women in the police. That's amazing. Still, that's well and good for the future, but now I'll make rabbit stew and a rabbit pie.'

'I can make the stew if you like,' I offered.

'Really?' Rosie said, echoed by Jack and Harry.

'Yep, show me what I can use, and I'll get it underway. It needs to cook long and slow.'

Rosie slid a wooden box from under a cupboard. It had onions, carrots and potatoes in it.

'That's all I got for now.'

'For how long?'

'Until the boys bring in more snow money.'

'You don't get any welfare?'

'Can't get the susso, 'cause we've got a roof over our head.'

'Susso?' I'd heard the word but wasn't sure what it meant.

'Sustenance payment. You gotta have nothing to get it. I was thinking it might be better to live in a tent and at least we'd have regular food.'

'I have to think of something I can do to help.'

'Don't you worry 'bout us, Mister Beringer.' She handed me a wet cloth. 'Wipe your hands on this. Sit by the fire. We've got bread and jam for breakfast.'

'I don't suppose you have coffee?'

'Sorry no, Mister Beringer, but I can make you a nice cup of tea.'

'That'd be great. And please, call me Ashley. Can I call you Rosie?'

'Yes, we don't need to stand on ceremony.'

The boys giggled their heads off.

Rosie flashed them a look. 'What?'

'You, Mum, acting all proper like, putting on airs.'

Rosie's face flushed with colour. 'I'm not putting on airs. There's naught wrong with having manners. You should learn some.'

'Can I look at your cards again, Ashley?' Jack asked.

I slid my wallet across the table. 'Sure thing.'

Jack carefully removed the cards and laid them on the table in neat rows. He grouped the coins and notes together and examined each fold in my wallet to ensure he hadn't missed anything.

He rubbed the wallet between his fingers. 'There's something else in here, but I can't get to it.'

'I reckon you've got everything.'

'No, there's another coin I reckon, stuck in the lining. See, feel that?' He took my hand and guided my fingers to the spot in question.

The memory hit me. 'Oh, you bloody *ripper*!' I pulled out the lining and squeezed the item out through a tear in the material. It hit the table with a thunk. There was a collective gasp. The sun broke through the clouds, and a ray of sunlight shot through the small window and illuminated it brighter than a gift from God.

There it was. I'd tucked it in my wallet two years back and forgotten about it. It had wormed its way into the lining and out of my mind for just as long.

'We've hit the jackpot, folks, thanks to Jack.'

Harry gasped. 'It's a bloody gold nugget!'

'Yep. Forgot I put it there. Must be two years back. I was prospecting in Western Australia using a metal detector. Twenty-eight point seven grams of pure gold. It's beautiful, isn't it?'

I lay the nugget on my hand and it extended from the bottom of my finger to the first knuckle. I grinned. 'This should buy us a few things.'

Rosie's eyes grew wide. 'Oh, my. You know what? All I want is some bug poison. There were two huge cockroaches on my bed this morning. Surprised you didn't hear me shriek.' She shuddered. 'Never seen 'em such a size before.'

Oh, shit. The roaches that came through with me. *Shit.*

This lot could've been roached in their sleep. Fuck me. Tapakah's minions had made their way back to 1935 using me as a taxi. Christ. What were the ramifications of that? One cockroach could produce 35,000 offspring. The planet was screwed. This would seriously fuck with the space-time continuum, let alone poor Rosie and her boys.

'Ashley? Are you all right? You look like you've seen a ghost.'

'Yeah, it feels like it.'

'Here, I'll make you a cuppa.'

I couldn't think about it. Didn't want to think about it. There was nothing I could do. I changed the subject. 'Where do I go to turn this nugget into cash?'

'Newman's in Collins Street,' Rosie said. 'It's next to the Old Royal Bank. That'd be the closest. It's a fifty-minute walk to town from here. That's where Eric went with his find. There are local assayers, but I reckon you'd be safer with a city one.'

'What's the price of gold? Anyone know?'

Jack threw a newspaper on the table. 'Here's the Argus, Mister.' He flicked through the pages and pointed a grubby finger at a page. 'It says right there.'

Rosie looked over my shoulder. 'Eight pounds, fourteen shillings and ninety-one pence an ounce.'

'I reckon this is close to an ounce. What's the average workers wage?'

'Depends, but I used to get three pound a week. Blokes get more.'

'So, this nugget is worth around three weeks work.'

'A lot more if you're canny with the money,' Rosie said.

'Okay, we'll go to Newman's, get cashed up, and then I'm going to take you all out somewhere special. Where would you like to go?'

Rosie shook her head. 'No, Mister Ber … I mean, Ashley, save the money. We don't need to go nowhere.'

'Yes, you do. Where would you like to go?'

'The Windsor Hotel!' Jack shrieked.

Harry jumped up and down on the spot. 'Yeah, that's the best place in town!'

'I've been to the Windsor. It's still around in the twenty-first century. I walked past it on the way here. I'd love to see what it's like now.'

'Can we, Mum? Please let him take us. *Please.*' Jack got down on bended knees and looked up at her with big brown eyes. His technique reminded me of Boo.

She smiled. 'How can I resist that face? We'll have to dust off our best bib and tucker. Jimmy left a blazer and waistcoat and other stuff, if you want. He was a big bloke; they should fit you. You won't get in dressed like a bum.'

I feigned a hurt look. 'Thanks, Rosie.'

She looked flustered. 'No, no, I didn't mean—'

I laughed. 'I'm kidding with you. I do look like a bum.'

'We all do,' she said sadly.

'Where do you wash up?' I asked.

'There's a tap out the back. There's a washing bowl on top of the tap. Here's a towel.' She handed me a threadbare piece of cloth. 'Soap's out there.'

'Thanks, Rosie.'

'I'll get the clothes sorted. Newman's won't be open today, it's Sunday. We'll go tomorrow.'

'Then maybe you can show me around a bit today?'

Jack looked pleased with the idea. 'Yeah, Mum, we could go for a picnic on the river, show Ashley the new bridge.'

'All right, we can do that. We'll get the stew on, have breakfast, and then head off.'

I opened the door and steeled myself for the wash. It was bitterly cold outside. I lifted my T-shirt and examined the bandages. They were stained with what looked like rosé. I thought of Maggie. Wine and Maggie went together like beer and — more beer.

The tap had stuck and groaned miserably as I twisted it. A muddy trickle shuddered into my hands and I splashed my face. That would do me. I dried myself with the tattered towel as cold, wet washing whipped up against me. What I'd give for a long, strong, hot coffee. A hot shower. Bacon and eggs with toast and lashings of butter. Drugs. Clean clothes.

Maybe the Maestro could find me, bring me back. I'd wanted to disappear, but not like this. Would I ever get home?

A pair of wet trousers slapped me hard across the face. A rooster cackled hysterically somewhere down the lane, and the wind sang mournful notes through the corrugated iron fence. It shrilled the same sound over and over.

Noooooooo … Noooooooooo … Noooooooooo … Noooooooooo.

* * * * *

 *Maggie*

'Will Billy be home when we get there?' I asked Tapakah.

'He has half a day off school to spend time with us, as he's heading away to camp tomorrow.'

It felt like a million years since I'd been in East Melbourne. I hadn't been away long, but so much had happened my head was spinning. I couldn't wait to see Billy.

We pulled up outside the house and the front door opened. Billy ran out and threw his arms around me as I staggered out from the car.

'I'm glad you're back, Miss! It was awful without you and Mister Tapakah.'

'It's good to be back. I missed you heaps, Billy. Are you okay?'

'Yeah, but I don't like Miss Lilith much. You're not going to leave us again, are you?'

'I'm not going anywhere.' I looked at Tapakah. 'I'm here to stay.'

Our eyes met and he acknowledged my statement with a look. A flicker of a smile played around his mouth as he put his arms around us.

'Who would have thought?' he said softly.

'Indeed.'

---

[28] *Maggie's Playlist: Never Going Home — Blue Shaddy*

Tapakah showed my engagement ring to Billy. 'I have wonderful news. Maggie and I are engaged.'

Billy jumped up and down. 'I knew it! I knew it! You two are meant to be together. Lilith said it would happen after Ja—'

'Billy!' Tapakah cut him off and glared at him. 'What did I tell you?'

Billy's little face looked crestfallen. 'I must never repeat staff gossip.'

Tapakah guided us towards the front door. 'Exactly. I'll have a word to Lilith as well. Let's go inside.'

So much for happy reunions. What was that about? Poor Billy. I felt sorry for him. Tapakah was way too harsh. And what was Billy going to say that made Tapakah shut him down like that? I'll have to have a word. Well, maybe not. Judging by the furious look on Tapakah's face, approaching him now would not be a wise move.

I guess we were both still on edge. I knew Tapakah worried for my safety. He was always on high alert now, his eyes scanning everything. I'd started to do it too, looking up in trees and the tops of buildings, expecting to see the pale and serious face of a sniper pointing a .50 cal Barrett M82 at me.

What the hell? Where had that come from?

I looked at Tapakah. 'What's a .50 cal Barrett M82?'

He wheeled around and stared at me. 'What did you say?'

'I said what's a .50 cal Barrett M82?'

'It's a shoulder-fired, semi-automatic sniper rifle. It has an effective range of 1800 meters and can penetrate a tank. Why on earth do you want to know that?'

'It came out of my head. I must be familiar with guns. Well, I do know about guns, we've established that. But rifles too? What the hell was I?'

'You may have been in the police force, or the army.'

'But I'm not fit enough.'

'You were rather sick, remember? Maybe you lost your

fitness.'

'I don't feel like I was ever fit. Why would an unfit girl be weapon savvy? It worries me.'

'Maybe you were a recreational shooter. Why are you thinking about this?'

'I'm worried about snipers and who's after me.'

'Let's get inside then.' He pushed me through the door. 'I'll find out who's behind this. I promise.'

Inside, I came face to face with the woman in my flash back. There was the pursed mouth, arched brows and evil eye of Lilith. I gasped.

She gave a small bow. 'Welcome back, Maggie. Tapakah.'

I expected to hear a click as her heels snapped together. Put her in uniform, tuck up her hair under a peaked cap, and you'd have instant Nazi. I felt sick.

Tapakah rubbed his temple. 'Lilith. I want a word with you before you go.'

Lilith's neck and head twitched, and as she turned, I swear her eyes rolled back in her head. I caught sight of her reflection as she marched past the hallway mirror. Her eyes were black.

I froze, felt my heart pound in my throat. I'd seen Tapakah's eyes do that. So what was Lilith? Was she a hybrid too?

She turned around. 'What's wrong, dear?' Her eyes had returned to their normal stink eyed appearance.

'Nuh … nothing,' I mumbled. 'Just tired, is all.'

'You look like you've seen a ghost,' Tapakah said.

'It feels like it. I'm going to bed.' I pushed past Lilith. I couldn't stand to be near her. I felt a sense of humiliation and shame around her, yet I had no idea why. She gave me the creeps. God only knew how Billy coped here on his own with her.

I raced up the stairs and into the bedroom. I shut the French doors, drew the blinds, stripped off my clothes and fell into bed. I would hibernate here until she left. My eyes felt heavy as soon as my head hit the pillow. I ached everywhere. I wondered if I would ever feel normal again. It was all catching up with me. My eyes started to twitch as I drifted off to sleep.

I awoke to the sound of gentle breathing. Tapakah lay next to me, the sheet around his waist. He always kept the temperature at twenty-four degrees Celsius. He said it was his "optimum external temperature". I didn't mind; it was heaven for me too.

Soft light played across his face and body. A five o'clock shadow highlighted his sensuous mouth. I studied the curve of his shoulders, the square of his jaw. His muscular chest had just the right amount of hair. I wondered if he'd had any "manscaping" done. It seemed too perfect. Faint lines ran along his ribs. I'd seen them open like the gills of a fish when he'd nearly died. I shuddered at the thought. His tussled locks spilled out across the pillow. I reached out to touch their softness.

I wanted to jump on his bones right then and there. I could never get enough of him and felt constantly aroused in his presence.

His eyes slowly opened and locked onto mine. I dissolved into their blackness.

His voice was husky with sleep. 'You look like you want to eat me.'

'I do.'

'What's stopping you then?'

'Nothing.' I slid over and took his nipple in my mouth. It was already hard, and I made it harder. He groaned. I slid along his belly, tucked myself between his legs and kissed the inside of his thighs. 'I haven't done this to you before.' I took him in my mouth. He gasped, arched his back and moaned with pleasure. Everything was new to me. From the sound of it, I guessed I must be doing all right.

He was going to come any minute; I could feel it, and I mentally prepared myself for whatever was to come. I mean, he wasn't human. I didn't know what the hell would come out of there.

BANG! BANG! BANG!

An urgent pounding on the bedroom door made us jump.

Billy yelled, 'I'm sorry, Mister Tapakah, the police are here. Detective Inspector Fox wants to ask you a few questions. He wouldn't go away, and I've gotta leave to go back to school.'

Tapakah slammed his fist against the bedhead and snarled, 'You've got to be kidding me! This is the second time the police have done this to us.'

'Bwuudy ell.'

'Don't talk with your mouth full, Maggie. It's impolite.' Tapakah lifted up my face and kissed me. 'This is definitely to be continued.' He leapt out of bed.

I tried to keep a neutral expression on my face. 'You can't go down there like that.' *What a waste.*

Tapakah laughed. 'Your expression is priceless. I'll deal with you later.' He opened the bedroom door and spoke to Billy. 'Tell Inspector Fox I'll be there in a minute. Give him a beer or something. I'm going to have a quick shower.'

'Okay.'

Tapakah muttered as he dashed to the ensuite. 'A very, very cold shower,'

He paused in the doorway, his body a stunning silhouette. I stared, drinking in the curve of his muscular legs and arms, the ridge of his spine running between the muscles of his back, all nicely finished by perfect pair of buttocks. Oh, my.

Tapakah spun around. 'Don't you know it's rude to stare?'

I swear he had eyes in the back of his head.

Buck naked, he stared, devouring me with his eyes.

He was seriously hot, and I was seriously aroused.

Cold shower here I come.

---

[29] *Maggie's Playlist: You Make Me So Hot — Barbara Lynn*

"And they worshiped the dragon, for he had given his authority to the beast, and they worshiped the beast, saying, "Who is like the beast, and who can fight against it?" — Revelation 13.4

The staircase creaked three times as Tapakah flew up the stairs. There were fifteen steps, and he took them five at a time. I pretended to be asleep when the door opened. I so wanted to pick up from where we'd left off. I planned to attack him as soon as he got back into bed.

'Maggie, wake up,' he whispered.

I opened my eyes and he stood looking down at me. Fully dressed.

'Fox is gone. He was almost apologetic. Not sure why he even bothered. I'm sorry. I've just had a call, an urgent meeting. I have to go, but I shouldn't be too long. Then we can pick up where we left off.'

Damn, damn, and double damn.

'What is it with us? How come we can never get it together?' I asked.

'It's incredibly frustrating. I'm going to book the deluxe suite at the Windsor this weekend. We can lock ourselves away with no interruptions, okay?'

'Yeah, okay. Has Lilith gone?'

'Yes, she's gone.'

'Excellent. Oh well, catch you later then.'

'You're miffed.'

'Not miffed. Don't care.'

'Yes. You do.'

'Don't.'

'Do.'

'Don't.'

Tapakah smiled. 'You win. I know you always like to get the last word.' He sat on the edge of the bed. 'You're being petulant, and petulance is a punishable offense.'

'Oh, yeah, what law would that be?'

'Tapakah's law!' He flung back the bed clothes, shoved an arm under my waist and flipped me across his knee. His hand slapped across my bare bum, and I cried out with shock.

'Ow! That *hurt!*'

'You love it.' He brought his hand down again.

'Ow!'

I struggled and kicked. He flipped a leg over mine and pinned them tight. His right hand caught my wrists.

'See what happens when you're petulant? You can't escape me, and I still have a spare hand.' He brought it down with a crack.

'Ow! Stop it!'

'You really want me to stop?' He rubbed my stinging buttocks, then slipped his fingers between my legs. 'Your body seems pretty happy to me,' he said as his hands worked their magic.

'The ... this wuh ... will only... encourage ... ongoing petulance.' I gasped as he brought me to orgasm.

I lay spent and comatose across his lap. He stroked my hair. 'I trust that will keep you happy until I return.'

'Mmmmm,' I groaned.

Tapakah laughed, flipped me back over onto the bed and covered me up. He bent, kissed me gently, and then he was gone.

* * * * *

'Hoo-Whee that was sensational.' I staggered down the stairs one at a time and stopped at the bottom step. There was a noise coming from the front door.

Scratch. Scratch. Scratch.

Scratch. Scratch. Scratch.

Woof!

Beans! It had to be. I rushed along the hall and flung open the door. Beans launched herself into my arms.

'Yay, you're back!' I tried to avoid the pink tongue frantically trying to lick my face. I looked outside hoping to see Ben, but there was no one there.

'Come on, Beans. I'll get you some tucker.' She leapt from my arms and raced into the kitchen.

I served her a portion of chicken and vegies; it was her favourite fare, next to fillet steak and lemon tarts. I sat at the kitchen bench watching her demolish her food in three seconds flat. Once every molecule had been removed from the bowl, she jumped onto the chair opposite me and sat with her head resting on the table.

I laughed. 'You shouldn't be up here.'

She sat and stared. It was quite disconcerting.

'I've got no more lemon tarts, and you've had a bowl of leftover roast chicken. It doesn't get much better than that.'

'Phffft!'

It was a sneeze that dismissed my assertion.

'If roast chicken doesn't rock your socks, you must've had it pretty darn good where you came from. And stop staring, it's rude.'

Beans stayed put but rotated her eyeballs to the side.

'You are one funny dog. I'm going to take you to the vet tomorrow and—'

At the word *vet*, Beans leapt off the chair and sent it skidding across the kitchen floor and into the fridge. Her legs scrabbled on the tiles as she ran for her life. The last thing I saw was her tan bum and black tail as she skidded down the hallway.

I ran after her as she took a sharp left and slid into the hall coat stand. The coat stand tipped, dragged by the weight of the coats. It balanced on two legs for a second, before collecting an antique plant stand. The vase on the plant stand pitched into the air. I took an almighty leap to save it.

The vase was extremely large and old. Knowing Tapakah's taste, it was probably expensive too.

Everything was in slow motion. I was a soccer goalie going for the ultimate save. I was airborne — I had it! As I flew, my elbow collected a set of crystal glasses on the hall cabinet. The sound of smashing glass came from behind me, and a crash as something else hit the floor.

I clutched that vase in a Vulcan death grip and held my hands high as I descended. My chest was going to take the worst of it. This was going to hurt. A lot. I headed towards the polished boards and let out an involuntary shriek in anticipation. My ribs cracked, and the air whooshed out of my lungs as I hit the deck.

I'd landed inches from the front door. I couldn't breathe; I was dying, but the vase was intact. I'd done it!

The vase was exquisite. A soft yellow glaze at the top and bottom highlighted the muted blues and reds of oriental flowers. The middle band of the vase resembled an ancient Chinese screen, with holes cut in intricate patterns. The screen was the colour of jade and emphasised a central gold-rimmed panel with blue flowing water and two swimming fish.

I wasn't into antiques, but this was a masterpiece. As I contemplated the beauty of the treasure I'd preserved, the front door flew open, hit the top of the vase and shattered it into a million pieces.

'Maggie! What's the hell's going on in there? Jesus, are you okay? What's happened?' Tapakah stuck his head around the door and squeezed inside.

I still couldn't get the breath to speak. The ceramic shards had cut my hands. I lay on the floor and groaned, surrounded by broken artifacts and the assorted flotsam and jetsam of our flight along the hall.

'Is someone in the house? he whispered. 'Were you attacked?'

I shook my head and managed to gasp, 'No, just me.'

Tapakah gave a sigh as his shoes crunched over the debris, breaking the vase into even smaller pieces.

'Here, let me help you up.' He hooked his hands under my armpits and hoisted me up as easily as a child.

I cried as a stabbing pain hit me in the side. 'Ow! *Ribs*!'

'Can you walk? If you've hurt your ribs, I don't want to carry you.'

'I can walk.' He held my arm and guided me through the trashed hallway and into the kitchen.

He pulled out a chair. 'Sit.'

I sat and dripped blood onto the table. He pulled out a first aid kit from the kitchen drawer and filled a bowl with water. He took my hands in his. 'Let me have a look.' His face was stern, and I assumed he was angry.

I sat in silence as he bathed and dressed the cuts. He still didn't speak.

'I'm sorry,' I said. 'It was an accident.'

'Accident? I thought you were being attacked. Jesus, there was a commotion, breaking glass, things slamming, you screaming. I couldn't get in fast enough.

'I wish you hadn't tried so hard.'

'What do you mean?'

'Well, the vase would still be in one piece.'

A quote from Mark Twain popped into my mind. "If you tell the truth, you don't have to remember anything." I decided I needed to fess up about the reasons behind the smashed vase. I took a breath, which hurt, and told Tapakah everything from go to whoa about Beans, Ben and the fight with the thugs out the front.

Tapakah remained silent the whole time I spoke. It was freaking me out. His eyes were dialled up to uber intensity and never left mine. I was being interrogated — strapped to a chair with a light shining in my face — all without him uttering a single word.

'So, there it is, Tapakah. That's the story behind the vase. I busted my arse trying to save it, for naught,' I said sadly. 'I can see you're angry. I'm sorry, I'll pay for the vase.'

The stern expression vanished as he laughed. 'Jesus, I'm not angry, and forget the damn vase. You couldn't afford it anyway. Promise me you'll never risk your safety for *things*. You could've been seriously hurt.' He watched me rub my ribs. 'It seems I'm in debt to Ben and Beans for taking care of you with those thugs.'

'I did my bit too,' I said.

'I know that. I have CCTV out front.'

'Ss … so … you knew about everything already?'

'Yes, there's not much that escapes me. I'm glad you fessed up.'

Shit. I should've realised he'd have had cameras. I couldn't believe he wasn't angrier.

'Can you stand?' he asked.

'Yes,' I said, getting up on my feet.

He hugged me. 'I was worried sick, not angry. I imagined the worst standing outside that door. I'm relieved you're okay. It's never a dull moment with you around, is it?'

'I was going to say the same thing about you.'

He smiled and drew me in for a kiss. It was gentle, but passionate and urgent, filled with unspoken words. My knees went weak. I had to reach for the back of the chair to steady myself.

I opened my eyes to see a little dog staring at us from around the corner of the door.

'Beans!' I pulled away from Tapakah.

Beans spun around and disappeared.

'Tapakah, it's Beans. She's gone again.'

'The mystery dog. Don't worry, she'll be here somewhere. I'll find her. I have a way with animals.'

'I mentioned the word *vet* and that's what sent her off in a panic. I wanted to check if she's microchipped to find out who really owns her. If she's a stray, can I keep her? I miss you when you're not here. It would be company.'

'I miss you too. I hate being away from you.'

'Why can't I come with you, help you? You can put me to work.'

Tapakah shook his head. 'It's not possible.'

I extracted myself from his arms. 'I'd better clean up the mess. Billy will be back soon.'

'I'll help you.' Tapakah grabbed a dustpan and brush from under the kitchen sink.

'I think a shovel would be more useful. And seriously, I'll pay for the vase and the other stuff I broke.' Goodness knows how. I didn't have a cent to my name. Everything I had was his. 'I'm going to get a job. I will pay you back.'

'No, you won't. You saved the vase. I broke it.'

'Was it expensive?'

'It was a steal at one point five.'

'One point five hundred?'

'One point five *million*.'

He reached over, put a finger under my chin and gently pushed upwards. 'Close your mouth, Maggie, you'll catch flies.' He laughed at the expression on my face.

'Oh, that's insane. I'll be working until I'm ninety and then some.'

'You don't have to work. I told you that.'

'No, it's not right. I hate feeling dependent on you. I hate it. I must have money somewhere from my previous life. It's probably sitting in a bank account somewhere and will continue to sit there because I have no idea who the hell I am — was.'

'Relax. You've been ill and you don't need any stress.'

'But this stresses me. I don't want to be dependent on you. I'm going to get a job.'

'Doing what?'

'I have no idea. I don't know what I'm qualified for. Maybe I'll start as a waitress and see what happens.'

'I don't want you waiting tables. You're better than that.'

'There's nothing wrong with waiting tables. Good wait staff are hard to find, and I'd be great at it.'

'I'm not saying you wouldn't be. Take a few weeks off first. Frank agrees that you should take it easy for a while. Can't you wait another month?'

I couldn't resist those dark eyes, and he looked so worried. I didn't want to worry him more. He had enough on his plate.

'Okay. For you, I'll wait.'

He looked relieved. 'Thanks. Everything will work out. Be patient. And now we need to find that dog.'

Billy came into the kitchen and threw his school bag on the floor. 'What dog?'

'I found a dog. I've named her Beans, but she became scared when I said the word *vet*. She ran off and hid somewhere.'

'Oh, cool!' Billy said. 'I'll find her.'

'She's only a small dog. Black, white and tan.'

'How was school?' Tapakah asked.

Billy kicked at his school bag with his shoe. 'Yeah, it was okay.'

'Just okay?' I asked.

'I'd rather be with Tapakah,' he said softly. 'Like before.'

'Yeah, I miss him too.'

Tapakah hugged us both. 'Oh, stop it you two. Who knew I

was so popular?'

'Why can't I have my own teacher at the lab, like before?'

'Because you need to have a normal life, be out in the world with other children.'

'But I hate it. I want to go back to the lab.'

'Things have changed. You can't. Security has increased, and I'm not always there. I travel more now. And it really wasn't the best environment for you.'

'I know it wasn't all good, with everything that happened, and I miss Ja—'

Tapakah cut him off. 'Billy! What's wrong with you? That's *enough*! Go to your room. I'll talk to you later.'

Tapakah's expression was thunderous, which seemed to terrify Billy. He turned and ran up the stairs to his room. I'd never seen him look so scared. The thump of his feet on the staircase was interspersed with gulping sobs.

'Jesus, what was that about? Billy didn't do anything.' I headed for the stairs to check on him.

Before I had one foot on the bottom step, Tapakah was at my side. He moved so fast it was as if he'd teleported. He gripped my arm and his eyes blazed.

'Leave him.' He pulled me away from the stairs. 'I'll talk to him.'

'But he's *terrified*.' I tried to pull my arm free. 'Let go. I want to make sure he's all right.'

'No.' He squeezed my arm harder and propelled me back into the kitchen. 'This is my business, not yours.'

'Why's he so scared of you? What was he going to say to make you react like that?'

'I have rules, and if you break those rules there are consequences. Billy knows that.'

'What rule did he break? What consequences?'

'Confidentiality. He's not permitted to mention the lab.'

'But he's a kid, for Christ's sake. You can't lay that trip on him, put him in your secret lab for months and then expect him not to say anything. He's a *child*.'

'He's smart and he has an old head on young shoulders. I can expect that, and I do. A breach of confidence could jeopardise everything.'

'But he was only talking to me and you. What's the big deal?'

Tapakah stared at me for a moment and proceeded to speak. I interrupted him as the penny dropped.

'Oh, that's it. It was something *I'm* not supposed to hear. Some of the bad shit I'm not permitted to know. You need to tell me. How can you expect a young boy to shoulder that sort of demand? He obviously knows what went on, and I don't. It's not right, and it won't work.'

He stared me down. 'It is right, and it has to work.'

I stared back. 'It's wrong and it won't work. Let go of my arm. I'm going to check on Billy.'

He tightened his grip. 'No. I forbid it.'

'Forbid? *Forbid?*' I hated that word. 'Don't treat me like a child. You're an arsehole!'

A spark deep inside my head ignited and burst into flame.

He pressed on my shoulders forcing me into a chair. 'Sit.'

I couldn't hear properly. Tapakah's voice echoed somewhere in the distance, odd words bounced around in my brain.

'You don't understand … you … safety … precarious … obey … own good…'

His words were a hot north wind in my ears. They fanned the flames in my head. He supplied the fuel and ignited it. The spark inside my head exploded into wildfire.

Beans peeped around the corner as my world dissolved into a red haze.

 # The Dark Force

"They were told not to harm the grass of the earth or any green plant or tree, but only those people who have not the seal of God on their foreheads." — Revelation 9.4

I knew I wouldn't have to wait long to set Maggie off.

The rage inside Tapakah was *delicious*. So much of it and so many variations. I fed his thoughts with paranoia, treachery and betrayal, and his rage spiked to new levels of intensity. Just how I liked it.

And the boy. An abundance of fear, terror and sadness. Perfect for dessert. I spiked his mind with doubt, insecurity and despair.

Tapakah liked beautiful things. I would destroy them. I feasted on his sharp pangs of emotional pain as I directed Maggie to trash his priceless antiquities. *Delectable.*

Maggie was beautiful. I would destroy her too.

Eventually.

The ultimate pain for him and her. The ultimate delicacy for me. Maybe I could have a taste now, a morsel, a tidbit of things to come.

Maggie held a knife. I took her hand and slowly ran its edge along the front of her arm, from shoulder to wrist. Her skin opened in a river of red.

Panic. Agony. Distress. Shock. It tasted delicious.

Tapakah gave me horror, terror, disbelief and fear. That

tasted better.

I made the boy watch. That was icing on the cake.

Tapakah shouted at me. He screamed at her. The boy cried. This was fun.

Maggie had Tapakah pinned against the wall, hand around his throat. I cut words into his chest with the knife. Well, she did it for me.

Tapakah screamed. 'What do you want? Why are you doing this? I'm not human. You promised!'

'I'm doing it because I can, and actually, you're half human. Plus, I don't like your plan, Tapakah. You're double crossing me. You want to replace my angry, unhappy humanity with peaceful hybrids. That can't happen. You said you would create chaos. But you want to create chaos to eliminate it. You want to starve me out.'

'It's insane. Stop this!' he shrieked at me.

Oops, Maggie must have nicked a vein. Blood spurted over her face, but she kept right on going. Good girl. Remember to dot your i's and cross your t's.

'Oh, and the mark. Cut one in his right hand, and in yours, of course. Don't forget the boy.

Now. Where was I? Oh yes. 'Planet Earth is my farm, Tapakah. Not yours. The humans are *mine*. They must be. Or else why would they exist?

'Humans are geared for self-destruction. They destroy themselves, each other and the planet. No other creature destroys its own home. Humans are beyond nature.

'Ego, self-interest, greed, violence and delusion; it's their default operating system. It keeps everything spinning. Did you know that sixty percent of humans live in a constant state of dissatisfaction? Why would humans be hard wired for negativity if they weren't supposed to produce negative emotions? They're designed for this. They're designed for me. We live in perfect harmony.

'It's humans who are the monsters, not me. They're too stupid to realise the trap they're in. The one they have created. Only rare individuals have seen the truth and found freedom. Too few to be of concern to me.

'Allow me spell it out for you, Tapakah, in simple terms so you understand. More humans equal more food for me. More humans equal more stress. More war. More violence, equals, yes, you guessed it, more food for me.

'When the population of the world reaches ten billion, that's when the real fun begins. If you think things are bad now, wait until that number ticks over.

'So, you see, Tapakah, I can't let you take that from me. You can continue to build your little hybrid empire; I don't have a problem with that. It could even help. But your plan to eliminate five billion people from the planet? That will seriously interfere with my food supply. You must shelve it, Tapakah.

'I am the spawn of humanity's mind. It created me. It keeps me alive. I encompass and feed on them all.

'Consistent destructive human behavior over time has changed human's physiology to the point that two thirds of the neurons in their amygdala are geared toward negativity. Sixty seven percent of their words convey negativity. Seventy four percent of the words they use to describe people are negative. I plan to increase those numbers. I like numbers, and statistics don't lie. Humans are hard wired with a negativity bias in their brains.

'More humans. More pain. The world is my oyster. Humans are my cattle. I feed on them. Their negativity keeps me alive.

'How can it be otherwise? I am steeped in the energy of two hundred thousand years of human violence, bloodshed, anger and fear. My power is such that soon I will become flesh and walk amongst them.

'You are but a speck of dust I can eliminate at will. Though I am partial to your uniqueness, take this as a warning. You are forbidden to interfere. On your knees, Tapakah!'

Maggie grabbed his hair, kicked his knees out and forced him to the ground.

'What are you, Tapakah?'

'Dust.'

He said it through gritted teeth, but he did say it. 'Excellent.'

'And what do you say to me?'

'I … I'm sorry.'

'And what else? What are the rules?'

'I … I'm forbidden to interfere with your food supply.'

Tapakah's fists clenched and his body shook with rage and humiliation. I enjoyed seeing him grovel. The emotions were unique. I liked how he tasted. In a sense, his emotions were the purest I'd ever experienced. Maggie's weren't bad either. The two of them were extremely rare. I'd keep them for top shelf enjoyment.

'Excellent. That wasn't so hard, was it?'

'No,' he croaked.

'The Crystal Keepers call me the Dark Force. You can call me Abbadon.'

'Yes, Abbadon.'

'Cross me, and you will beg for death, but death will run from you. Enjoy your torment. Make sure you do as you're told. I look forward to our next encounter. This was only the entrée.'

---

[30] *Maggie's Playlist: Evil Ways — Santana*

Maggie

Someone said Maggie.

They whimpered. *Maggie. Maggie. Maggie.*

Maggie? I think maybe I was Maggie. Wasn't I?

I was on my knees in a pool of blood. The kitchen knife was covered in it and felt slippery in my hand. A puddle of blood flowed slowly towards a heater duct. I used the knife to push it away. The blood reminded me of thick gravy. I hated thick gravy.

I noticed a pair of expensive leather shoes in front of me. They were covered in blood too. Someone was standing there, right in front of me.

I looked up. It was Tapakah. His shirt was gone. I'd liked that shirt.

He'd changed into a blood red T-shirt with bloodier, redder words scrawled across it. *I Will OBeY!* I hadn't seen that one before. I didn't like it at all.

A small boy huddled in the corner. He had his arm across his chest and his hand sandwiched under his armpit. He was the one making the noises I could hear. The sobbing.

Tapakah knelt and tied his torn shirt around my arm. I already had scars. Now, it seemed, there was another.

'Stay with me, Maggie. Come back to me. Focus on me. Please, don't go.'

He kept saying the same thing over and over. It was annoying.

I drew patterns in the congealed blood with my finger. It reminded me of ... something.

* * * * *

Tapakah

Maggie's eyes were far way. I knew that look. She was sinking back into catatonia.

Jesus Christ.

'Maggie, please, I love you. Look at me! Stay with me, you have to stay with me.'

She met my gaze. Green eyes meeting black.

The green looked so green and the white so white — staring out of her blood drenched face. Still beautiful. Always beautiful.

A spark of recognition. She held my gaze.

She surveyed the carnage around her and whispered, 'Oh, Tapakah. What have I done?'

Maggie started violently as the front door burst open. She dropped the knife. It skidded across the floor.

There was a man. A behemoth. I'd never seen anyone as imposing. Close to seven-feet-tall, massive physique, bald, with eyes like blue ice.

What the hell?

I recognised the man who entered behind him. Fox. And the woman — you couldn't forget her — the Maestro. And the smallest, the most frightening of them all, Dromeus. Frightening because of what he held in his hand. His gaze fixed on mine. It burnt into my brain. All attention was on me as he raised his arm.

'Please, Dromeus. I beg you. Don't do it. She's happy, really, happy. Don't destroy what we have. *Please!*'

His response was an ice-cold stare.

This was it.

Maggie would be lost to me.

I knelt in front of her and she looked at me. 'Know this, Maggie. Remember this. I'm sorry. Sorry for everything. Remember. I love you more than life.'

'I love you too. Why are they here?'

'To give you your life back.'

'I don't want it back. I have a life. With you.' She clutched my hands and her eyes filled with fear.

There was a *thunk* as the crystal hit the ground. It rolled purposefully through the blood towards her.

'Not anymore, Maggie. It's all over.'

---

31 *Maggie's Playlist: It's All Over Now Baby Blue — Russell Morris*

Appendix — Maggie's Playlist

1. The Beginning of The End — Klergy, Valerie Broussard
2. Secrets — OneRepublic
3. Lost & Found — Eye Cue
4. Changes — David Bowie
5. Bad Choice — Kathy Valentine
6. Me and You and a Dog Named Boo — Lobo
7. Secret Agent — Rory Gallagher
8. Barista — Pamela Machala
9. I Want Your Sex, Parts 1 & 2 — George Michael
10. Before He Cheats — Meg Birch
11. Runaway — Del Shannon
12. Every Breath You Take — The Police
13. Better Than Revenge — Taylor Swift, Homeless Brother — Don McClean
14. You Can Run but You Can't Hide — Solomun Burke
15. Memory Lane — Adeaze, Come on Get Higher — Matt Nathanson
16. The Ugly Truth —Matthew Sweet
17. Fire Your Guns — ACDC
18. Died and Gone to Heaven — Tommy Castro
19. Get to the Chopper — Dum Dog Run
20. Never Tear Us Apart — INXS
21. Take Me Away — Avril Lavigne
22. It's All Over Now — Rod Stewart
23. Get Out of My Head — Firewater
24. Basket Case — Green Day
25. Time is Running Out — Muse
26. Out of Control — Rolling Stones
27. Long Time Traveller — Wailin' Jennys
28. Never Going Home — Blue Shaddy
29. You Make Me So Hot — Barbara Lynn
30. Evil Ways — Santana
31. It's All Over Now Baby Blue — Russell Morris